Y0-BPW-262

THE WHITE MAN'S WORLD

SETH was getting through medical school with his parents' help. He was determined to let nothing get in the way of his becoming a doctor—not even his feelings for Nadine.

LIVVY had been Seth's girlfriend before Seth met Nadine. She'd wanted nothing more from him than the pleasures of lovemaking and she was still available whenever Seth wanted her.

JASON was responsible for the overwhelming success of Nadine's singing career. He discovered her at a folk festival and carefully mapped out her rise to the top. In the hours of loneliness that came with her drive for stardom, Nadine was often tempted to turn to Jason for the affection she so desperately needed.

ALAN FAITH was the youngest, best-looking, and most popular TV talk show host in America. When Nadine began dating him, she became the envy of millions of women. They would have felt differently if they'd known what Alan was really like.

Where Running Waters Meet

Julie Ellis

Exclusively published by
KAPPA BOOKS, INC.

This story is based on fictional characters in fictional settings and locations as created and developed by the author. Any resemblance to actual persons, living or dead, locations or specific occurrences in history is purely coincidental.

© 1997 by Julie Ellis

All rights reserved under International and Pan-American Copyright Conventions. No portions of this book may be reproduced or electronically transmitted without the written permission of the publisher.

Published by: Kappa Books, Inc.
Fort Washington, PA 19034

Manufactured in the United States of America.
ISBN: 1-56682-049-9

CHAPTER ONE

Nadine Scott stood on a street corner in the humid heat of the Chicago morning. Duffel bag slung over one shoulder, guitar tucked under one arm. Burnished gold hair stained dark at the temples with perspiration. Her shift clung uncomfortably to her tall, narrow body. She tugged at the neckline as her brown eyes somberly surveyed the low buildings before her. Depressing gray tenements alternated with dirty red-brick ones. All of them were time-scarred and unloved.

A two-family house with a patch of tenderly nurtured grass–freshly painted, windows sparkling–appeared alien here. Across the street a bulldozer, like a giant prehistoric monster, methodically munched at the earth. A sign indicated a high-rise apartment project for the elderly would appear soon on the site within a year.

From one sagging tenement a woman leaned precariously out of the window.

"Alice, you come up here–you know you ain't supposed to be down there on that sidewalk!"

A girl darted past Nadine into a doorway partially obstructed by a wino swigging from a bottle. A transistor radio blared out the number-one rock record in the country. At the end of the block, before the rubble of an ancient mansion, kids dug into the ruins.

"Aw, ya screw your mudder!" an early teenager jeered at another while both paused to stare in contempt at a blue-and-white squad car that inched menacingly down the street.

The area wore the stench of defeat, of hopelessness. This was Eddie's Chicago.

She walked slowly down the block, ignored by most, jostled by some, stared at by others, conscious of the Indian faces that predominated over blacks and Puerto Ricans and occasional whites. All of whom wore an expression of sullen resentment that Nadine recognized.

Her eyes sought anxiously for house numbers. Her heart thumped. She was approaching her destination.

One month ago, she sat alone on the dirt floor of the dome-shaped windowless adobe hut that was home for the eight members of her family. Her slender golden hands clutched the guitar which Eddie had sent to her when he had been in Chicago scarcely two weeks. No tears were in her eyes. Indians learn, early in childhood, the futility of tears.

She stared without seeing at the arid, alkaline earth that was the floor of the hogan. She heard, with a matching anguish within herself, the high-pitched wailing that emerged from Eddie's hogan, a hundred yards to the west. Eddie's women, his mother, his grandmother, his sisters, wore close-cropped hair now, and their long buckskin dresses covered gashed legs, as tradition required.

Eddie had been dressed and painted, his body wrapped in a robe, and now the procession of mourners carried him to a hill on the reservation to place him on the scaffold, as had been done in death with their ancestors. She had not become part of the procession. Part of her still refused to believe that Eddie was dead—Eddie who was so strong, so tall, so handsome.

One month ago she had walked away from the hogan, away from the village. Chicago was a thousand-mile hitch, but she knew she must see this place where

Eddie had lived; she must try to understand.

"Tall buildings, Nadine, rising clear into the sky," Eddie had written. "You never saw anything like this city. And right in the middle is this beautiful lake—and parks!"

For a few minutes, leaving the Greyhound terminal, she had seen the tall buildings gleaming in the morning sunlight, the shop windows laden with fine clothes. Elegant cars moved in the morning rush hour. Incredibly well-dressed people walked purposefully along the sidewalks. That was the Loop. But then she had climbed up to the Elevated, and rode thunderously into Eddie's Chicago.

A pair of Indian youths lounged against a semi-denuded vintage Ford and inspected her boldly in a way that was more American than Indian. Her blonde hair labeled her white to these boys, but the small, solemn girl standing at the curb, studying her Navajo jewelry, comprehended.

"You lookin' for somebody?"

"Yes." Nadine smiled quickly at the child. "This address." She pulled out the creased, soiled envelope that had lain in her duffel bag since she'd left the reservation, an envelope ready for a letter that was never mailed.

The little girl leaned forward to squint nearsightedly at the envelope, preening in her pride at being able to read.

"It's the house next to the corner." She pointed to a decaying building which matched those about it. "Go to the top floor." Her eyes were bright with curiosity. "You gonna live with Mama Stringfield?"

"I'm going to ask about a friend," Nadine explained quietly.

"Did your friend live with Mama Stringfield?" the little girl demanded.

"Yes," Nadine acknowledged painfully. "For a while."

Nadine stared at the house with a feeling of sickness. But it was no worse than the hogan. Better. She was spoiled since Leila Edwards picked her up when she was hitchhiking and gave her a job as a mother's helper for the month of impatient waiting. Leila Edwards was rich—she had two cars and a dishwasher and a color TV. She'd felt guilty living in that fancy lake house, but the money bought her ticket to Chicago.

She didn't know what it was like inside those houses before she had met Leila Edwards. Here also they would have water in pipes; they wouldn't have to walk a quarter of a mile for every drop of water. They would have electricity and telephones and beds.

"I've got electricity in my room. And a bed of my own," Eddie wrote in his first letter. "Not a crummy little cot, like we thought was so groovy at boarding school. A real bed. And I can look out the window and see half of Chicago standing tall against the sky. When I get a job, we'll have a whole apartment for ourselves. Three rooms, Nadine!"

Nadine paused before the house, gearing herself for the moments ahead. An elderly Indian rested his rump against a car while he rolled a cigarette, wrapped up in a world of his own, seeing no one. A pair of subteen Indians played catch across the entrance. Their eyes were far wiser than the eyes of children on the reservation.

Nadine's glance moved slowly up the front of the building. So many broken window panes. But in the hogans they didn't even have windows, just the small hole in the ceiling which allowed smoke to escape when a fire was set in the middle of the room against the winter cold. She tried to concentrate on a time-desecrated shade, pulled down secretively against the morning sunlight. At the next window one white face leaned incongruously from the window. Someone like her perhaps, Indian mother, white father.

Nadine walked reluctantly into the narrow, dark foyer. She recoiled from the ugly stench of stale wine, urine, garbage. She put a hand on the paint-famished, shaky railing, and began the upward trek.

A kind of relief closed in about her when, from a half-opened door at the top of the second flight, a torrent of Navajo surged into the hallway. She felt wrapped in the security of familiarity. A flight further up, she nearly tripped over a calico cat, who meowed querulously and scampered downward.

Doors were ajar because inhabitants hoped, futilely, for some relief from the sweltering humidity that sat upon the city. From behind one door came the wail of a Janis Joplin record. A favorite of Eddie's. Her hand tightened on her guitar as she remembered.

At the top floor Nadine tensed in anticipation, searching for the number Eddie had given her. There, the front apartment. Trembling, she approached the door, knocked. She turned her eyes down the corridor. They froze on the open doorway to the toilet that was shared by the floor. The light was a drab twenty-five-watt bulb regulated by a pull-chain extended with a piece of string and left lighted by the last occupant. Eddie had died in that toilet.

The apartment door moved open a few inches. A small, squat woman stared out.

"What do you want?" The voice was laced with distrust. Nadine slowly turned around.

"I'm Eddie's girl," she said softly. "I came to find out what happened to him."

The woman pushed the door wider ajar, squinted suspiciously. Misled, Nadine guessed, by her blonde hair.

"You no Indian," the woman reproached.

"My mother is Navajo. In the tribe I am Small Blonde Daughter. Eddie and I came from the same reservation–in Arizona. A month ago we buried Eddie. I have to know what happened to him."

"I am Mama Stringfield," the woman in the sleazy calico dress, who was elderly by Indian standards, early middle-age by white, introduced herself with an impassive face. "You come inside. We talk."

Nadine walked into the kitchen of the apartment, a small, square room with plaster cracked across the ceiling and along the walls. The paint dirt-and-food stained, peeling. A decrepit gas range, on which an iron pot boiled up a mess of potatoes, stood at one side of the kitchen, beside a small, enamel-pocked refrigerator. A rectangular table was covered by an unexpectedly attractive plastic tablecloth.

"Why did Eddie die?" Nadine asked urgently.

Mama Stringfield stared sharply at her.

"Didn't the social service people tell you? Eddie shoot heroin. All the time I tell them is no good. But they do anyway. Hank find him, out in the toilet. We call police, was too late." She spoke in a monotone, relating facts. "We got two rooms more. Eddie slept in this one here, "

The second room held four single beds, pushed together as though one huge king-sized bed because of lack of space. Two beds were clumsily made up, the other two occupied. On one lay an older Indian, an empty wine bottle on the floor. He snored loudly, oblivious of their presence. On the adjoining bed sat a stern-faced Indian in his late teens, head bent over a book. He glanced, smiled briefly, and returned to his book.

"Jim go to school. He try for high-school equivalency test." Mama Stringfield stumbled over the word, as though it had been recently learned. But she was proud of this younger lodger.

Eddie had talked about taking a high-school equivalency test. He'd dropped out of high school, despite all her pleas that he stay, because of that ugliness last fall, right after school opened. Suddenly, she was back on that bus again, on a muggy September morning, sitting beside Eddie en route to the high school in town....

"Hey, buddy boy, you and Pocahontas git up, give them seats to white boys," the greasy-haired, smirking driver ordered them. Nadine had hated him on sight because of the way his eyes had stripped her when she'd climbed aboard. "Indians git up when white folks stands."

"You gonna make me?" Eddie shot back, his eyes blazing. His hands tightened into fists.

The driver spun about menacingly in his seat. Half a dozen inches shorter than Eddie. Fifty pounds heavier.

"Yeah, now git up and save me the trouble."

"Eddie do what he says." Nadine shoved anxiously at his elbow. "We'll complain to Mr. Kendrick at school. Eddie, please!" Panic laced her voice because the driver was lifting himself from his seat.

His face flushed dark, Eddie rose from his seat, shoved his way to the rear of the bus with Nadine at his heels. The white students tittered. Every Indian on the bus humiliated, infuriated. But outwardly acquiescent.

"You shouldn't have told me to get up," Eddie reproached angrily under his breath.

"Sssh," Nadine exhorted. "We'll tell Mr. Kendrick. He'll talk to the bus people."

All through boarding school Eddie had been a "bad Indian", thrown out of one school after another because he resisted being treated as a fifth-class citizen. At the bottom of the heap, he'd ranted in frustration. Below the blacks, the Puerto Ricans, the Mexican-Americans, the migrant workers.

Eddie was on probation at the high school. He'd talked out against racial intolerance. Civil rights had made some outward changes. The Navajos could go into town without facing signs in stores that blatantly read: "No Indians or Dogs Allowed." The Indian stalls in public bathrooms had been eliminated. Indians were allowed to sit downstairs at the movies. But nothing had changed in the minds of folks in town. They were still those "damned, no-good Indians."

Before going to their classes Eddie and Nadine diffidently presented their complaints to the principal, wanting to believe he would do something about this.

"Of course, I'll talk to the bus company," Mr. Kendrick said emphatically. "We don't permit that sort of thing."

But the bus driver continued to order Indian students to give up their seats to white classmates. Eddie and Nadine assailed Mr. Kendrick's office again and again in indignation. He was always too busy to see them. They wrote letters to the school board, to the local newspaper, to their assemblymen. Nothing happened.

Fuming with frustration, Eddie dropped out five weeks after the term began.

"I'll study at home," Eddie said, seething with rage. "I'll take the high-school equivalency tests."

"In here we got another room." Mama Stringfield's voice brought Nadine back to the present. A faint pride glowed in the landlady's eyes as she led Nadine into a bedroom where two women sat working on a rug. No joy in their faces. Not even curiosity at Nadine's appearance. They were intent only on the rug spread across one of the double beds that filled the room. "Come into the kitchen. I give you a cool drink," Mama offered with unexpected compassion. "Hot town, Chicago. In the desert is hot but not like this." Contempt in her voice for the city that had replaced the reservation in her life. With the sleeve of her dress she wiped away the beads of perspiration that glistened on her face.

In the kitchen Nadine sat on one of the rickety cane chairs. Mama Stringfield opened the vintage refrigerator. Cold air belched forward as she reached inside for a pitcher. She poured a purple liquid into a tall glass, and brought it to the table to place before Nadine.

"This house is terrible," Mama conceded with resignation. "Still, no worse than the others. Last month they raise the rent again, twenty-five dollars. Do nothin', fix nothin'. Look." She pointed to the roaches that climbed boldly about the sink. "Them we feed, too. At night the rats come out."

"Why did Eddie stay?" Nadine's throat was painfully tight.

"Plenty don't stay," Mama reminded. "All the time the relocation people send me the young from the reservation. They stay week, month, six weeks."

She shrugged tiredly. "Then go home. Some, like Eddie, too proud to go home. Eddie keep sayin' 'I find a job, you'll see.' But instead he find the needle in his arm. You go in bars around here, you see Indians like Eddie. Too proud to go home, not know what to do here. No place in white world for Indian. Don't you know yet?" Mama demanded with sudden intensity. "We sit and wait, till we die. No place in white world for Indian."

Nadine drained the tall glass of bitter liquid, distasteful to her despite its welcome chill, because it would have been impolite to reject this show of hospitality. Then she rose to her feet, reaching for duffel bag and guitar.

"You stay Chicago?" Mama Stringfield asked. "You want place to sleep? I got room. Stay here cheap."

Eddie had sat on one of those beds in the room shared by the men. Here he wrote his letters to her. Those letters with such big promises. He had sat at that table in the kitchen and eaten a meal of potatoes.

Eddie hadn't lied to her. He saw beyond this place. He saw that other Chicago, in which she traveled this morning. Eddie meant to live in that world someday. But he couldn't do it alone. He needed help. There was none. Only the needle in the arm that made life bearable. The needle that killed him out there in that toilet.

"I'll be going back home," Nadine said.

"You change your mind, you come back," Mama Stringfield urged. "Place to sleep and I feed, too."

"Thank you." Nadine managed a small smile. "I'm taking the bus home."

Nadine walked out into the hall, trying not to look at the dimly lit toilet. She felt so close to Eddie at this moment, remembering with poignant clarity the night

Eddie had confided his determination to cut out of the reservation. They'd walked in desert solitude, comfortably distant from the hogan, hand in hand beneath the spill of stars.

"Nadine, I'm going to ask for relocation," he said tensely. She stared at him in shock, consternation. "What's here for us? I won't stay here and become like my father, my brothers! What kind of job can I get in town? Only to fill in when a white man's sick. And for half the pay," he said bitterly. "In the city, in Chicago, it'll be different. People in cities don't think like these pigs. Nadine, I'll find a job. You'll come to me. We'll get married, live like human beings.

Meaning, not like Indians. To most people Indians were not humans. Even though, Nadine recalled with a flash of humor, that Pope back in the sixteenth century made a public announcement that "Indians are human beings." Miss Lawrence, back at boarding school, had talked about that. Trying to make them feel being an Indian was important.

"I'm scared, Eddie," Nadine admitted. "But whatever you say I'll do. Go to the Board. Ask them to relocate you."

"I'll take a Greyhound bus out of here," Eddie said jubilantly, "and then I'll send you a ticket. Remember when we were kids, how we used to watch the Greyhound buses?" Her eyes softened reminiscently. The Greyhound bus had been the magic carpet of their childhood.

"Do it quickly," Nadine urged, battling panic. How would she survive till Eddie sent for her?

"I'll start pushing the Board right away," Eddie promised. "I'll make it out there," he swore, a vein in his forehead distended with emotion. "I don't care if I break my back working. I'll make it, Nadine. We won't bring up our kids on the reservation."

"Eddie, take me with you," she pleaded impulsively–the Board wouldn't relocate her, she was barely seventeen. "Eddie, let me go with you. We'll manage." That one hundred forty dollars a month relocation money seemed a fortune, more than her father earned in a month.

"You stay here and get your high-school diploma," Eddie ordered tenderly. "As soon as I can, I'll send for you. Maybe in Chicago you'll even be able to go to college." He grinned broadly. "Jazzy, huh?"

"Oh, Eddie!" Her eyes shone.

"So you stay here till I send that Greyhound bus ticket to you, hear?"

In the darkness of the desert night, soundless except for the occasional noise of a small animal, Eddie reached for her. She trembled in his arms with a fresh urgency because he was going away. To Chicago or Minneapolis or San Francisco, one of the relocation cities. Tonight his mouth was impatient on hers. His hands moved about her tall, slender frame with the passion of youth.

Eddie knew she wouldn't let him do everything, Nadine reminded herself. Right at the beginning, when this new feeling first flowered between them, she had made it clear they could not sleep together. He could kiss her, touch her, do what he willed, except that final act.

Her stepfather was good to her. He treated her the same way he did her five half-sisters and half-brothers. But she was forever conscious that she was the product of her mother's sin. Only half-Navajo. In her third year of high school, her mother had slept with a white boy and conceived her. Until her own wedding ceremony she would take no chances of getting pregnant.

"Nadine." Eddie's voice was tormented, enhanced by the knowledge of impending separation. "Nadine, you won't get pregnant. I promise."

His breathing was hot on her cheek. His hands fumbling at her small, high breasts. His thighs pressing hungrily against hers. She felt the hardness of his excitement, and shivered faintly.

"No," she rejected, even while her hands tightened at his shoulders. "Like all the other times, Eddie. We can wait. We can."

She drew him down to the still warm, desert earth. Wanting his arms about her, the length of his body pressing against hers. Wanting all of him. But remembering her mother.

For a while, after Eddie left the reservation, she had felt hope. When Eddie boarded the Greyhound bus for Chicago, she stood before the small station, ignoring the broad stares, the obscene remarks of the station hangers-on, until Eddie was aboard the bus and it was lumbering out on to the road. Then she went to where Mama waited with the wagon.

Sitting there on the wagon with Mama, she'd felt so triumphant. Eddie was going to Chicago, into the world that would provide a home for the two of them. How handsome he was. How determined! So certain that, away from the meanness of the small towns around the reservation, people would be different. He would find a job because he was deserving. But Eddie had come home in a pine box. Dead from an overdose of heroin.

She walked slowly down the dark stairway,

remembering Eddie's determination. His strength. Twice he'd been sure he had jobs; both had fallen through. But then this new one came up, better than the other two.

"Nadine, it's a groove," he wrote. "I'm going to work at this garage. I took some kooky test—they say I've got a great aptitude for working with engines. I'll make almost as much in a week as I get for a whole month in relocation money. In no time at all I'll be sending for you."

Questions she had asked herself a hundred times were still unanswered. When did he go on drugs? When the first job, the second, fell through? When a white boy stepped forward and took what was rightfully his? When he couldn't stand staring at the ugly closed-in walls, with roaches and rats crawling up them? But he hadn't taken to drugs to die. To live. To see him through until he walked out of this Indian ghetto and felt himself a man.

No! She wouldn't go back to the reservation. She was staying in Chicago. Eddie hadn't run. He'd looked for help, be he looked in the wrong place. She wouldn't stay up there with Mama Stringfield. She would find another place somewhere around here.

She had twenty-seven dollars left from the money Leila Edwards had paid her. It would be enough for a bed in an Indian place. Enough to eat on until she found a job. She was young, strong. She could work.

Eddie's dream would live in her. She would make it into the Chicago Eddie had seen. The white man's Chicago.

CHAPTER TWO

Nadine walked out of the evil-smelling hallway into the uncomfortable humidity of the city streets. She would never be quite the same after today. That filthy kitchen upstairs.

Eddie said he sat at the kitchen window and looked out upon the city. Not his city. The prison city, from which he sought escape in drugs. A desperate need to escape reality at intervals, when reality became too painful.

Eddie had to dream to live. He was the New Young Indian, he'd declaimed, who was going to break barriers for his people. But Eddie dwelt in ugliness, smothered in this new trap. In a way, death was his escape.

Eddie hadn't tried to cop out. He hadn't meant to die. Nadine clung to this realization. He had taken an overdose by accident. The needle in his arm was to tide him over the rough moments. Eddie still believed in the impossible dream.

Nadine walked aimlessly, knowing she walked in an extension of the reservation. Children played ball, hopscotch on the sidewalk, shrieked humorously among themselves. The sidewalks were their home for the summer. Wistfully, Nadine remembered the beauty of a desert night, the striking uncluttered blue of a day-time sky.

A group of teenagers slouched against a car at the corner. An Indian woman, so drunk she could barely remain vertical, was wheedling money from a male companion, a black man. The women on the reservation never drank, Nadine thought with a touch of pride. Some of the men buried their sorrows in cheap wine and homemade raisin whiskey, but never an Indian woman.

She walked for blocks, recoiling from the monotonous repetition around her. Smelling, feeling the poverty, the lost dreams, the bitterness that made this a new kind of ghetto. More than ever, she was acutely aware of the necessity to hoard her money. How would she find a job in this jungle? A whisper of panic welled in her. It was inconceivable to consider walking into one of those fine buildings on the Loop and asking for a job. Here. Among her own kind. This was where she must look for a job. But she wouldn't stay here forever. It was only a starting point.

Nadine slowed down before a small luncheonette with red neon sign advertising tortillas and chili. With guitar under one arm, her duffel bag clutched in hand, Nadine walked to the door of the luncheonette, opened it, walked inside.

No air-conditioning here. An ineffectual fan oscillated atop a cabinet that showed off a display of doughnuts, cakes, and pies with sagging meringues. At the closer end of the counter two Indians and a black, all males, straddled stools and ate from thick china plates before them. Behind the counter a tall Indian girl, her waist-length reddish-black hair in a thick braid down her back, washed down a work area. She wore an air of arrogance, of faint defiance. High cheekbones, velvet dark eyes, square jaw. Her body narrow, gaunt, yet sensuous.

"What are you having?" The girl was scrutinizing Nadine while she mopped at the patch of counter before which Nadine sat.

"An orange drink and one of those." Nadine pointed to the sugar-covered doughnuts.

The girl served Nadine, her eyes resting speculatively on the silver jewelry which hung about Nadine's neck.

"You visit a reservation this summer?" the counter girl inquired, faintly supercilious.

"I lived on a reservation," Nadine said with quiet emphasis, comprehension washing over her. The girl was trying to categorize her, unsure, because of her hair, if she were Indian or an American girl slumming. "I'm Navajo." She lifted her head with pride, though much of the time Nadine resented the stigma this became in the white world's eyes.

The girl grinned.

"I wasn't sure. I thought you might be one of those social-service chicks. Some of them pull this bit of mixing in the neighborhood, for a 'better understanding' of the problems," she drawled. "Bullshit."

"I'm looking for a place to live around here." Nadine strived to sound casual. "Something cheap."

"Nothing's cheap, baby," the girl laughed. "It's just a little less rich around here. There's a woman in my building, she takes in girls. Eight bucks a week for a bed and you can use the kitchen. You might go over and ask if she has any space." She leaned over to rip off a scrap of paper from a pad, foraged for a pencil. "It's close by," she said while she scribbled the address. "You go down the corner, that way." She pointed south. "Then over one block to the right. Her name is Clarice Dawson. Tell her Joanna sent you."

"Thanks, Joanna." With a grateful smile Nadine read the address, then slid the paper beneath her glass while she nibbled at the doughnut.

"You being relocated?" Joanna asked, the arrogance gone.

"No, I'm here on my own," Nadine admitted. She had enough for three weeks at Clarice Dawson's, if she ate home. Just buying beans and potatoes and a jar of instant coffee. In three weeks she must find a job.

"If Dawson can't take you in, you can bed down on the floor in my place," Joanna offered after a minute's deliberation. "I keep a sleeping bag for emergencies. Come back and let me know what works out."

Nadine left the luncheonette, headed for the house in which Joanna lived. Feeling less alone now. She found the house with no difficulty. A replica of the dreary, gray building in which Eddie had lived. Clarice Dawson, a Sioux came to the door with one child in her arms, two small ones trailing at her skirt.

"Joanna sent me over," Nadine said quickly. Again she saw Indian eyes darkening with suspicion. "I'm looking for a place to live. I just came from Arizona." Mrs. Dawson would translate that to read "reservation."

"I got one bed," Mrs. Dawson said with a broad smile. "This chick went home last night. Homesick," she shrugged this off, but her eyes were appraising Nadine. "It'll cost you eight a week, and you can use the kitchen, so long as you keep things clean."

"Can I see it?" Nadine asked, and the woman's smile dimmed.

"Why not?" she shrugged. How old was Clarice Dawson, Nadine wondered. No more than thirty, probably, though she looked older. "We live here in this room." Mrs. Dawson gestured to a room at one side of a minute foyer where a boy of ten or eleven sprawled across one of the two double beds, engrossed in a comic book. "The girls sleep in there."

The room at the other side contained three set of double-decker bunk beds. Corrugated cartons sat at each end of the bunks, obviously containing the personal belongings of those who slept in the beds, while dresses were hung on nails about the walls.

Much used but brightly printed café curtains hung at the two immaculately washed windows. The sheets were worn thin but clean. Clarice Dawson had not collapsed completely into hopelessness.

Nadine gazed about wistfully, recalling Eddie's letters, "We'll have three whole rooms, just for ourselves." But the beds were clean, Nadine reminded herself, and the linoleum on the floor freshly scrubbed.

"I'd like to take it," Nadine said hastily, because Clarice Dawson spoke impatiently to the baby and she suspected delay in sealing this arrangement was responsible. "Starting right away." She shifted the guitar so that she could dig into her duffel bag for the eight dollars.

"The top bunk by the wall." Mrs. Dawson extended a hand for the money. "Somebody moves, you can take another bunk."

Nadine rested her guitar on the bed, as though it were a child, unpacked her two changes of wardrobe, and folded the items neatly in the carton near her bunk. Clarice Dawson had returned to the kitchen. The sound of Johnny Cash filled the small apartment, while Clarice washed clothes in the kitchen sink and refereed a battle between two of her children.

Nadine pulled forth a much smaller replica of her duffel bag from within the larger one. In here was stowed her bankroll and a lipstick. With this in tow she left the tenement flat to go downstairs again, nagged by a compulsion for activity, yet uncertain which way to turn.

At least she knew where she'd sleep tonight, Nadine

acknowledged with relief. Later, she would go into one of the grocery stores and buy what she would need to eat, and think about a job.

She had tried to find a job back home, knowing she wouldn't. In a city like this, where did you go? Where did you look? Eddie had said relocation people were supposed to help him, but they didn't. She couldn't go to them. She wasn't being officially relocated.

Pushing down the panic which was constantly ready to bubble to the surface, Nadine turned in the direction of the luncheonette. Joanna had said, let her know about the bed. Maybe Joanna would know about a job. She'd just walked into the job with Leila Edwards. Maybe it could happen that way again.

She quickened her strides. At the door she hesitated. A man, white, was behind the counter now. Was he Joanna's boss? All right, she would go in and buy a cup of coffee.

She walked inside and sat down on a rear stool.

"Coffee," she said quickly.

"How'd you make out?" Joanna asked.

"I'm going to stay there," Nadine reported, and hesitated. The white man was down at the other end of the counter, heatedly arguing with a male Indian about the possibility of Bobby Kennedy running for president one day.

"It's like I tell you," the white man was insisting grimly. "A poor man's got no chance in politics in this country no more, whether he's white, red, or black. The rich man buys himself what he wants. You heard the talk about how the Kennedys were already holding a conference about building Bobby for the White House, before JFK was even buried there in Arlington. What chance does a poor man stand, the way they throw money around in campaigns? Them that has "it," he emphasized with a pound of his fist.

Nadine leaned forward urgently.

"You wouldn't know anything about a job?" she asked Joanna quietly. Her eyes desperate.

"Jobs are hard to come by," Joanna said warily, her voice low. "How much schooling have you had?"

"I graduated high school," Nadine said with pride. "In the top ten percent of my class." Joanna was impressed, she noticed with pleasure.

"I'll ask around," Joanna promised. "But you can't be too particular."

"I'm not," Nadine shot back defensively.

"You could apply for welfare," Joanna pointed out, "but there's a waiting period."

"No," Nadine said quickly. "I have to find a job."

"I'll ask around," Joanna promised, moving briskly toward a customer who was settling himself on a stool. "Come up to my pad tonight. Four-D."

The room was small but lively. Bright red throw covers on single beds which sat at right angles to each other. Printed red curtains hung on either side of the windows. Nadine sat with bare feet tucked beneath her, while Joanna grilled franks in the vintage broiler.

"You can go down to the Loop and try for a sales job," Joanna pointed out thoughtfully. "With that hair you could pass for white, you know that. But you'll have to dress sharp or you're out from the start. I'd say, take anything you can get, save up a couple of decent outfits, then try Marshall Field or Carson Pirie Scott."

"Okay." Nadine nodded enthusiastically. But why did Joanna stay here? She was so bright and attractive and she knew the angles.

Joanna swung away from the stove with a wry smile.

"You wondering why I don't practice what I preach?" Joanna jibed. "You forget one thing, I'm Indian, all the way. All those fancy civil rights acts they're passing might be putting more blacks into decent jobs, but it's not doing anything for Indians. You know about Watts–how much more depressed can a black area be than Watts? But the average black out there earns sixty-eight dollars a week, the average Indian thirty dollars a week." She smiled wryly. "I'm great on gathering statistics."

"Eddie was like that," Nadine said quietly, and saw the glint of inquiry in Joanna's eyes. "My boyfriend. He's, he's dead."

Joanna's eyes were compassionate but she didn't question.

"Back on the reservation my father was active in trying to better conditions. I helped him send out letters to our congressmen and our senators, complaining about how rotten conditions were on the reservation. We tried to get the BIA to get some action for us." Joanna shrugged. "You know how far that got us. Finally, we had to stop–the local fuzz began to harass my father. It was after that I came here on relocation, about a year ago. I was so damn sick of that American concentration camp.

"I know." Nadine stared somberly into space, repulsed by the memory of the reservation, yet achingly lonely for her family.

"There were ten of us," Joanna said softly. "When I was small, we were so damn poor. Not that it's much better now," she conceded. "But in those days I was always hungry. I'd eat anything–bits of wood, bark– anything I could put in my mouth. Oh, I hated the ugliness when we went into town! Remember the signs in the stores? The looks on people's faces, like we were dirt? Civil-rights acts didn't change that."

"Back home they still flinch when an Indian has the brass to go downstairs in the movie," Nadine remembered.

"Did they ship you off to boarding school, Nadine?" Joanna asked, her eyes bitterly reminiscent.

Nadine nodded, frowning in memory.

"When I was seven. God, I used to cry myself to sleep every night. Once an aid tried to comfort me. They switched her to another dorm. Everything was supposed to be impersonal. But even then I was thrilled at the prospect of going to school. Mama used to say 'learning is a gift.' But after the school hours, there was nothing, and every night I'd pull the covers over my head and cry."

"It was so wrong!" Joanna shot back violently. "To take young kids like that away from home, leave them stranded in a cold situation. At home we had love. Maybe we didn't have much in the material way, but baby, we had love. So they take us and put us into their 'military installations'," she continued with contempt. "The building where I lived, all through elementary school, and the school building, too, had been condemned forty years earlier! Wow, I was always in trouble because I wanted to be me, Joanna. I hated all their regulations that reduced you to a number. We were in jail, without ever having committed a crime. Except that of being born Indian."

"Eddie was like that," Nadine whispered. "Always in trouble for trying to be himself. Always the 'bad Indian'."

"When I was ten, I tried to run away from

boarding school." Joanna's eyes were black coals of rage. "They caught me and dragged me back. For punishment I wasn't allowed to go home for Christmas. I'd been waiting a whole year for that!" Joanna moved back to the range to flip the franks over. "I hated every one of those sons of bitches."

"I was close enough to take the bus home," Nadine said wistfully, "but this wasn't allowed. They didn't even like it when Mama managed to come and see me once in a while. I used to be a nervous wreck when I knew she was coming, for fear she'd arrive and they wouldn't let me see her because of some demerit. That happened all the time in our dorm."

"Honey, there are only two routes for an Indian. Either you kill yourself and you get it all over with, or you try to fight your way out of the trap and go all the way up. And that's what I mean to do, Nadine. Some way or other, I'm escaping the trap." She chuckled at the earnestness in Nadine's eyes. "I know I'm not making jet-age progress, but I'm here and I'm not tied down to BIA any more. When I came to Chicago, I figured they'd help me find a job for sure. Everything was going to be groovy. So for weeks I'd sit in that damn BIA office every day from eight to five, hoping they'd send me out on a job, and then I sharpened up. I went out looking on my own. I met a fellow at an Indian bar. He knew about a job. That one lasted a few months, then I found the luncheonette job. The money is shitty. They'd pay a black girl twice as much. A white girl wouldn't work there. Still, it's better than relocation money, though not much. But I belong to me."

"Joanna, what do you want to do? I mean, deep down?" Nadine asked quietly. "Besides having a good place to live and fine clothes to wear. What turns you on, Joanna?"

Joanna stood tall and straight in the doorway to the closet kitchen. The intensity on her face mesmerized Nadine.

"I want to go back to school. To college. I want to earn a degree that'll let me teach. On a reservation. Teaching my people. In September I'll start night classes. That's why I can stand living here, working in that luncheonette."

Nadine frowned, squinting into space. Caught up in secret guilt, Eddie and Joanna both so dedicated to their own people. Her people. She wasn't, not in the same way.

"I don't know where I'm going." Nadine spread her hands in an eloquent gesture of uncertainty. "With Eddie I knew. I don't know any more."

"You'll find out, baby," Joanna said gently. "Come on now, chow time."

Nadine lay in her bunk and felt a kind of claustrophobia as she listened to the night conversation of her roommates. The air was sticky, thick with city smells. One of the girls, in black bikini pajamas, was standing at a window, trying to wrap the café curtains around the rod to allow more air into the room.

"Oh, come on, stop knocking yourself out," scoffed the fat but pretty Cherokee who'd introduced herself as Maria. "All you're letting in is stinking air. Everything's rotten in this town. Look at what's happening to Lake Michigan. It's not fit for swimming any more! Back home the water's so clean you can see to the bottom of the ponds."

"I don't see you running," the girl in the bunk above her jibed. "Home, I mean."

"Home," said the fat girl, "is a beat-up bus some folks abandoned. Roast all summer, freeze your ass off all winter." She shook her head resolutely. "I won't ever go back." But fear hovered in her eyes.

"We all say we won't go back," Maria reminded, half-hanging out of the window in search of relief from the heat. "But most of us go back. One way or another."

"Get in from that window," the quiet girl who said she was Shoshone ordered shrilly. "You could fall right out!"

A clammy coldness closed in about Nadine. Eddie went home, involuntarily, in a pine box. She shut her eyes tightly, as though to sweep away the brutal reminder of the long trail of escapees from the reservation who ultimately returned. No, she wouldn't go back. She would find a way out of the Indian trap. She must make it out there in the white world. For Eddie, as well as for herself, and for Mama.

Restless, Nadine climbed out of her bunk, reached for her guitar. It was like holding Eddie, when she held his guitar in her arms. Her lover, her child.

Nobody could sleep in this enervating heat. Nobody here would mind if she sang one of her own songs, which talked about people like themselves.

Experimentally, she touched the strings, caught the glimmer of interest on Maria's face.

"Sing," Maria urged.

In the flat across the way a beer-sodden pair was shrieking invectives at each other. Downstairs, a child cried querulously in the oppressive humidity. And in Clarice Dawson's improvised, miniature dorm, Nadine sang about an Indian girl who fled the reservation.

Nadine moved about with an increasing confidence

in her surroundings, yet conscious of a persistent uneasiness. Everywhere she asked for work. Anticipating rejection before the words were out of her mouth because this was becoming a pattern. Yet the pattern must be broken!

Toward the end of the week a manager of a cleaning store decided he might have an opening for her. She nodded eagerly when he mentioned salary. It was far below the legal figure, but almost as much as Joanna earned. She knew not to complain about that.

"I need a girl who's quick–and friendly," he said, his eyes overbright.

"Oh, I'll be nice to the customers," she promised naively.

"And nice to the boss," he reminded, pulling her to him in the tiny room that was his office. "You take care of old George, he'll take good care of you." He reached out a hand to close in about her breast. His breathing heavy, he moved in to her, pressing against her. "Come back tonight, closing time. We talk about this."

"No!" Her eyes flashing, Nadine shoved him away. "You keep your job!"

"Your decision," he shrugged. He wasn't yet sure that she was turning him down. "If you change your mind, come back at seven, I'll be here."

"I won't!"

Nadine hurried out into the summer street again. She was beginning to be disconcertingly conscious of the frustration she saw on all sides. The lost hope in the eyes of those who peopled her new world. The reservation look, repeated over and over again in the ghetto.

By the conclusion of her second week in Chicago

Nadine was frantic. Her hands were trembling when she handed over another eight dollars, twenty-four now, in all, to Clarice Dawson. In the afternoon she walked across to the neighborhood library. Finding a kind of solace at sitting at a table, reading a magazine which recognized no distinction between white, black, or red faces. Joanna's flat was littered with old magazines and library books.

Every evening, at Joanna's insistence, she went to the pad to share whatever Joanna prepared for her. Joanna's roommate worked part-time at an Indian bar, and she loathed being alone in the pad.

Nadine reached out to knock on the door. She stopped halfway, Joanna was not alone. She was talking to a man. Nadine hesitated, instinctively ready to retreat.

No, she'd better at least drop in for a minute. Joanna had said earlier, be sure to come up. Chicken was on sale at the supermarket. They would feast on chicken tonight.

Nadine knocked, an excuse to leave quickly already forming in her mind.

"Come in," Joanna called out, seemingly in rare high spirits.

Joanna was in the kitchen, fork in hand, leaning over a large black skillet on the range. A young Indian in chinos slouched precariously in the window.

"Don't do that!" Nadine ordered involuntarily, and instantly blushed.

"I won't jump," he chuckled, swaggering to his feet. His eyes moved from Nadine to Joanna, back to Nadine again with candid pleasure.

"Change your mind and stay?" Joanna taunted humorously.

"I told you I have to cut out," he reminded reproachfully. "You're a suspicious chick."

"Nadine, this is Hank Crawford. Nadine Scott," Joanna introduced.

"Hi," Nadine smiled uncertainly. Why was he staring at her that way?

"Nadine Scott?" he repeated oddly.

"That's right." A voice ricocheted in her mind. Mama Stringfield's voice. "Hank find him, out in the toilet." Nadine's throat was tight. Her mind shied away from questioning him. Yet she must. "You knew Eddie Shaw? she stammered. "You knew him?"

"Nadine, guess what!" Joanna moved forward, unaware of the overbearing heaviness in the room. "My roommate's cutting out. She's joining some kind of commune out West. So what about moving in here with me? And she can probably shove you into her job at the bar," Joanna's voice petered out as her eyes went from Hank to Nadine.

"Tell me about Eddie," Nadine whispered.

CHAPTER THREE

Nadine's eyes looked into Hank's while he painfully sought for words.

"Eddie and I lived at the same pad. Mama Stringfield's." Hank's voice wore an air of guilt, because he was alive and Eddie was dead. "He was a great guy."

"What happened to that wonderful job he wrote about?" Nadine whispered. Feeling painfully close to Eddie at this moment because Hank, who had known him here in Chicago, stood three feet from her. "He was so sure of it."

Hank shrugged cynically.

"When's anything sure? The man told Eddie the job was his, after he took that aptitude test and scored so high. A hundred bucks a week, the man promised. Then this group comes along. They carry on because the man don't have any black boys in the shop, and they start to picket, see? Black power, baby, that beats out red power." Hank hesitated. "But it was an OD. Eddie didn't mean to cop out. He wasn't like that. He kept talking about you, and how he was going to make it big. He was sure he'd hit, sooner or later."

"That's the story of my life," Joanna cut in abruptly. "Always later." She smiled determinedly at Nadine. "Honey, put on some plates. That chicken's almost ready. Sure beats beans or tortillas. Sorry you can't stay, Hank," she drawled.

"I've got something big going," Hank boasted with a broad grin. "Jo, you got a phone yet?" His eyes searched the room. "Can I call you here?"

"What Indian gets a phone in this turf?" Joanna jibed. "I tried. I figured I could swing it if I watched my outgoing calls. I went over to the phone company office, and you know what the girl told me? I'd have to put down a one hundred fifty dollar deposit because my folks were all the way out there in Colorado. They were scared I'd run up long-distance calls when I got homesick and there wouldn't be anybody around to pay the bills. Balls! If I lived at Lake Shore East Apartments, with all that glass and that way-out swimming pool on the top, they'd ask me for a twenty-buck deposit."

"Maybe someday you'll live at the Lake Shore East," Hank said, swaggering slightly, his eyes holding Joanna's. "Maybe I cut out of school in the ninth grade, maybe I haven't been doing too great the two years I've been in Chicago, but I see something big coming up." He stared ahead with a glow of triumph about his face. The look in his eyes the look which Nadine remembered in Eddie's. "I can't talk much yet, but I've just made myself a jazzy connection."

"Hank, are you going out on the street to push dope?" Joanna demanded with contempt.

"Honey, you know me better than that," Hank protested. "You mix with dope, any way at all, you're halfway dead already. This is business." He hitched his chinos higher with an air of bravado. "I'll drop around, Jo," he promised. "See you, Nadine."

Hank left. They could hear his footsteps in heavy descent. Joanna crossed to open the door, hopeful of a breeze. From across the way came Nadine's favorite cut of the Beatles' *new Sgt. Pepper* album—"She's leaving home."

"As I was telling you," Joanna leaned forward intently. "Bunny's moving out tomorrow. She's flipped for this Sioux she's been making it with for the last three months. They're cutting out for Minneapolis. Tomorrow she'll take you over to the bar where she works evenings part-time. I figure you should be able to inherit the job."

"Hey, that would be groovy!" Nadine's eyes shone. That kind of job, serving drinks in an Indian bar, shouldn't be too hard. "Oh, Joanna, " Consternation clobbered her. "I just paid Clarice Dawson a whole week's rent!"

"Forget it," Joanna said briskly. "Bunny's paid up till the end of the month. You ride free until then."

Bunny's boss was happy to have Nadine replace her. The turnover, he acknowledged, was tremendous. At the wages he paid, Nadine wasn't astonished. Still, she was grateful. It would be money coming in every week.

Nadine moved her meager belongings into Joanna's pad, and settled with a sense of belonging into a new pattern. She worked from six to eleven each evening. Two or three evenings a week Joanna would pick her up after work and they would go to a coffee house that was popular with young people of varying ethnic backgrounds—the Casbah.

Nadine was struggling to save on her minuscule salary, constantly shocked at the staggering prices of necessities. Joanna was saving to take a night course at the university. Nadine realized that Joanna was sleeping with Hank. Half-a-dozen times she'd seen Hank with a flashily dressed white woman in her early thirties, who obviously considered Hank her private property. When Nadine tried to tell Joanna, she had been cut off. Joanna knew.

Quite unexpectedly one day Joanna discovered Hank's big connection. Hank had become a runner in a numbers racket.

"This is the life," he gloated, when Joanna

confronted him on one of his regular visits to their pad. "I get a twenty-five percent cut out of every buck I collect, plus a fin for every thirty-buck hit one of my customers makes. Plus tips when somebody hits big. This is living," he said expansively, an arm about Joanna's slim waist.

"It's against the law," Joanna reminded bluntly. "And when a red man gets picked up by the fuzz, it's doubly hard. Hank, cut out!"

"Jo, you're worried about me," he crooned, bringing Joanna to him. "I'm doing this for us. So you'll have that shiny white Cadillac convertible and a classy pad. Give me time, baby."

Hank was swaying with Joanna now, moving his thighs impetuously against hers. A hand cruising about one breast. Nadine turned her head away in discomfort, headed for the kitchenette.

Nadine stood at the small corroded sink with her back to them, and washed the dishes Joanna had stacked there earlier, recoiling from the passionate whispers in the other room.

"Nadine," Joanna hovered in the doorway. "Why don't you run on over to the Casbah? To hell with the dishes. Hank and I'll come over in a little while."

"Sure." Nadine managed a nonchalant smile. They couldn't wait to hit the sack. The mental picture of Hank making it with Jo was disturbing . "I'll hang around the coffee house for a while, Jo."

Nadine walked out of the dimly lit foyer in the glare of the night. People hung out of their windows, in hope of relief from the late summer heat wave. The fuzz cruised up and down the streets in their blue-and-white squad cars. On the next block a paddy wagon sat before a rundown tenement while a pair of cops shoved a couple of drunks from doorway to wagon.

Nadine walked swiftly, face stern, to avoid any unwanted invitations. Conscious of her blondeness. The Casbah was actually at the border of their own turf. A kind of meeting ground for the offbeat, the searching. A handful of Indians, some blacks, mainly white and black students who gravitated to the area in the evenings.

With a comforting sense of kinship, Nadine walked into the semi-darkness of the coffee house, knowing she would be recognized and welcomed. She inched her way through the tiny tables to an empty one at the rear. Here she could nurse one cup of their insanely expensive coffee all evening. They understood. Or Hank would show up with Jo and throw around his numbers money.

A gaunt, pale boy with shoulder-length flaxen hair and the liquid accent of Georgia in his voice sat on a stool in the spotlight, and sang about a childhood on welfare while he accompanied himself on a guitar.

"That's my thing, kids," he said quietly, when the earnest applause died down. "Who else has somethin' to say? For Chavez in California or blacks in Birmingham or reds on the reservations? Come on, kids, sing it out." His eyes searched the darkness, his hands holding out the guitar.

Nadine rose to her feet, moved compulsively toward the slight young man who extended the guitar with luminous eyes.

"Come on, honey," he encouraged softly as Nadine hesitated at the edge of the spotlight.

With long strides she went up to him. Wordlessly, she accepted the guitar and sat on the stool. Her burnished gold hair fell in silken limpness about her face, her shoulders. Her stern nose accentuated the high cheekbones, the mouth, a sensual curve.

She closed her eyes, remembering Eddie. Remembering how his face shone when she sang the words that told about the dreams of an Indian girl and boy. Her voice was low at first. So low there was a rustling among those at the tables in the rear. And then her voice swelled, grew rich with intensity, filled the small room that was suddenly still.

Afterward, the applause terrified her, and sent her scurrying out of the spotlight.

"Hey, you're great," the southern boy said with respect as he accepted the guitar. "Sing something else."

"Another night," Nadine stammered, tense with self-consciousness, and he didn't coax her.

Nadine settled herself at her table. She felt exhilarated, loved, fulfilled. She had never sung for strangers before. Only for Eddie, and her own people.

Twice in a row, on Nadine's night off, Hank showed up with another Indian in tow. It was always tense. Nadine rejected these efforts to involve her in the socializing. She could never forget. She had denied herself to Eddie.

Nadine was singing almost every night at the coffee house. No pay, but she found meaning flowing between herself and those who sat out in the darkness. For a little while she was wholly alive.

Joanna took Nadine around Chicago, showing her the city. Into the Old Town to mingle with the bohemian crowd, with whom both Joanna and Nadine felt such an affinity. For a picnic in Ravinia Park, with paper bags carried from their own pad, because the delis in the vicinity of the park were prohibitively expensive, Jo warned. To the Economy Bookstore to browse, and cautiously to buy, used books. One Saturday noon they took the Elevated down to the Loop, strolled along the busy streets, walked into the elegant main floor of Marshall Field on North State.

"Look at the way they stare at us," Joanna whispered contemptuously when they lingered to inspect a counter display of costume jewelry. A saleswoman with high, stiff coiffure pointedly watched them. "Like they're sure we're going to steal something and run."

Nadine's eyes clashed for an instant with the saleswoman's. Her heart pounded. She felt a compulsion to strike out at the woman. Her slender hands balled into furious fists.

"Let's get out of here," she said tightly. "I hate this stinking place!"

But striding down the aisle to the front, Nadine was conscious of a compulsive will to walk through this imposing store and buy with wild abandon. With disdain for price tags. Next month, Jo said, Marshall Field would start hiring clerks for the Christmas business.

Summer was on the wane. There were pleasant days now, at intervals, with a delightful breeze from the Lake. Days when Nadine would take her guitar and go to the park to sit on the grass. Here was the gathering place of the young. Singing was her passport in this park existence, yet she shied away from making contacts that carried beyond the park. It was sufficient to sing with these students, share their lunch and their stimulating thoughts, and return Uptown for her night job at the Indian bar.

A week before her mother's birthday, Nadine took five dollars, a huge sum on her wages, and shopped for canned food because she realized nothing would be more welcome in her mother's hogan. Cans of tuna, sardines, beef stew, bought after comparison shopping that carried her from supermarket to supermarket. A small salami picked up at a kosher delicatessen in a fringe area. A giant-sized Hershey bar because her mother dearly loved chocolate. Joanna, knowing about the project, contributed a bag of hard candies and a dozen packages of gum for the children, and accompanied Nadine to the post office.

No letter, no card accompanied the package. But Nadine walked out of the post office with a sense of touching home. Mama would understand. She couldn't write Mama until she was doing well, justifying her running away. But small gifts would keep Mama posted on her welfare.

Joanna kept trying to bring fellows into Nadine's social life, but Nadine hedged. Still uptight at the prospect of even the slightest touch. Joanna was exhilarated by her night course at the university, insisting that Nadine join her next term. Going back to school, Joanna declared, was the beginning of a new life. Yet along with Joanna's avowed exhilaration about school, Nadine felt a fresh tension in her, a brittle humor which was out of key.

Nadine and Joanna sat over a spaghetti dinner, in that brief, nightly interval when Joanna came home from the luncheonette and Nadine had not yet left for her job at the bar. A job which she disliked with mounting intensity. The boss has warned her last night to be less imperious. "A girl workin' in an Indian bar has got no room to give herself airs," he'd said meaningfully.

"I wonder where Hank is?" Joanna restlessly twirled a forkful of spaghetti with glint of vague dislike on her face. "He said he'd be around tonight."

"His social life is catching up with him," Nadine suggested bluntly. Last night Hank had been at the bar where she worked, with the flashily dressed blonde. Uncomfortable but defiant in her presence.

"Hank knows I have a class tomorrow night, damn

him!" Joanna abandoned the spaghetti with a shrug of distaste. "He's supposed to be here."

"Did you eat at the luncheonette?" Nadine asked curiously. Normally, Joanna ate with gusto.

"Are you kidding? " Joanna scoffed. "They watch me like a squaw in a grade-D movie, the last hour I'm behind the counter. My deal calls for lunch, no dinner. I'm just not hungry."

"I wouldn't let Hank spoil my dinner," Nadine derided gently.

Joanna looked tired. Circles were beneath her eyes, a tired droop to her sensuous mouth. Uptight about that busty blonde. "Whitey," Hank's friend Alfie called the blonde in derision. Behind Hank's back.

"I'll have some coffee," Joanna said, pushing back her chair. "Maybe that'll wake me up. Coffee for you, baby?"

"Sure." Nadine frowned at the way Jo's eyes kept moving toward the door, anticipating Hank's arrival.

They were idling over a second cup of coffee, on this first cool evening of early autumn, when Joanna stiffened to attention, listening to the heavy footsteps tramping up the stairs, turning down the corridor toward their door. Joanna was on her feet before the knock sounded.

"Come in," Joanna called tensely, an air of expectancy in her posture.

The door opened. Alfie walked in. Joanna braced herself.

"Where's Hank?" she demanded, her eyes fastened to Alfie's face.

"Some little trouble, Jo," Alfie said uneasily. "He got picked up today. Running numbers."

"Oh, God!" Joanna's voice was anguished. "I warned him! This neighborhood crawls with fuzz!"

"It's gonna be okay, Jo," Alfie uneasily. "He's down there now, waiting for his bail to be put through."

"Who's standing bail for Hank?" Joanna shot back.

"The white chick," Alfie said contemptuously. "She's part of the numbers scene. Hank says don't worry, he'll be over later, soon as he can cut out." Joanna sniffed scornfully. "Hank says he won't serve time. His boss has everything fixed. This was some new cop on the beat. Hank'll just have to cool it for three or four weeks. He sent me around so you wouldn't be uptight because he didn't show."

"Thanks," Joanna said bitterly. "I won't be uptight."

"I'll blow," Alfie said, relieved that his mission was over. He sent a long, hopeful glance at Nadine, who ignored him. "See you around...."

Joanna sat down again, drumming on the table top with her fingernails.

"That stinking son of a bitch! Why does he have to mess around with the numbers? Doesn't he know there's no percentage in that except for the bankers?"

"Hank will get off," Nadine reminded gently. "He's got the connections. That syndicate he works for makes payoffs all the way up to the top."

"I have to talk to Hank," Joanna said with an urgency that brought Nadine up sharply. "I've been suspicious for three weeks. Nadine, I'm pregnant."

"Jo, maybe you're wrong," Nadine looked at her, not believing. "Jo, you're mixed up on dates."

"No," Joanna brushed this aside impatiently. "I'm so regular you could use me for a calendar on a desert isle. We got careless two or three times. I'm pregnant, and I don't know what the hell Hank is going to say."

"He knows it's his baby," Nadine protested.

"Will he care?" Jo countered. "I keep telling myself beautiful stories about Hank. But I'm scared.

I'm scared he'll run like hell."

"Jo, talk to him," Nadine exhorted, and paused. "Maybe, maybe you don't have to have the baby. There are doctors, Jo, who–"

"If it'll make Hank marry me, I'll have the baby," Joanna admitted defiantly. "I know I'm out of my mind when it comes to Hank. I know what he is. But I want him, Nadine."

"What about college? What about going back to the reservation to teach? That was all that mattered, you said!"

"Right now I'm on this kooky trip." Joanna closed her eyes for a moment. "All I remember is how it is with Hank in the sack. I could kill that frigging blonde for letting Hank screw her. I want it all for myself, Nadine." Joanna took a deep breath, tried for a smile. "Now, baby, you'd better cut out of here and get to work. One of us has got to show some sense."

The evening dragged painfully for Nadine. Her mind shot through with images of the encounter between Hank and Joanna in Joanna's pad. She harbored little belief that Hank would marry Joanna. One night in the sack with Hank zonked and careless and Joanna's whole life, all the years ahead, could be wrecked.

With relief, Nadine left the bar at the end of her shift, headed back through the brightly lit streets, with their overabundance of cruising police cars, an ever-present paddy wagon doing curbside business.

Approaching the house, she glanced upward. A small light shone through the spidery window shades. From habit Nadine knocked in case Hank was inside with Jo. She frowned, visualizing the look of smug sensuality that etched his face when he lounged about the room inside, with the bed still wrinkled and warm from his coupling with Joanna.

"It's open–" Joanna's voice, with an edge of desperation.

Nadine walked inside. Joanna was on her feet. Tense.

"Was Hank here?"

"He was here," Joanna conceded bitterly. "I'm probably wrong, he said, probably just late. Nadine, he doesn't want to believe I'm pregnant." His voice rose stridently.

"He'll know soon enough," Nadine looked at the neatly made bed with a wry smile.

"He'll cut out," Joanna said flatly. "He has already hinted that his boss wants to move him Downtown." She sighed heavily. "Why kid myself? Hank won 't marry me. He's after an easy piece of tail. So I asked him, how about money for an abortion? And that dark face of his bleached right out to white. Who's got that kind of loot? He knows this old broad three blocks over. She knows what to do, Hank said. But not for me." Joanna hammered on the shaky card table with one fist. "I'm not going to end up on a slab DOA because of some butcher!"

"Jo, have the baby," Nadine whispered. "Jo, my mother did." But never could her mother tell her who her father was. Someday she'd find out. Someday.

"How can I?" Jo shot back. "I won't go on welfare. I'd rather take the suicide route."

"No, you wouldn't," Nadine said with calculated calm. "You've got too far to go, once this mess is cleared away. You'll do what has to be done. We'll manage. You're big boned, you won't show for months. Work as long as you can, then I'll take over your job. I can swing both for three or four months, until you've had the baby and you're back on your feet."

"What about the baby?" Joanna's face was stormy. "We can't raise a baby." Her face a kaleidoscope of emotions. "My folks," Joanna whispered. "They won't be happy about this, but it's my baby and they'll take him. Nadine, I'm terrified of a butcher, I don't want to die! If I could have an abortion in a hospital or a sanitarium, all right, but Hank's not footing the bill, even if he could raise it. So this is the only way out. If you think we can swing it, Nadine."

"We'll swing it," Nadine turned to her with rash young optimism. "You'll go on to school for the rest of the quarter. You'll have that much credit." She hesitated, knowing Joanna's pride. "You'll have to go to County Hospital."

"I'll live through that," Joanna assured her dryly. "County Hospital is a way of life, for the likes of us." A contrived flippancy in her voice. "I hope you know what you're letting yourself in for."

"I know we can swing it," Nadine said calmly.

But she wouldn't be able to try for that job at Marshall Field, Nadine remembered unhappily. She'd be tied down here for the next seven months, hating every minute of it.

"You know what I hope?" Joanna broke violently into her thoughts. "I hope his damn prick falls off!"

CHAPTER FOUR

Nadine and Joanna shaped themselves into a new existence, with a tacit determination to survive. No outward difference in their way of life, except that Hank no longer regularly invaded their pad. In these early few weeks of her pregnancy, Joanna was constantly sleeping, falling off in the midst of a newscast.

When they were not at work, they stayed in their flat and read. Or went to the park, in the glorious Chicago autumn, and read. Joanna, who normally scorned the bestseller lists as being Establishment, spent hours engrossed over *Topaz* and *Night Falls on the City*. Nadine automatically following Joanna's lead. And, always, the two girls poured over masses of newspapers which Joanna brought home each evening from the luncheonette.

At regular intervals Joanna talked defiantly about buying a small, reconditioned TV, but they knew they didn't dare spend an unnecessary cent.

"I've got television all day at the luncheonette," Joanna conceded after a lengthy conference about their ability to pay for a reconditioned set on time. "Who needs more? What do you hear these days? Crap! Like that Eric What's-his-name." Her voice deepened with rage. "In one breath he says Martin Luther King may be one of the most noble Americans of this century, and believe me, baby, I wish we had a red man of Martin Luther King's caliber to lead us, and in the next breath he's saying that King ought to go to jail when he defies a court order! Give me a man like Fulbright who says what's on his mind, even if it's against some of our fancy members of Congress. An the day George Wallace dies, I'll pop a bottle of champagne, even if it takes the last cent I have."

"When are you going to the clinic?" Nadine asked gently, because Joanna was hedging. "Jo, you have to sign up."

"Next week." Joanna stirred restlessly. "God, I hate the County Hospital scene!"

"You know how many babies die on the reservation," Nadine reminded somberly. "You know most of it comes from the way the mothers lived before the baby arrives. You have to get the right things, take vitamins." Nadine had gone to the library, brought home some books on prenatal care, and earnestly read them.

"Baby, I know all the statistics," Joanna reminded bitterly. "I was the chick who helped write letters to congressmen. But Indian statistics don't mean a damn to the government. Oh, they know how to search out the Indians when they need soldiers for their wars!" Her eyes moved to the snapshot of her brother Roger, seventeen months her senior, recently scotch-taped to the wall, in his newly acquired infantry uniform. "But it doesn't matter how many Indian kids float around the reservation without ever going to school." She rose restlessly to her feet. "Come on, Nadine, let's go out and walk a bit."

"You'll be swearing about climbing the stairs when we come back," Nadine warned, but she was already reaching for the poncho she'd made for herself. Understanding Joanna's need to escape from their room.

"At least I'll sleep," Joanna pointed out grimly. "Oh, tomorrow I want to go to the library. Don't flip if I don't show up by the time you leave for work. You know Pete McGregor, my instructor in the course. He's given me a list of books he thinks we ought to read." Nadine glanced up sharply, gratefully, at the inclusive "we."

"Give me the list," Nadine offered. "You'll be too bushed after work. I'll go when I wake up. What they don't have I'll reserve." The library was becoming their second home.

"Groovy, baby," Joanna approved. "This is like a private course. All the books I've always wanted to read. Of course," she acknowledged with a chuckle, draping a sweater about her shoulders, "what I don't dig I'll forget. You'll probably read every word of every book," she jibed with good-humored affection.

"McGregor must be a jazzy character." Nadine enjoyed this vicarious sharing of Joanna's course.

"Pete's sharp. Not establishment at all. When we all sit around after coffee, after class, its great. He's about sixty, with this kooky beard, and he always needs a haircut. But when he talks, the kids listen."

Down on the street Nadine and Joanna walked with quick strides, sharing a need for motion. Nadine knew where they'd wind up. At the coffee house .

Always, on her night off, though each week they swore this would be the last because Jo had to get up at seven and she was so tired.

They pushed their way through the closely placed, small tables to a vacant one at the rear. With a cheerful "hi" to people they knew. Within minutes a gaunt blonde youth who managed the impromptu entertainment was at their table, offering the guitar to Nadine. With a half-anticipatory smile, Nadine rose, accepted the guitar, and moved to the small clearing where the spotlight quickly enveloped her.

Head back, hair tumbling about her shoulders, Nadine closed her eyes and began to sing. Her repertoire was slight, specialized, always her own songs, varying from time to time, as she labored over lyrics, changed, added.

She sang two songs familiar to the habitués of the coffee house, hesitated a moment, and launched onto a third and final song. The story of an Indian boy alone in Chicago, who died of an OD in a hall toilet. She felt the intensity of the listeners about her. All of them knowing the Indian boy could have been black or white or brown or yellow. He belonged to them.

As usual, that silence when she finished, a silence that spoke loudly of touched emotions, and then the unstinting applause. Tonight almost deafening, with cries for "More, more." But Nadine refused to return to the spotlight.

She was too shaken, too moved over sharing Eddie so openly with others.

"That was great," Joanna whispered with respect, when Nadine was settled at their table again.

A waiter was scurrying to bring them food and a carafe of coffee, the unspoken financial arrangement for Nadine's appearance as an impromptu entertainer.

"You've been working hard on the one about Eddie. I didn't even know you'd completed it."

Nadine frowned.

"I'm not satisfied with it yet."

Joanna leaned forward urgently.

"Nadine, you must do something with your singing. It could be your road out."

"No," Nadine said quickly, her heart pounding. "I just want to sing. Not as a job."

"I read somewhere the other day, I think it was in *Time*, that the Beatles just turned down one million dollars for a single day's work. Just two performances, in the same day, at Shea Stadium in New York."

"I read that too," Nadine said somberly. "Think what we could do for our families with even one thousandth of that. The Beatles," she continued hurriedly, "turned it down because of some electronic problem. They can't figure out yet how to present the '1967 sound onstage,' they said."

"Zowie, that loot!" Joanna shivered ecstatically. "Can you even imagine that kind of money? Like Richard Burton. He goes out and buys this place for a million bucks because that's the way Liz Taylor likes to travel!" Joanna paused, gazing intently at Nadine. "Baby, you've got a gift. Don't sell it short."

"We have another project on hand," Nadine dodged. "Giving your baby a good start."

"Mama was so sweet when she wrote." Unexpectedly, Joanna's voice thickened with emotion. "Not one word of reproach about how the hell did I let myself get caught, in a day when any girl can buy a diaphragm or go on the pill? Just tell her when the baby comes and she'll take a Greyhound out here to pick up the baby and take him back home. She'll love my baby, as my father will. But more than ever, I must make up to them for all the rottenness on the reservation. I've got to go back to school, get my degree, return to the reservation to teach. Can you imagine their pride, Nadine? That'll mean more to them than bringing them a million dollars."

They lingered for a while, listening to some highly charged but badly written poetry on campus unrest. Joanna was yawning broadly, though apparently glad to be here.

"It's late," Nadine said finally. "Let's go, Jo."

Nadine and Joanna lived a strangely isolated

existence, except for those hours when each was at work. Joanna was having trouble with waistlines, resorting now to oversized safety pins. Nadine took it upon herself to make Joanna two maternity tops.

After much prodding from Nadine, Joanna took a morning off from work and went with Nadine to register at the prenatal clinic. Not at County Hospital, but at a small, private modern hospital, usually outrageously expensive, about which her boss knew. The hospital accepted a few welfare and other indigent patients.

"Wow, look at that jazzy joint," Joanna flipped when they approached the brick-and-glass structure, and followed the sign that led to the discreetly located clinic.

"For the cattle," Joanna pronounced, while they walked to a registration desk. "So we don't nauseate the delicate stomachs of the paying clientele." The clerk stared sharply at Joanna as she moved ahead in place.

"Aren't you taken care of by the Indian Bureau?" the short, firmly corseted but still bulging woman demanded with a look of suspicion.

"I'm taken care of by Joanna Rogers," Joanna shot back with a touch of arrogance that elicited a sharp look from the clerk's eyes. "I work for a living. Now do I sign up at this clinic or don't I?" Joanna's face said she'd be likely to complain to the press if she were refused.

Nadine waited while Joanna filled out the registration card, with vocal annoyance at some of the questions. Then the two girls sat on a bench until Joanna's name was called. Two minutes later, Joanna strode back into the waiting room, head high, eyes hostile.

"I have to come back at nine tomorrow," Joanna reported. "The bastard didn't even see me. I was a clinic card to him."

"You'll be back at nine tomorrow," Nadine insisted firmly.

Autumn was blending into winter. Joanna urged Nadine to buy a coat in one of the thrift shops.

"Baby, you don't know what cold feels like until you walk on Chicago streets when the temperature dips down to twenty-two and the wind blows in over the lake."

The landlord was cheap about supplying heat. Then the furnace went on the blink. When Joanna called to complain, he boredly said, "So turn on the gas stove."

Thanksgiving was a dreary, desolate day. Nadine and Jo felt especially conscious of the distance between family and them. With the approach of Christmas Nadine fought against the alarming onset of depression. Joanna, too, was bogged down by fits of dark despondency that frightened Nadine. Nadine recalled uneasily that Joanna had suffered a breakdown while in high school.

She coaxed Joanna into applying for psychiatric help. A sympathetic but helpless clerk told them frankly, with the backlog of applicants Joanna would be lucky to be interviewed in eighteen months.

"Christmas is a rotten time when you're away from home," Nadine comforted Joanna. It was Christmas Eve. They sat around a tiny table tree contributed by Joanna's boss because the restaurant would be closed on Christmas Day, "and who needs a Christmas tree after Christmas?" he'd pointed out.

"Jo, remember Christmas time at boarding school?"

"I'd rather not remember boarding school." Joanna shifted about in search of a comfortable position.

"I'd have to remember all the subjects I took like 'Laundry' and 'Housekeeping,' where we did the headmaster's laundry three times a week and went into his house to clean up as our field work! I'd have to remember some of the rotten matrons who made a habit of trying to set the bad Indians against the good Indians because they got their kicks out of the riots. I'd have to remember the damn discipline. Bells all the time, every time you took a breath. The set hours for everything. We weren't human."

"The worst part," Nadine said quietly, "were the nights when you were little. Seven years old and all those miles from home. Lying in the darkness and crying into your pillow. Knowing it'd be months before you'd see home again. And nobody cared. Nobody at the boarding school."

"They've got no right to drag kids away from home that way!" Joanna protested violently. "Half the kids don't even speak English. How do they expect those kids to keep up? By the time you hit the fifth or sixth grade, unless you're a mulish Indian, like you and me, you don't give a damn about school. All the excitement about learning has fizzed away. You're just serving time till you can go home again. We've got to have schools on the reservation. That's where I want to teach."

"You will, Jo," Nadine encouraged.

"Will I?" Jo's eyes squinted in contemplation. "Or am I breathing in some esoteric drug nobody's identified yet? A new form of pot, LSD? Why do I dream, Nadine?"

"Let's turn on the news," Nadine ordered briskly, and walked to the small radio that was their lifeline to the world. They hadn't been listening to the news for the last two days. Joanna had been on a strike against news, and Nadine humored her.

The air ricocheted with static, and the two girls half-listened while Nadine went to the range to reheat the coffee left over from their spaghetti dinner. And then, with shattering suddenness, the news acquired a personal impact. Nadine and Joanna clung to the words of the announcer.

"...a meteorological monster dropping a devastating blizzard onto the Southwest, venting particular hardship on the Navajo Indians living in substandard hogans on the reservation. The six states have been declared a national disaster area."

"Joanna!" Nadine stood with percolator in hand, her eyes glazed with alarm.

"Sssh," Joanna ordered tersely, leaning forward to listen to the special report from the local station.

In the mountains, temperatures had dropped to an incredible twenty-five degrees below zero, the newscaster reported, with snowdrifts running up to twelve feet high. The temperature in the desert had been much lower than normal. Highways were closed down. Traveling and communication at a standstill.

"Jo, I have to go home." Nadine's voice soared unnaturally high.

"Cool it, baby," Jo exhorted quietly. She rose to her feet awkwardly, took the percolator from Nadine. "Listen."

"The snowdrifts stretch on endlessly, beyond anything one can imagine," the newscaster continued. "And now the Federal weathermen predict fresh blizzards. The known dead total fifteen, most of them on the Navajo Reservation." Joanna reached for Nadine's hand, held it tightly. "Arizona state officials fear that many more have frozen to death. Starvation stalks on every side. But already, hundreds of Army, Navy, and Air Force men are in action. Helicopters are aloft and crews are dropping food and supplies, tons of hay for the stranded livestock. 'Candy drops' have been made for the twenty-two thousand Indian boarding school students stranded during the holidays. Helicopter crews are watching for pleas for help written in the snow. On the ground plows work around the clock...."

"I have no right to be here!" Nadine balled her hand into fists. She was white with the shock. Trembling. "I belong on the reservation with them!"

"Baby, the government's dropping food by helicopter. You heard him. It's rough, but your folks are bright. They'll survive," Joanna insisted with enforced calm.

"Not even a telephone, to call up and find out!" Nadine blazed bitterly.

"Why are we alive? Why don't they just kill us off and be done with it? What does genocide mean to Americans?"

"We have a right to live!" Joanna lashed back. "This is our country, more than any other American's."

"Jo, I have to try to get back."

"Nadine you can't get through. You heard the radio. Everything's blocked off by the snow. Not even if you were white and rich could you get through now!"

"But, Jo, how can I just stay here, not knowing? Oh, Jo, I ran out on them." Her voice broke.

"Your mother is glad," Joanna said forcefully. "At least you're making your escape. What happens to you in Chicago will shape their future. Can't you see that? You're their hope for tomorrow."

"Jo." Nadine was struggling to control her voice. "If they pull through this storm, I'll do anything to make it up to them. Anything!"

"Write home," Joanna urged. "Your mother'll write back as soon as the mails are going through. Let her know where you are."

Nadine's arms closed at her breasts. Her eyes wore an odd glint.

"Jo, do you honestly think I could make a lot of money singing?"

"I think you can make a bundle. Maybe not right away," Joanna conceded with candor. "You'll have to fight for it, push your way up there, but you've got the quality, baby. That crowd in the coffee house told you that."

"I've got to do it." Nadine's eyes burned brightly. "For Eddie. For mama and the family. For all Indians who need to see what can happen to a red girl in a white world." She lifted her head with pride. "Jo, I'm dying my hair black. I want no part of the white in me. I'm Navajo, Jo. Navajo."

CHAPTER FIVE

It was well into January by the time Nadine heard from her mother. No word of protest, no rebuke.

"It was bad for a while," her mother wrote. "But your father took the mule and went out to the trading post for groceries. The mule wouldn't go, but your father did. We had food, my daughter. We are well."

Joanna was all involved in Eugene McCarthy's announced candidacy for the presidency. Nadine agreed avidly with Joanna's enthusiasm. It was a time of learning, of waiting, Nadine acknowledged, and tried to rout out restlessness.

Dr. Martin Luther King, that most nonviolent of men, was planning a spring march in Washington. The *Pueblo* has been seized. Things were going badly for the Americans in Vietnam. Nadine remembered that her oldest brother would be eligible for the draft in five years.

Early in February, Nadine insisted that Joanna quit work completely, only then learning that the current doctor on duty in the obstetrics clinic had also ordered this. Joanna tired easily. Nadine was astonished at the drain of her strength in working both jobs.

There was little time for anything other than working and sleeping but, despite her exhaustion she practiced her small but growing repertoire of songs. She was increasingly critical and impatient with herself.

Nadine and Joanna had made a pact that she would make no effort to crack the music field until Joanna had delivered the baby and was on her feet again. After that it would be nothing but music. Despite her chronic weariness, Nadine faithfully showed up at the coffee house once a week. Waiting all the other days for that brief period of perfect communication between her and the audience.

By the end of February, not even the prospect of an evening at the Casbah could drag Joanna from the flat on nights when the temperature slid into the teens and the wind howled through the streets. Nadine was anxious about Joanna's recurring despondency.

Nadine walked back through the icy night, shoulders hunched against the cold, ignoring the occasional males who sauntered up with sexual suggestions. Glad tonight for the patrol cars that rolled along the street.

At her building Nadine automatically glanced upward. As she'd expected the lights were on. Joanna kept the lights on even when she was sleeping these days. She hated being alone in the apartment. For all their efforts the place was still roach, and mice, infested.

Arriving at their landing, she thought Joanna was listening to a radio commentator. Then she realized Joanna was talking to someone. She listened, curious. Hank! With a burst of anger, she knocked on the door. From habit not using her key when Hank was around.

"Just a minute." Jo's voice, with a fresh lilt.

It was as though the calendar had rolled back more than half a year, and she was here at the door waiting for the couple inside to arrange themselves and admit her.

The door opened, with Joanna wearing an anxious imploring smile. Hank stood in the center of the room, drinking a can of beer.

"Hi," he greeted her with cautious high spirits.

"Hi."

Nadine stared briefly at the mussed-up bed. Involuntarily, her eyes moved accusingly to Joanna. But despite Joanna's anxious smile, her eyes shone. There was a glow about her.

"You must be frozen," Joanna said solicitously. "I have fresh coffee perking. Unless you'd rather have beer. Hank brought a few cans."

"Coffee," Nadine said tersely, avoiding eyes.

"I'd better be going," Hank said warily. "I'm living way Uptown these days."

"Good night," Nadine said with cold, contained fury. and occupied herself with taking off her coat.

Joanna walked with Hank into the hall. Nadine went to the gas stove, hugged herself before its faint warmth, waiting for the liquid to bubble golden into the top of the percolator. She didn't turn around when Joanna returned to the room.

"You're sore," Joanna reproached quietly.

"Hank's got a nerve," Nadine said, without looking at Joanna. "Coming here now."

"He's had a lot of trouble." Joanna shrugged, hesitated. "He said he was sure I'd got rid of the baby. Somebody told him that."

"Sure they did," Nadine derided. "So what's he going to do about it now?"

A flicker of pain brushed Joanna's face.

"I told him to stay away." Joanna's voice was bitter, confirming Nadine's suspicion that Hank was just passing through her life. "But just tonight I, I couldn't turn him away."

"But, Jo, when you're so far along," Nadine protested.

"It's not too close," Joanna said quickly, and frowned. "I know how it looks, Nadine, that son of a bitch comes back and I let him screw me. But I haven't been near anybody in months, you know that. And it won't hurt the baby. We were careful." She reached for two mugs, put them on the wedge of the counter beside the range, poured the rich golden liquid.

"My mother let my father do it till a week or two before each baby came, and nothing ever happened. I used to lie awake and hear them. The other kids slept, but not me. Nadine, I couldn't turn Hank away!" she burst out. "What the hell else have I got right now? Sometimes, I think I'll go ape before I drop this kid! It's like that black woman in the next pad. She took her welfare check and bought herself a TV set for Christmas. She'll eat beans and potatoes the next month, and some nights she'll go hungry. But she's got her moments of joy with that TV set, and that's how she holds on. Her mother screamed when she saw the set, but Nadine, I understand." Her voice was low, urgent "Everybody has to have something. For her it was that TV set." Unexpectedly, Joanna chuckled. "Baby, don't worry about Hank and me. I'm already pregnant And for a little while, with Hank, I was alive. It was groovy." Her face glowed with a defiant exultation, "For a little while I had a reason to stay alive."

"What kind of a man is he to come back this way?" Nadine challenged, but part of her mind was thinking of what Jo had said with such conviction. Eddie had to have something. Unfortunately, it was drugs.

"You know Hank." Joanna shrugged. "He was in the neighborhood, and in the mood. It didn't take any persuasion, Nadine," she conceded honestly. "I was so damn hot I was ready to take off my clothes before he touched me. For a minute, just a minute, I thought about throwing him out. Because I look so lousy with this belly. But you know, it didn't mean a thing to him, except we had to plan around that belly." Her eyes rested wisely on Nadine. "I'm shocking the hell out of you. It kills me, the way you've managed to stay out of the sack."

"Technically," Nadine pinpointed her relations with

Eddie, "I've never gone the whole way with a fellow. But Eddie and I—we did everything else. It was great." Suddenly, she had a compulsion to talk. "He wanted to do it that way, too, but I always said 'no'." She gazed earnestly into the mug of strong, black coffee Joanna had handed her. "I don't think I can let anybody now— ever."

"You will," Joanna insisted. "You've been turned on. If Eddie was in this room with you alone, right this minute—would you say "no?"

"I'd let him!" Nadine's voice was suddenly husky. "You know I'd let him!"

The two jobs were beginning to take a toll on Nadine. She was exhausted, sleepy. Impatient with difficult customers, where earlier she had been able to ignore the occasional racial slurs brought on by her compulsion to stress her Navajo background.

Joanna had been typically vocal about the presidential commission report, which said that "Our nation is moving towards two societies, one black, one white, separate and unequal."

"Let's make that three!" she hooted indignantly. "When is somebody in this country going to remember red people?"

The last day of March, a white customer at the bar where Nadine worked made a crude overt pass. Nervously, Nadine dodged him. He tried again. She knew why white drinkers came to the bar—to pick up a girl to take to a cheap hotel room in the area. She was tired, irritated, watching the clock, though it would be hours before she went off duty.

"Come on, baby!" The burly drinker leaned forward and thrust a dirty hand down the front of her dress. "Be nice to me, girlie!"

"Stop that! Stop it!" She shoved aside his hand with a glare of revulsion, reached for a glass of beer, and flung it in his face.

"You little bitch!" he yelled. "Hey, Bill!" he gestured for the owner.

Bill–furious, white-faced with apprehension–dashed forward with a towel to try and dry up the customer, who carried on in foul-mouthed indignation.

"What the hell's wrong with you?" Bill yelled at Nadine. "You wanna start a riot? The fuzz'll close me up!"

"He put his hand down the front of my dress!" Tears stung her eyes. "You saw him!"

"You're fired!" the owner yelled. "Here." He strode to the cash register, pulled out five singles. "Get the hell out of here and don't come back." And then he turned to placate the still-swearing customer.

Trembling, Nadine went into the back for her coat, and then hurried out the side door into the night. Oh, she'd been really bright, she chastised herself. At least, she'd brought money home regularly. But she wouldn't let anybody touch her like that!

Nadine worried about the effect on Joanna, yet once inside the flat, she spilled out the story of the ugly encounter at the bar. "What are we going to do, Jo?"

"That was a long run, baby. Most girls last three or four weeks. Besides, you're ready to fall apart, trying to hold down two jobs. Oh, I wish this kid would get born!" Jo sighed with impatience. "They get you out of the hospital in three or four days, I hear–if you come in through the clinic. In two weeks I'll be back at work." She hesitated. "You hang on to the luncheonette job, baby. Though I think you ought to stop once I'm working again and make a stab at breaking into singing. We'll squeak through on one salary if we have to."

Unexpectedly, she laughed. "God, we sound like an old married couple."

"You go back to the luncheonette," Nadine decided seriously. "I'll look for a night job, then I can make rounds about singing in the daytime." She hesitated. "One of the fellows at the coffee house gave me a list of agents to go see. He says it's tough, but I ought to try."

"Before you go," Jo chided affectionately, "let me give you another hair-dye job. What kind of Navajo balladeer has blonde roots?"

Nadine knew Jo was struggling to keep from falling into a heavy depression, and she was concerned. Twice since Christmas Jo had made the trip across to the college to talk to Pete McGregor about the possible scholarship. Pete was hopeful, but cautious about the outcome of his campaign.

"He's trying," Jo reported, churning with restlessness. "But there are so many students who are in on this minority kick. Oh, come on, Nadine, what chance have I got?"

"Pete wouldn't he trying if he didn't feel there was a fair amount of hope, Jo." Nadine strived to be logical. "It takes time."

"All I've got right now is time!" Jo burst out impatiently. "Every day seems a hundred hours long. I can't even read any more. I wish I could take some pill, and this baby would be born."

"Another five or six weeks," Nadine soothed. "You'll survive."

"I promised Pete I'd work on some promotional material," Jo remembered. "He's starting a 'Students for McCarthy' program here."

"Once the baby's born, we'll have time to work with them." Nadine watched Joanna for some flicker of enthusiasm. Usually, talk about Gene McCarthy brought a glow from her. Especially now, Jo needed to be involved in a cause. "I like that man McCarthy," Nadine said with sudden intensity. "He makes me feel better about tomorrow."

"They'll crucify him," Joanna predicted morbidly. "You'll see."

"Did you know he writes poetry?" Nadine's eyes were luminous. "I heard somebody reading something of his at the coffee house the other night. It made me realize how much I have to learn."

"You've got plenty of time," Jo said with a touch of her old assurance. "You'll make it big."

They started at the sharp pounding on the door.

"Coming," Nadine called out, and crossed to the door, The welfare recipient who'd spent her check on a TV set hovered, pop-eyed, in the doorway.

"Hey, you kids don't have a TV—you know what just happened?"

"What, what?" Jo demanded avidly. "'Truce in Vietnam?"

"The first installment," their neighbor chortled. "LBJ just announced on television he ain't seekin'—and won't accept—the nomination of his party. Now ain't that somethin' to sing about?"

But Pete McGregor had said, Nadine recalled secondhand, that Lyndon Johnson would probably go down in history for bringing about more reform for the poor than any president.

Nadine climbed the stairs to the apartment, glad to be out of the blustery April wind that swept through the streets. She'd stopped at the small grocery down the block—with their outrageous prices—because today she was too tired, too cold, to walk nine blocks to save twelve cents.

Joanna had the radio on. Near the landing, Nadine identified the recording. A recent Bobby Dylan release, "The Battle of Frankie Lee and Judas Priest."

Nadine unlocked the door, and then walked in with a prepared smile because Joanna was so persistently morose these days.

"I bought a can of soup," she reported. "And powdered milk." She always insisted that Joanna drink milk every day. That rarity on the reservation.

"I'm not hungry," Joanna said distastefully. "No matter where I sit, I can't get comfortable today." She dropped onto one end of her bed, still rumpled from an earlier attempt to nap.

"Have some soup, anyway," Nadine persuaded, and shivered. "Wow, it's cold outside!"

In a few minutes they sat down at the card table with the bright plastic cover Nadine had bought at the thrift shop. The soup was hot and tasty, the toast properly crisp.

The radio was too loud, but Nadine realized that in some fashion this assuaged Joanna's restlessness. They talked over the blare of recorded music. Joanna was scheduled to go to the clinic next day. She was on an every-two-weeks schedule now. Joanna hated the impersonal clinic, and spoke with contempt about one of the nurses who was unsubtle in her bigotry.

"I'll bet she makes a guy show her his birth certificate before he screws her to prove he's of the Caucasian race," she drawled.

"More coffee?" Nadine rose from the table to go to the range.

"God no!" Joanna grinned. "The more I drink, the more I have to run to that ice-cold john." She sighed. "Which is right now."

Nadine went to the radio, lowered the volume,

settled down with a fresh mug of coffee. In a few moments Joanna returned. Something about her face captured Nadine's attention.

"I seem to have sprung a leak." She spoke low-keyed. "That means I'm in business."

"Not right away." Nadine smiled. Joanna was playing it cool, but Nadine saw the tic in her left eyelid that betrayed her tension. "With a first one it always takes a while, remember? Any contractions yet?"

"No," Joanna said, and suddenly leaned forward, wincing. "Yes!"

"When did they tell you to come in to the hospital?" Nadine was moving across the room for the clock.

"When the contractions are running about six or seven minutes apart," Joanna reported. She leaned back in her chair, her face strained. "I'd better pack my toothbrush." She tried to be flippant.

"Oh, Jo, we'll be sitting here for hours timing contractions," Nadine teased gently. "We'll probably be here till morning."

"This one may have other ideas," Joanna warned with a grim smile. "It's going to be a rotten night to stand out and wait for a bus."

"We'll take a cab," Nadine decided recklessly.

"Are you kidding?" Jo was derisive. She stared at the percolator, still half-full on the stove. "They told me to stop eating once the contractions started, but a cup of coffee won't hurt—"

"I'll get it." Instantly Nadine was on her feet. She poured coffee, brought it to the table, and launched into a casual monologue about what had happened at the luncheonette during the day. Joanna was hunched over the table, frowning with a fresh contraction.

"Baby, I think we ought to cut out," Joanna said quietly.

"But the contractions have just started," Nadine protested. "They're still running twelve minutes apart. You said they warned you not to come in too early. It always takes time with a first baby."

Joanna lifted her eyes to Nadine's.

"It's not the first, Nadine," she whispered, and smiled wryly at the shock on Nadine's face. "The first was when I was fourteen and at boarding school. I had that one alone in the girls' bathroom. He was dead–it wasn't quite seven months. Nobody had even guessed I was pregnant."

"Jo, you should have told the doctor," Nadine reproached.

"I couldn't!" She closed her eyes for a moment. "I never talk about it. Nadine, you know what it was like at boarding school." Her voice thickened with remembered frustration. "Lonely all the time. Always bogged down with rules. Once in a while they'd let the girls and boys get together. We all stood around in this big room. You could manage to hold hands, but move close together, and the matrons blew the whistle. Anyhow, I met this boy–a Sioux–and he turned me on like crazy. No boy ever touched me until we sneaked out to meet that night. There we were, out in the barn, screwing like crazy–and a matron and two aides walked in. I was expelled, then sent off to another school. I didn't even know I was pregnant until I was four months along, then I was too scared to tell anybody."

"Oh, Jo." Nadine shivered with compassion.

"I got these terrible contractions one night and I ran to the bathroom. I didn't even realize what was happening at first," she mocked herself. "And then the baby was coming–I caught him myself, sitting there on the toilet seat. I was so scared. I was sure he was dead. I didn't know what to do. I started to scream, and they all came running. That's when I had the breakdown–after they sent me home from there."

"Jo, it could have happened to any girl at boarding school." A vein was distended in Nadine's throat as she spoke. "It could have happened to me."

"Baby, I think we ought to cut out," Jo said briskly, battling another contraction. "It's going to take a while to get across town."

Nadine clutched her coat together at the throat, her head bent over as Joanna and she trudged against the blustery wind that zinged along Sheridan Road. Joanna swore at her own slowness.

"We'll never get a cab here," Joanna warned, shivering in her coat which didn't quite fit across her swollen belly. "We'd better try for a bus."

"No," Nadine said with a new stubbornness. "You're riding to the hospital in a car."

Nadine anxiously searched the slow stream of traffic. Not a cab in sight. This was a bad hour. She glanced uneasily at Joanna. Too late to phone for a cab, to stand shivering in a doorway till it arrived. Just ahead, she spied a police car moving toward them.

On impulse, Nadine moved away from Joanna, stepped off the curb. She imperiously flagged the car, which pulled to a stop. The cop at the wheel rolled down the steamed-up window.

"Could you drive us to the hospital?" Nadine asked urgently. "My friend's in labor."

In seconds, the police car was at the curb. One cop was out of the car, hurrying to Joanna, reassuring her while he helped her solicitously into the car.

"We all get training in delivering kids," the cop at the wheel said cheerfully as they sped through the night with siren screaming, "but we'd just as soon leave that to the doctor."

The cops deposited them at the admitting entrance to the hospital. At the door, Nadine waited sympathetically while Joanna doubled up with another contraction.

"Okay." Joanna smiled shakily. "Let's get in out of this damn cold."

The middle-aged woman at the desk looked impatient when Joanna presented herself for admission. She'd been interrupted in the midst of what was obviously a personal conversation. "Your card, please," she said coldly, without respect. Consternation rode over Jo's face. "Oh, God, in the rush I left it behind at home!"

"Shall I go back and get it?" Nadine offered because the woman at the desk was frowning in annoyance. "Jo, where did you leave it?" she pushed, because the woman was tapping impatiently with long, lacquered fingernails.

"Look, I don't have it," Jo told the woman, striving to be polite but firm. "My name is Joanna Rogers, I've been coming to the clinic for months. Can't you send for my chart?"

"Who's your doctor?" The woman behaved as though Jo were trying to force entry into the hospital.

"Who knows?" Jo flared. "There's a new one every time I come to the clinic." But she frowned in concentration. "Berkstein," she remembered triumphantly. "I heard the nurse call him Dr. Berkstein, the last time."

"Please sit down outside," the woman ordered. "I'll call you."

Nadine reached for Jo's hand as they walked together into the waiting room of the admitting office, deserted at this hour. Ten minutes later, while Nadine and Jo waited restlessly, a girl about two or three years older than Jo arrived, surrounded by husband and mother. A wheelchair was brought in. She was escorted upstairs, husband and mother trailing behind. The woman at the desk strode out of the admitting office, through the waiting room, and disappeared into the rear of the hospital.

"How long does it take them to find a chart?" Nadine demanded, uneasy because Joanna's contractions were closer. She'd timed them with Jo at five minutes on the wall clock. Perspiration beaded Jo's forehead now. Her knuckles were white when she clenched her fists with each contraction. Nadine rose to her feet, a new defiance m her. "I'm going to find that woman."

"No!" The urgency in Jo's voice stopped her. "Stay with me."

Five minutes later the woman returned. Instantly, Nadine was on her feet.

"You have to admit her," Nadine said tightly. "Unless you want her to have the baby right here in the waiting room."

The woman recoiled with distaste.

"We can't find the chart anywhere," she explained uneasily. "They're painting the chart room and there's been some disorder in the files."

"What am I supposed to do?" Jo demanded. "Have you ever delivered a baby?"

The woman whitened. Nadine's eyes held hers. With a fresh contraction Jo made no effort to conceal her discomfort.

"We have rules, you know," the woman said petulantly, and squinted in concentration. "Take her over to Emergency," she decided. "While the chartroom clerk searches. I'll call over there and explain. It's out this door, to the left, all around to the back. You'll see the sign."

Out into the cold again, with the wind cutting

sharply against their hot faces. Nadine held Joanna's hand firmly in hers, stricken to see Joanna minus her cool, her bravado. They made their way through rows of shrubbery to Emergency.

An ambulance backed up. Attendants removed a woman in a lustrous mink coat, supine on a stretcher. Nadine turned away, sickened at the splash of blood across the woman's face. Inside, nurses dashed about to receive the new arrival. A call echoed on the loudspeaker for a doctor. Nobody was at the desk.

Nadine deposited Jo on a bench near the desk, stood there determinedly as though to force someone to give them attention. A heavy-set, elderly woman sat opposite, with her visibly terrified daughter on one side and an embarrassed son-in-law on the other.

"A basin, please," the woman called out loudly. "Somebody had better bring me a basin."

The daughter stumbled awkwardly to her feet, to go for help. The son-in-law looked away. An aide dashed forward with a basin. A little too late.

"Mommie, I want to go home," wailed a scared four year old with a gash above her eyebrow. "I want to go home."

"In a little while, darling," her mother soothed. "As soon as we have the cut fixed." But she lifted the child into her lap.

The phone rang shrilly on the desk, but everybody seemed to be involved with the woman who had just been brought in. The phone continued to ring. A nurse, muttering with impatience, charged out of a room to pick up the phone.

"Yes, Miss Renoir is here," the nurse said briskly. "She's being treated."

"Cecile Renoir," Joanna whispered in sudden recognition. "That was the broad in the ambulance."

Nadine looked at her inquiringly, the name ringing no bells. "She's jet-set, baby. So rich it makes me turn green to think about it"

The nurse was off the phone, hurrying back to the room where Cecile Renoir lay.

"Miss!" Nadine was on her feet, color staining the gold of her high cheekbones. "My friend is in labor. The admitting office said they were calling you about her."

"Yes." The woman glanced at Joanna briefly. "She's to wait here until they can locate the chart. She can't be admitted till they have some identification that she's a patient."

"Her contractions are four minutes apart," Nadine said tightly. "Do you want her to have the baby sitting there on the bench?"

The nurse hesitated. Jo was bent over, eyes shut tightly in pain, fighting not to cry out. And from the room Cecile Renoir screeched loudly.

"I tell you I want a plastic surgeon! Get one here immediately! I know my face is cut up!" An imperious but terrified voice, almost out of control. "Get the plastic surgeon!"

"Take her in there," the nurse ordered Nadine, pointing to an examining cubby opposite Cecile Renoir's room. "She'll be able to lie down there. I'll bring you a gown in a moment. We'll send her over as soon as the chart comes through."

Nadine and Joanna walked to the tiny examining room. The door opposite was wide open. Cecile Renoir lay stripped on a table with a team of doctors and nurses bustling about her.

"In here," Nadine said with a forced smile for Joanna, and pushed aside the entry curtain.

"I never took the natural childbirth course," Joanna

reminded grimly, "but true to reservation fashion this kid might arrive that way."

Nadine helped Joanna onto the slab, feeling herself perspiring, from nerves and the elevated thermostat in the hospital. If Joanna had been "Female, Caucasian," Nadine told herself bitterly, she wouldn't be here on an emergency-room examining table missing clinic card or not.

Joanna lay back, her face drained of color, biting her lips to keep back the sounds that threatened to escape. Outside, the elderly woman was violently sick, over and over again. The little girl was crying, pleading to be taken home. Cecile Renoir continued yelling in the kind of language Nadine was accustomed to associating with the bar customers.

The nurse pushed back the curtain to hand over a hospital gown, and disappeared. Nadine helped Joanna into the gown and neatly folded up the discarded clothes.

"I'm going to ask about a doctor," Nadine said when they had waited twenty minutes, during which Joanna chided herself for being spoiled. An earlier-generation Indian would have squatted on the dirt floor and dropped her baby onto a piece of much-washed cloth. Now the look on Jo's face frightened Nadine. The contractions were coming one on top of another. "I'll just be a minute, Jo."

"Stay!" Joanna cried out sharply. "Nadine, the baby's coming! Oh, my God!"

"What's going on in here?" A small, officious nurse stuck her head in the cubicle with a glare of annoyance.

"My baby's coming," Joanna shot back fiercely. "I'm holding his head in my hands!"

"You'll have to leave!" the nurse told Nadine briskly.

"Dr. Kingston!" Her voice carried above the outside din. "Dr. Kingston! Delivery in Examining Room C!"

Nadine stumbled back into the waiting room. A tall Negro doctor, presumably Dr. Kingston—was striding toward the cubicle where Joanna was delivering her baby. A nurse stepped forward, her face white with shock, to put a briefly detaining hand on his arm.

"Dr. Kingston, did you hear? Martin Luther King has just been assassinated!"

Nadine sat down in the waiting room, not looking at anything, trying to assimilate what she'd heard. Joanna was bringing life into the world. And Dr. King—probably one of the country's most noble men—was dead. And that insolent woman with the cut-up face—Cecile Renoir—was screeching for a private suite, her personal physician, and a plastic surgeon.

Nadine reached into her duffel bag for a piece of paper and pencil. Words moved together in her mind about the tragedy that had descended upon the world. The black man had lost his leader. The red man had yet to find his. Perhaps the child being born in Examining Room C would be that leader. Some red child being born this minute might lead his people out of the hell, the desolation of being fifth-class citizens....

CHAPTER SIX

Seth Coles rested his tall, slender frame against the wall of the corridor, opened his sheepskin-lined jacket. He thrust one large well-shaped hand through the length of dark, tousled hair that fell low on his neck, and gazed into the room where Pete McGregor sat talking to a girl.

Damn, he had to see McGregor before he flew back to New York. He'd promised the local group he'd tie up McGregor's support. But if he missed the ten PM out of O-Hare, he couldn't get another until one AM. And by the time he got into New York it'd be five. He'd never make it to classes.

With the competition what it was in medical school he was working night and day to keep his grades at top level. The folks would flip if they knew he was out here, involving himself in this scene. He'd get all that jazz about how they were sacrificing themselves to put him through med school, how these days med school was a privilege of the rich.

Today had shook him. His hand touched the tiny transistor radio jutting out of his jacket pocket. All day he'd followed the funeral down in Atlanta. He'd caught part of it on television. The two hundred thousand whites and blacks who had followed behind the mules and the old farm wagon that creaked down the Atlanta streets with the body of Martin Luther King. Coretta Scott King, beautiful in her grief, the mother figure in the tragedy that involved them all. The usual black faces of the Ebenezer Baptist Church congregation sprinkled with the faces of white leaders, visibly moved by this second assassination in one decade.

Olivia had been churning to go down to Atlanta. He'd wanted to go. Right now, though, it was more important for him to be here with Pete McGregor, talking up the McCarthy campaign. The country was in such desperate need of a leader. Gene McCarthy could be that man.

Seth glanced apprehensively at his watch, and then moved his body for a view of the interior of the room. A slight, dark-haired girl sat with her back to him, talking urgently to McGregor.

"I thought everything was going to be all right," the girl was saying intensely. "The baby was fine, the doctor said Jo was all right. Her mother came in from Colorado, saw Jo at visiting hours, and took a plane back with the baby. Jo didn't want her traveling all that distance on the bus with the baby. They left and–" Her voice broke, "Jo just fell apart–" Pete leaned forward to cover her hand with his. "They've transferred her to County, to the psycho ward! She told me to come to you, Mr. McGregor. She said there was nobody else. She'll really go nuts if she has to stay there!"

"We'll bail her out," Pete McGregor said firmly, one hand toying with his beard as he squinted thoughtfully. "I have a friend who's a psychiatrist. I'll buzz him–" He glanced at his watch. "I can reach him in about twenty minutes. If he thinks it's okay, we'll have him sign Jo out. We have to go through this routine." He hesitated. "But we have to be sure she'll be able to cope, Nadine," he warned. "She'll have to see the psychiatrist regularly."

"She'll be fine if she gets out of that awful place."

"Wait for me in the lobby," McGregor instructed with quiet assurance. "I have an appointment with a young fellow from New York–he should be here any moment. I have to talk to him for a while, then I'll pick you up. Better still," McGregor corrected himself, "go over to the cafeteria and have some coffee. Then we'll cab over to County. And don't worry, Nadine, Jo'll come through this."

Seth propelled himself into view, smiled tentatively as Pete McGregor spied him, and waved. He'd never met McGregor, but there'd been some highly charged correspondence. On sight he liked the man.

The girl rose and turned to walk toward the door. Slim, sensational carriage, Seth noted. A quality about her that turned him on, as though she'd pressed a button. For an instant, as she walked through the door, their eyes met, and he felt a rush of excitement deep within him that he told himself was ridiculous.

"Excuse me–" A breathy voice with a wistful yet sexy quality.

Seth strode into the classroom where Pete McGregor was on his feet in welcome. Back in New York they'd been most impressed by what they heard about this guy. It was important to tie up with him if they were going to build unity. At this stage, with RFK making noises about jumping into the pond, this was essential.

"You're Coles," McGregor said with quiet pleasure. "Sit down."

Seth was impressed by the way Pete McGregor settled down to basics. He explained his own activities in the eleven-plus hours he'd been racing about Chicago, discussed the groups with whom he'd met, outlined what his own group hoped to accomplish by organizing.

"We knew we had to do something besides marching on the Pentagon. It was beautiful, down there on the October march," he admitted with a reminiscent gleam of satisfaction in his eyes. "But the physical type of protesting—the marching, the picketing—wasn't doing much more than providing us with an emotional outlet. I guess at the beginning most of us didn't think we had any chance at all of putting McCarthy in—we were mainly hopeful of pushing LBJ out and giving somebody else a chance to stop the Vietnam war. But now everything's different." He squinted reflectively. "If we work hard enough we might—we just might—put Gene McCarthy into the White House." He sighed heavily. "What a stinking shame the eighteen-year-olds won't be able to vote in November!"

McGregor questioned earnestly, made suggestions, wrote down notes for his own references. Always cutting through to essentials, Seth noted with admiration. For a few minutes they talked about the terrible loss of Martin Luther King, and then McGregor was glancing at his watch and Seth remembered the girl sitting in the cafeteria. Remembered the way she looked.

Tired but exhilarated, Seth took the airport bus for O'Hare. Glancing over his shoulder as the bus sped through the streets, Seth took a last look at the sweep of the Chicago skyline, with the John Hancock Building rising so impressively above the surrounding buildings. It was supposed to be higher than the Empire State.

He settled his long legs as comfortably as he could in the cramped quarters of the bus, gazing with distaste at the ugly steel girders that crossed the river with unattractive regularity. That was the Merchandise Mart over there, owned by the Kennedy family. He frowned.

There were few points on which Seth agreed with his parents, particularly these days, but mom and dad were both strongly for Gene–he found satisfaction in that. Dad swore he'd never forgive the Kennedys for the way they steam-rollered Adlai Stevenson. In a way, the McCarthy kids were the new Stevensonians.

The bus was moving beyond the city, passing the modern, new high-rise apartments, the fancy motels. The Marriott there was a lush sight. Seth suppressed a yawn. Exhausted, but happy about his meeting with Pete McGregor.

On the plane he dozed until they landed at Kennedy. One AM on the nose, New York time. He boarded the airport bus with an eagerness to be done with this day. He'd take any bet that Livvy would be waiting at the pad for him. No patience, that chick, he thought, resigned and tired. She'd want to know every minute detail of what happened since he flew out this morning.

Seth cabbed down from the terminal to Fifth Street, dropped the cab at the avenue, and walked across Filth to the sagging tenement where he had inherited a fifth floor walk-up. Miraculously, still only forty-seven bucks a month. A wino ducked out of a doorway at his approach, with an open hand–the familiar plea. A pair of hippies, obviously stoned, walked arm in arm.

He glanced up at the entrance to the building. The pad was dark. Livvy must have gone back to her place. According to the college records, Livvy commuted between Ardsley and New York City. The college knew nothing of the jazzy high-rise apartment on West Ninth which she shared with two other coeds of widely different political convictions.

Seth walked cautiously into the dark, unlocked foyer. He started up the stairs, lighted at intervals with twenty-five-watt bulbs, swore under his breath when he nearly slid on a wet mass of garbage.

Behind a door on the first landing, the late late show was kept to a discreet quietness. Two flights up–on the floor below his own–the pair of lesbians who worked in an off-off-Broadway nudie show were screeching invectives at each other. If they didn't cool it soon, the cops from the precinct down the street would be banging on the door.

At his pad, Seth fumbled in his pocket for the keys. First the Siegel, then the conventional lock. He reached for the knob, turned it, shoved the door wide, moved cautiously into the kitchen to grope for the light chain.

"Hi–" He started at the low, languorous drawl that emanated from the living room which held the double Hollywood bed he'd inherited with the apartment. The closet bedroom served as his study. "I thought you'd never get home."

"I made great connections," he chided, turning on the overhead kitchen light

"Want a beer?" Livvy tossed back the covers and sat up, naked. A small, perfect figure whose potential Seth well knew. But she was already scrambling into his robe, nestling at the foot of the bed against such a moment as this. His landlord was notoriously parsimonious about the heating, finding it to his advantage to pay fines at regular intervals rather than provide the heat the law demanded. "I brought up beers when I came over. I was feeling rich."

"Coffee," Seth substituted, stifling a yawn.

Livvy was going to hit the sack. He could read it in her smug, hazel eyes, in the deliberate show she was making of pulling the robe tightly about her naked body. Personally, he could have omitted tonight. He had to be up at seven–one day was all he could afford to miss at classes.

"You won't sleep if you drink coffee," Livvy warned, but she was moving into the kitchen to put up water for instant.

"I don't intend to sleep for a while." He grinned because Livvy was making that quiet inventory of him that told him exactly where her mind dwelt. God, this chick was ready half a dozen times a day! She said this was what came out of her two years in analysis. Before that, she was all hung up about sex. "Damn, it's cold in this shithouse." It was the ugly cold of a house that hadn't been sufficiently warm in years. "I'll bring out the electric heater."

Seth pulled the heater—which did shocking things to his Con Ed bill—out of its hiding place, plugged it into action. After the rigors of today, he craved some comfort. Damn, that wind in Chicago had been raw!

Livvy stood by the gas range, waiting for the water to boil. She'd put up just enough to fill the two mugs. She wasn't wasting time.

"Seth, you happy about McGregor?"

"I think he's great."

As they drank coffee Seth outlined what had been discussed, winding up with a report of his personal reactions to Pete McGregor.

"There was a great-looking girl talking to McGregor. Wonder who she was," he teased.

"Oh, shut up," Livvy murmured provocatively.

She undid the robe, letting the sides part to show the small, high breasts with the incredibly large nipples.

"You're going to catch cold," he jibed. But his eyes clung to the view of her, remembering how it could be with Livvy.

"You'll catch pneumonia," he pursued, and cleared

his throat in the small signal that indicated his arousal.

"I won't," she promised, her eyes smug. "Strip, sweetie."

He slid his feet to the floor, careful to avoid contact with the electric heater. He'd thought he was bushed, too uptight about the meetings today, to think about making it. But with Livvy hovering that way, playing the scene out in her mind, he was conscious already of the rise of desire.

"I love your gorgeous blue eyes," she murmured throatily. Her gaze glued to his crotch.

"I notice," he chuckled, shucking off his jeans, now deliberately slow in removing his shorts.

"Oh, come on," she reproved, and climbed across the bed to tug at the shorts. One hand fondling provocatively.

"Hey, you want to waste that?" he clucked.

"Seth, let me do everything," she coaxed. "Please, baby."

"You getting bugged on this women's lib scene?" he taunted. But he allowed her to push him across the bed.

"I thought they were all bull dykes or ugly broads who couldn't get a guy to take them to bed without a pillowcase over their faces."

She stretched her brief length beside him, threw a leg across his thighs while her hands delved and her breasts grazed his chest.

"Baby, are you going to take all night to get this show on the road?" he protested moments later, because desire was rising hard and Livvy was content to nuzzle and touch.

"My show," she reminded firmly. "What's the rush? You have to catch a jet somewhere?"

"Livvy," he said thickly, his hands reaching toward her breasts. It drove her ape when he bit her nipples.

"Wait," Livvy ordered, her child's hands tightening at his thighs, her mouth parted, reaching. "You won't mind, baby," she soothed. And then she was silent.

His hands closed in about the short, dark hair, cradling her head while the wild heat rippled through him.

"Yeah, baby, yeah–"

And then he threw her over on her back–and it began all over again.

The alarm jingled raucously in the winter-morning drabness. Seth swore, reached over to silence it. Livvy lay naked, only her legs covered by the blankets. Without opening her eyes, she frowned her resentment of the intrusion.

"Hey, Livvy, rise and shine." For a moment, he toyed with the idea of waking her in the manner she liked best. No, no time. Besides, they'd had enough last night. No, Livvy never had enough. "Livvy." He ran a hand across her breasts. She smiled and murmured approval, eyes still shut. "You got an early class today?"

"Screw it," she turned over.

"You know better," Seth reminded. "You let your grades slide down, you're going to lose that jazzy pad." Her folks had been lowering the boom lately.

"Oh, Seth, I forgot to tell you." Her eyes opened. "Your old lady called last night." Seth frowned and went toward the john. "She was pissed off because I answered again. Is it against the law for you to sleep with a broad?" she mocked.

"What did Mom want?" He felt vaguely uncomfortable.

"She said to remind you about dinner tomorrow

night at the apartment. Your sister's flying in."

"I remembered," Seth lied, and closed the door of the bathroom behind him.

Damn, he muttered to himself, why did Mom always call when Livvy was here? Mom disapproved, though she tried to play it cool. To her he was cheating on his schooling every time he laid a chick. Hell, he wasn't getting married.

He still had two more years of med school, his internship, and residency ahead of him before he could be earning any decent money. Mom and Dad never let up about what it was costing them to put him through school. The bank loans, the staying on in the old rent-controlled apartment on Riverside to keep their expenses down....

"Seth–" Livvy called, interrupting his introspection. "I'm going to make it to Chicago with you with no sweat. My sister and her husband are cutting out for Europe in August. I'm going to stay at their pad. That makes it acceptable to the parents. They figure I wouldn't dare screw in that holy sanctuary."

"Hurry up," Seth ordered coming out, showered and shaved. "I'm throwing two frozen bagels in the oven. That's all we'll have time for if we're going to make it to class."

CHAPTER SEVEN

Nadine walked swiftly. She strode past the small groceries, the pawnshops, the secondhand stores, the missionary churches and taverns. Trying to blot out the ugliness that surrounded her because there was an aura of hopefulness in this lovely spring day.

She slowed down momentarily to inspect a clock in a small shop window. Jo would be home from the luncheonette by now. Tonight was one of Jo's evenings to go to the psychiatrist. They'd eat early so Jo could get there on time.

When Jo left, she'd go over to the McCarthy store-front headquarters and address more envelopes.

Nadine approached the entrance to her building, where a pair of teenage Indians were making a deal with a pusher. She turned hurriedly into the hallway.

Walking up the last flight, Nadine sniffed appreciatively at the aroma of simmering spaghetti sauce. They tried not to eat spaghetti more than twice a week, because of the starch. She used to wonder how Mama could be fat when they ate so badly. Now she knew—all the starches they ate. Beans and potatoes and tortillas to fill up the belly.

She reached for her key, slid it into the lock. Jo had the radio on. The Mamas and Papas wailed "Monday, Monday" into the room as she entered.

"Hi." Jo smiled at her while she drained the spaghetti with a plate across the mouth of the pot, and swore violently when a gush of steam hit her wrist.

"That smells great." Nadine slid off her coat with a smile. "Guess what? Good news. I've got a job!"

"Doing what?" Jo glanced up with a dazzling smile,

but her eyes were cautious.

"The money is shitty," Nadine warned, utilizing Jo's favorite adjective. "Waitress at the Casbah–but they want me to sing every night, too."

"But they're not paying you for that," Jo pinpointed. "Baby, they're getting away with murder. You're building up a following there. I know people who come just to hear you sing."

Nadine smiled wistfully.

"I'm glad somebody likes me. I bomb out with the agents."

"Those two-bit creeps you went to see?" Jo scoffed. "You're too damned good for them!"

"I don't know how to handle myself with them," Nadine admitted honestly. "I panic, just coming face to face with them." Remembering the raw pitches, the bold looks, the wandering hands she awkwardly dodged. "I can't make rounds, Jo."

"All those white faces?" Jo jibed.

"All the offers to go into the office and lie down," Nadine said bluntly. "The only job offers have been as a topless dancer." Nadine shrugged in frustration.

"Screw them! Someday they'll be groveling at your feet. Come on, let's eat," she ordered briskly. "I've got to go have my brains turned inside out."

"Anyhow, I like being in the coffee house," Nadine said slowly while they sat down at the card table before steaming plates of spaghetti. "I'll have a chance to try out new material." Her face glowed. "There's this great feeling–between them and me, when I'm up there singing. A kind of contact that tells me when I'm right and when I'm wrong."

"What are you working on now?" Jo stared at the folded-up sheet of paper protruding from Nadine's blouse pocket She went nowhere without paper and pencil within reach.

"A song about Mayor Daley," Nadine said somberly, and Joanna's eyes flashed.

"I'd like to cut off his balls and shove them down his throat!"

"I wish I were old enough to vote," Nadine said passionately. "I would vote against Mayor Daley. I would vote against anybody who preaches violence."

"Eat," Jo said with mock sternness. "I have to go to the shrink and you have to go stuff envelopes for McCarthy."

In May, Pete McGregor told a jubilant Jo she was making it into college on a scholarship. He'd also rustled up a summer job out there for her. She'd live in the home of a college professor and care for his two youngsters. When school opened, she'd remain as baby-sitter in return for room and board. Jo would have preferred by-passing the summer job, but didn't feel it politic to turn this down.

Nadine fought panic at the thought she would be alone in Chicago. Still, she rejected Joanna's suggestion that she gamble and move on out to California. She had a shaky foothold here. It was frightening to consider starting all over again.

"I won't be leaving until mid-June," Jo reminded, exhilarated at this final success, yet sympathetic to Nadine's uncertainty. "The rent will be paid up until the first of July—you'll have plenty of time to find another roommate."

"It won't be you." Nadine sighed unhappily. She hated the prospect of sharing the pad with a strange girl. "I'll probably wind up with some awful kook."

"I've had a few," Jo admitted with a wry smile.

"You use your head, baby—you're sharp. Don't take the first chick who looks interested."

But the ensuing weeks were colored for Nadine by the realization that Jo would soon be climbing aboard a Greyhound, California-bound. Then she would be alone.

Nadine flipped the hamburgers over, returned to finish up the tossed salad that was within their budget now that the cheap summer vegetables were coming in. The apartment was sticky with humidity, with the heat of a long day's sun beating on the roof directly above. Nadine pushed away the sweep of hair that rested along one high cheekbone, glanced at the clock. Jo ought to be walking in any minute.

Next week this time Jo would be on a plane bound for Los Angeles. The professor for whom she was going to work had sent the plane ticket. Pete had arranged that, Nadine thought with gratitude. How comfortable to have money! To fly across the country in a few hours.

How awful it was going to be here, how empty, without Jo sharing.

Nadine straightened up, listened attentively. That was Jo now, climbing the last flight in her thonged sandals.

"Hi,"" Jo wearily mopped at her forehead with a tissue. "That rotten boss of mine keeps swearing he's putting in air-conditioning, but it won't ever happen. All that stinking fan does is move the hot air around." She inspected the salad bowl with approval. "You're a good kid, Nadine Scott. This is a salad night."

"Plus hamburgers," Nadine reminded, pointing to the skillet. "It was on sale."

"You hear anything from that chick about sharing?" Jo slid out of her sandals with a sigh of relief.

"She's cutting out," Nadine reported. "Mama Stringfleld sent over a girl, too. But this one came in stoned. I said I had somebody. I figure when we go over to the Community Center tonight I'll put up a notice on the bulletin board. Bob Frazer said I could do that."

"Bob's a groovy guy." Jo moved to a chair by the window, hoping for a stray breeze. "He's doing great with the preteen group he's teaching Indian culture." Her smile was wry. "That's a gas, isn't it? A white, second-generation American has to teach Indian kids about their own background."

"Let's eat up and go," Nadine said, putting the plates of food on the table.

Nadine and Jo approached with a familiar sense of belonging the decaying mansion which had been converted into a Community Center. The doors were wide tonight, in deference to the humidity, the tall, narrow windows flung wide on every floor in hopes of some relief. At first, Nadine had come here to the Center with reluctance, at Jo's prodding. Now it was almost home. This was the night the coffee house was shut, and she took a class in painting.

Despite the heat which inevitably siphoned off a solid chunk of the regulars, the lower floor was bustling with activity. Nadine crossed to the bulletin board at the left, reached for one of the thumb tacks kept there in readiness and attached her notice.

"Hey, kids!" Bob Frazer–small, compact, with intelligent, compassionate brown eyes–beckoned them to his cubbyhole of an office.

They pushed their way across the once-elegant, marble-floored foyer to the door of the office. Bob urged them inside. A small fan sat on his desk, spewing out hot air, while papers fluttered reproachfully beneath improvised paperweights.

"You expect to stay open all summer?" Jo jibed affectionately, touching her damp forehead with a tissue. "Wow!"

"You bet we're staying open," Bob said briskly. "We've got a job to do here." He dropped into his chair, tilted backward, bracing himself against the peeling wall. "I'm working on an article about Indian relocation problems. I'll need a couple of brains to pick." His eyes moved from Jo to Nadine.

"I cut out in a week," Jo warned. "Up till then, pick."

Great." He swung to Nadine. "You available?"

"Sure," she said, fighting down an aversion to such activity. "I'll tell you whatever I can."

"I can't make a living at free-lance writing," Bob conceded with candor. "And support a wife and two and a half kids. But when something comes along about which I feel deeply, I get the old itch to put it on paper. Kids, I don't mean to be stuffy." He leaned forward earnestly. "I just want to be useful. Sometimes the written word packs a wallop."

"Anything you want to know, you ask," Jo said with sudden intensity. "You ask, and you tell it to the people!"

Nadine was glad when she had to leave for her art class. It evoked a sense of guilt in her, of futility, to sit here in Chicago and talk with Bob Frazer about how it was back home. Too sharply she envisioned the hogan, her mother, her stepfather, the kids.

"Look, Bob," Nadine heard Jo say as she left the small, airless room, "any Indian who comes to Chicago is a man without a country. There's all this jazz about jurisdiction you're under—the BIA's or the state's?

You're scared and homesick, and you hang out with other Indians, but they're in as bad a shape as you are."

Nadine and Pete McGregor saw Jo off at O'Hare. Jo beautiful with a new-found strength, a determination to make it this time. Pete drove Nadine back to the empty flat, talking all the way because he was aware of her depression and anxious to bolster her spirits.

"Go back to school, Nadine," Pete urged gently while they slowed down before the house. "Take some night courses. Come over and see me. We'll talk about it."

"Thanks, Pete," she said gratefully. Knowing she wouldn't go back to school. In the beginning she'd yearned to go to college, as Eddie had dreamt about this. But she knew now what she wanted. She wanted to write her songs and to sing them. Nothing else gave her that kind of happiness. "Thanks for everything."

Pete leaned across to open the car door for her, watched until she was inside the building before he drove off. Nadine walked up the stairs. Tomorrow LaVerne Hendricks–a Cherokee who'd been in Chicago almost a year–was moving into the pad with her. But opening the door, knowing Jo was already miles away from Chicago, she knew it wouldn't be the same.

Saturday, August 24, the hordes began to pour into Chicago by air, by train, by bus, by car. O'Hare and Midway spilled over with arriving passengers. The Greyhound and the Continental Trailways terminals disgorged crowds far beyond the normal summer outpour. The railroad stations churned with activity. All the major expressways were clogged with traffic. Cars sat bumper to bumper on the Indiana Toll Road, the Chicago skyway, the Dan Ryan Expressway, the Calument

Expressway, all offering their dramatic views for the travelers.

The hotels were geared for the onslaught of Democrats. Humphrey arrived and settled in at the Conrad Hilton. The McCarthy headquarters were set up at the Hilton. By Sunday night, it was prophesied, there wouldn't be an empty hotel room in downtown Chicago.

Sunday afternoon Lincoln Park swarmed with the young. Perhaps two thousand kids sprawled on the grass, listening to a folk-rock group play, while another thousand or two fanned about the perimeter, too restless to remain, but curious for a look. Among those on the grass, Nadine and LaVerne. Nadine with one arm cradling her guitar. An orderly crowd.

The word was around that there could be no scheduled entertainment because the permit for a flatbed truck to use as a platform had been denied. But there was no need for planned entertainment; the kids provided their own.

At LaVerne's prodding, Nadine rose to her feet in a moment of non-entertainment, fingered her guitar, began to sing. The faces of the listeners were rapt, the atmosphere electric. She sang the song she had composed in the waiting room while Jo's baby was being born. There were calls for quiet because the crowd was huge and there were no mikes, but in the stillness Nadine's voice carried.

She dropped to the grass again amid shouts of approval and cries for "more, more," but already another young troubadour had arisen to his feet to fill the air of Lincoln Park.

The Yippies were providing laughter with their placards. Their candidate, Humpty Dumpty, and a Yippie clown done up as a painted egg strolled through the crowds as the "next President of the United States." Mayor Daley's political machine was buffooned, along with Miss America and the Green Berets.

The afternoon gave way to evening, and the young were reluctant to leave the park, to abandon the closeness they felt together. Some drifted away, Nadine and LaVerne among them. The girls were hungry, food expensive in the area, they returned to the apartment. Not until next morning did they discover that the Yippies had been driven out of Lincoln Park, long after the eleven PM curfew, with tear gas, and that along with the Yippies and the kids, some reporters and photographers, despite displayed press cards, had been beaten.

On Monday the politicians carried on their business in the Chicago Amphitheater, out at the stockyards. The streets near–deserted except for the patrol cars and recently erected barricades. The local people in nearby residential areas stayed uneasily in their homes.

In Lincoln Park police cars prowled everywhere. Foot policemen in platoons were stationed every few hundred feet. The young gathered in the meadow, to sing, joke, harangue, make love. Nadine, wishing to be part of this and yet fearful, allowed LaVerne to prod her into the gathering. LaVerne said there must be a few thousand in the park, altogether. Kids from every state, kids who swore they'd be heard.

Close to midnight, the lights of police cars revolved ominously in the darkness while the kids stretched out on the expanse of grass, some of them with blankets, others walking around, tense with the emotions of the evening. All of them waiting. Expecting trouble.

Word passed with lightning swiftness, lending a new defiance, a kind of joy. Allen Ginsberg had arrived! William Burroughs, Jean Genet, Terry Sothern, Richard Seaver!

Suddenly, a cry went up. A police car was smashing through the flimsy barricade. The kids tossed rocks, bottles, whatever was at hand. Screams rose in the darkness. Invectives ricocheted.

"Walk! Don't run! For God's sake, walk!" yelled the kids who had been through encounters with the fuzz on earlier occasions. Panic would make the police ferocity worse and right now it was bad enough.

Nadine scanned the darkness for LaVerne. A minute ago LaVerne had been beside her!

"LaVerne!" Nadine called out. "LaVerne!"

Kids were running in every direction. Nadine moved, too caught up in the mounting panic. Clubs struck in the blackness. Tear gas. Nadine coughed, her throat stinging. Colliding with bodies in the darkness.

"The pigs got tear gas!" the cry was passed along. "Cover up your faces!"

Sputtering and coughing rent the air, blended with the outcries of the infuriated and the injured. Everywhere the flailing clubs. Run, Nadine's mind exhorted. Run!

Something struck her a sharp blow on the side of her face. She stumbled, lifted a hand to her face while she winced with sudden pain. She felt the sticky, alarming dampness of blood.

"Hurt?" a male voice asked **anxiou**sly, steadying her with a hand.

"Something cut my face," Nadine reported shakily. "It's bleeding—"

"Come on, let's cut out of here," he ordered, an

arm about her waist, prodding her through the jungle of battling bodies.

They pushed through the woods, across the lawn area, Clark Street their destination. They emerged, finally, into the night light of the street. Trembling, Nadine held a wad of tissues to the cut on her face.

"Let's get you over to Henrotin Hospital," her companion decided. "They'll be busy there tonight," he added grimly.

"No! No hospital." Remembering the night with Jo. "I'll go home, I'll be all right."

"Come over to the pad where I'm staying," he urged. "A fellow at the university loaned it to a bunch of us while we're here. I'll patch that up." He indicated the cut on her face with an encouraging smile. "With whatever talents a second-year med student can provide."

A cab cruised down the street and he hailed it. The driver pulled to a stop, inspecting them suspiciously. He frowned at the address. This was not where he wanted to go on a night like this, but Nadine's companion was already prodding her inside.

"Wow, that fuzz was on a rampage!" The tall, slim young man with unruly hair leaned back tiredly. "You see the way they were going after the TV guys? They didn't want a filmed record of that massacre. I saw some of them ripping off their name plates and their badges, even the unit patches. So the TV and the press wouldn't be able to identify them.

"I'm Seth Coles," Nadine's rescuer identified himself with a smile as they pulled up before a decaying pillared mansion. "From New York City."

"Nadine Scott." She smiled faintly. "Now of Chicago, before that Arizona." Her eyes met his with faint defiance. "The reservation."

"Why do you say it that way?" Seth reproached, leaning forward to pay the driver.

Her heart pounded, but she didn't reply. They got out of the cab in silence.

"It's just one flight up'" he said. "Nothing fancy—"

"I'm not used to fancy," Nadine shot back, looking around the dimly lit foyer.

Seth unlocked the door, gestured to Nadine to wait until he found the light cord in the middle of the room.

"Come to the bathroom," Seth ordered casually. "We've got some first-aid equipment there." He stared hard at her now. Oddly. Momentarily, she was discomforted. Then he smiled, a glint in his eyes. "How's Pete McGregor these days?"

Nadine's eyes widened with astonishment.

"I haven't seen Pete since June. He was fine then." Her eyes mutely questioned him.

Seth laughed gently at her bewilderment.

"I saw you with Pete at the school," he explained. "The day I flew out from New York to talk about McCarthy. I was waiting outside to talk to him while you were inside with him."

"That's why you looked familiar." Nadine allowed him to seat her on the edge of the claw-footed tub, waited while he rummaged in the medicine chest. "It seemed so crazy to me when I thought I'd seen you somewhere before, because I've never been to New York."

"This is going to sting a bit," he warned, reaching to touch antiseptic-soaked cotton to the scratch. "It's long, but it isn't broad or deep. You won't need any stitches." He held the cotton firmly in place, stopping the flow of blood.

She sat with eyes shut while he worked over the injury, knowing his small talk was to distract her from the sting of the medication. His bedside manner. He'd be great as a doctor. With some fancy practice one of these days.

"You should have a tetanus shot," he said somberly, when he was done.

"No," Nadine said quickly. "It was probably a soda can with a jagged edge."

"Let's go inside and I'll make us some coffee. Instant," Seth warned. "After that bash, we need it."

"I didn't think it would happen that way," Nadine said quietly. "I knew there'd be trouble, but not like that."

"The police state in action," Seth explained angrily. "Mayor Daley's pigs. Why shouldn't we stay in the park? What was wrong about that?"

"Do you think Daley's ever going to be elected again, after this?" Nadine hovered in the kitchen with Seth, finding comfort in his presence. "He's running in November, isn't he?"

"He's running, and he'll make it in," Seth predicted. "No matter how many kids get their heads bashed in. Daley controls ten thousand jobs that are worth fifty million dollars annually in Cook County—that's hard to beat. There's all the construction going on, the Loop El to come down, a new airport and more skyscrapers going up, the university complex expanding. Daley can make millionaires out of a lot of people in the construction field. He'll get in."

"Seth, how does it happen?" Nadine's eyes were dark with perplexity. "In a country like this! How could something like tonight happen in this country?"

"We've lost control, Nadine," Seth said seriously.

"We have a runaway machine. A handful of people hold control. We know what's wrong, we have the means to correct what's wrong! God, the technological knowledge that's misused! We know what brings about social disorder, crimes, but we let these things ride unchecked. Urban riots were predicted, we know the way to stop them is by providing jobs, decent housing, education. But nothing happens." He waved his hands in a gesture of hopelessness.

"The Indians have known that for two hundred years,'" Nadine reminded softly.

"We've got to fight for a change, Nadine, because without that we're lost."

"I've never liked cops," Nadine confessed. "Even when I knew there were good cops and bad cops. But after tonight—" She shivered. "It's like reading about what happened in Nazi Germany when the people lost control."

"Tonight, the police declared war. They announced they were taking over. A lot of college kids grew up in twenty minutes. They won't ever be kids again." He walked across to the refrigerator, opened the door with a speculative glint. "All that action made me hungry. Let's fix some sandwiches."

Seth fished out ham, cheese, liverwurst, found a loaf of bread in a cabinet above the stove. Nadine turned off the boiling water, and then measured coffee into a pair of oversized mugs that sat on a small shelf adjacent to the range.

"I hope my roommate's okay,'" Nadine said nervously. Taciturn, bitter LaVerne had been uptight about the appearance of the fuzz. "We got separated when the fighting started."

"Why don't you call her? The phone's in there" He

nodded toward the living room.

Nadine smiled faintly.

"We don't have a phone." Seth stared at her in shock. In his world everybody had a telephone.

"My folks are probably climbing the walls back in New York," Seth said reflectively. "If the news has reached there yet. There must be plenty of the press sitting around in hospital emergency rooms tonight. They're going to be fighting mad when they're patched up." He frowned, coughed into one hand. "That damn gas irritates the hell out of your throat. I got a taste of it in the school fracas—I didn't like it." He sighed heavily.

"I wonder how my folks are going to react to this whole scene? Brutality from the fuzz, the tear gas."

"They'll be worried," Nadine offered.

Eddie would have been proud of her for being at Lincoln Park tonight. Mama would be nervous, but she'd accept it. Mama had accepted so much that was bad in her life.

The coffee was made. Sandwiches ready. Nadine and Seth took the food and coffee into the living room, to sit on the edge of the Hollywood bed and eat from the steamer trunk serving as coffee table. The low wattage of the lamp bulb camouflaging the peeling paint, the stained floors.

"My folks are great, really," Seth said quietly. "They're all screwed up about what's going on in the world, but they can't see things the way we do. My older sister, Linda, is married, living out in Seattle; they figure she's set, but they worry about my kid sister, Audrey, and me. They're liberals, thank God for that, but the kids scare the hell out of them because they can't honestly understand, as hard as they try."

"Pete McGregor says that people are always

ripping into the kids, for their long hair, the way they dress, the way they don't want to accept what the Establishment hands out, because they feel we're a threat to their whole reality. They've built their lives a certain way and we challenge that. They're scared to death they'll have nothing to hold on to if we prove we're right."

"Reality for my folks," Seth said grimly, "is seeing me through med school. It's costing them a fortune. My father's an accountant, not a six-figure one. My mother teaches school, she calls that her trust fund." He smiled reminiscently. "Medical school fits comfortably only into the budgets of the rich. But Mom and Dad have this vision of me with a jazzy Scarsdale practice, a new Cadillac every year, and a seventy-five thousand dollar house. They shit green when I talk about practicing in Appalachia. Mom tells Dad secretly that this is a phase all med students go through, that I'll fall in line by the time I struggle through my internship. What's real for them is unreal, unsatisfactory, for me." He gazed curiously, speculatively, at Nadine. "What do you want, Nadine?"

Nadine frowned, suddenly self-conscious. Searching for words.

"To be me," she said hesitantly. "To do what makes me feel good inside." Still inarticulate, despite her minor success at the coffee house.

"I guess that's what we all want," Seth said quietly. "Strange, isn't it, how we bumped into each other in that madness tonight? I remembered you from McGregor's classroom. I didn't know your name, but I thought about you—"

"Yes, I remembered you, too," Nadine admitted. The way Seth was gazing at her disturbed her, added to her nervousness.

"You're beautiful," he said gently. "Even with a cut on your face and the sleeve of your blouse ripped and your hair all disheveled, you're beautiful."

Instinctively, she reached to brush the silken sweep of long hair into smoothness about her head. Her heart pounding because Seth was reaching to take the mug of coffee from her hand. She knew he was going to kiss her.

"Seth." It was a reproach her eyes denied. His mouth was firm but gentle on hers. Nobody had kissed her since Eddie. It had been so long. Over a year. And before Eddie there had been no one.

Nadine's hands tightened at his shoulders. As one they moved back along the length of the bed. The weight of him heavy on her slimness. His hands fumbling with the buttons down the front of her blouse.

"No," she said. But she didn't push him away. The phone jangled stridently. They froze.

"Oh, shit." Seth disentangled himself to reach for the phone. "Hello." He frowned, listening to the voice at the other end. "What the hell happened to you, Livvy? I looked all over for you—you'd cut out!"

Her face hot, Nadine swung into a sitting position at the edge of the twin bed that doubled as a couch. With unsteady fingers she rebuttoned her blouse. The moment was shattered. She was disappointed yet relieved.

"Livvy, where are you?" Seth pressed. "The emergency room *where*?" He listened, nodded, while Nadine rose unsteadily to her feet. Brushed with a wistful regret because for a few exquisite moments it had seemed that Seth Coles would belong in her life. There was a gentleness combined with strength in him that had reached out to fill a need in her. "How bad is it? What does the doctor say?'

She crossed to the table where she'd laid her purse, picked it up, ran toward the door.

"Nadine!" Seth's voice called out sharply while she moved through the door into the corridor. "Nadine—"

She hurried down the dimly lit, urine-scented stairs, impatient to put distance between Seth Coles and herself. Knowing he couldn't follow, with that girl named Livvy on the phone. Shaking at the closeness of their encounter. Feeling guilty, cheated.

At the bottom of the stairs she dodged an orange-and-black cat who meowed reproachfully at the nearness of their collision.

"Nadine!" Seth's voice echoed down the stairs. "Wait!"

Nadine bolted out into the night, took a long deep breath. Her throat still stung from the tear gas. She listened for a painful instant. Seth wasn't charging down the stairs. It was over.

She'd wanted Seth to love her. How could she, when she'd denied herself to Eddie? Eddie who was dead. Who could never love her. Seth Coles. He never happened. He was part of a nightmare.

CHAPTER EIGHT

At the hospital Seth lied competently. He was Olivia Mason's brother. She'd called for him. Livvy, her head swathed in bandages, was in a cubicle off the emergency room. A nurse brusquely informed Seth that Olivia would be taken upstairs in a few minutes for an x-ray, he couldn't stay. She bustled out, and Livvy raised herself shakily on one elbow.

"How do you like the damn fuzz?" she whispered contemptuously. "You should have seen some of the TV guys who were brought in with me. They took the worst clobbering of all."

"How's your head?" Seth asked anxiously.

"It hurts like hell. They think I may have a concussion, I get dizzy every now and then. Seth, call my old man in New York. Tell him to get me shifted out of here into the hospital where my sister had her appendectomy, it's a real country club. Don't scare him," she said dryly. "Just warn him he's got some bills to pay."

Seth and Livvy talked a few minutes about the news that came from the convention floor, then a nurse came in and threw him out, with Seth promising to call Mr. Mason. Back at his pad Seth phoned Livvy's home in Westchester County. Her father's answering service picked up, explaining he was at his house on Fire Island. Mrs. Mason was at Southampton. Dutifully, he asked for Mason's Fire Island number.

"Is it serious?" Mason demanded, irritated at being awakened at this hour.

"It looks like a concussion," Seth reported, hating the healthy Masons who had time for everything except being parents. "They're running tests. But Livvy wants out of that hospital. It's crawling with welfare patients," he added with malicious pleasure, knowing Mason would recoil.

"I'll call my older daughter's brother-in-law," Mason promised coldly. "He'll arrange for all the necessary medical care." He was silent a moment, perhaps feeling Seth's contempt. "I'll call Livvy in the hospital tomorrow when she's been transferred." But he wasn't flying out to see her.

By the time Seth got to bed it was early morning. Sunlight poured in through the unshaded kitchen window. "Happy birthday, LBJ," he thought to himself with dry humor. Back at the ranch– And then his thoughts focused, recurrently, on Nadine. Damn Livvy, did she have to call at just this minute? No chick ever turned him on the way Nadine did. How would he ever find her? She didn't even have a phone.

Next day three thousand of the young went to the Chicago Coliseum to take part in an anti-birthday party, which was sponsored by the Mobilization to End the War in Vietnam, while the old men carried on their business in the convention hall. Seth went with them. Dick Gregory wound up the anti-birthday party with a statement: "I've just heard that Premier Kosygin has sent a telegram to Mayor Daley asking him to send two thousand Chicago cops immediately."

That same night the worst battle of the week took place at Lincoln Park, with four hundred clergy and concerned citizens of the Establishment joining in. Tear-gas canisters crashed from all sides. Fires were lit. Again the fuzz advanced with clubs in hand.

In the fervent need to protest the brutality of the police, the nomination of Humphrey, McCarthy's youthful army, spearheaded by men like Paul O'Dwyer,

Richard Goodwin, and Theodore Bikel, marched from a rallying point close to the Hilton, up Michigan Avenue, with lighted candles, to be joined by the hippies and by the McCarthy clan in Grant Park. And Seth Coles marched with them.

Seth felt himself on a battlefield. The National Guard was everywhere. Army trucks parked on side streets. Jeeps barb-wired for action moved in the area about the Hilton. Searchlights blinded. Emotions ran high. Nobody here could ever be the same after this week.

Saturday, after thorough tests, Livvy was released from the hospital. Seth and Livvy bussed to an incredibly active O'Hare with its constant drone of loudspeakers, the rush of humanity on every side. They waited in the impressive arena of chrome and glass for their flight.

"We should have been armed," Livvy said violently. "We should have met the fuzz with bombs! We were idiots!"

"No." Seth was repulsed by her outburst.

"Seth, you don't get anywhere with words!" Her eyes glowed with distaste. "Bomb a few buildings back in New York, and you'll see things start to happen. The fuzz showed us the way, Seth. We'll give them back what they gave us.

"Sssh." Seth frowned, uneasy because the urgency in Livvy's voice was giving it a force that carried. People stared at them strangely.

Seth was relieved when their flight was announced, when they were settled in their seats, and Livvy was content to lean back and doze for the two-and-a-half hour flight back to New York.

He felt a kind of relief when Livvy said good-bye at

the Eastside Terminal. He got on the Second Avenue bus going downtown, and stared at familiar sights. God, that church at the corner of twenty-second Street was a beauty! The Church of the Epiphany. Such modernity was not expected among the aging apartment houses, the vintage schools, the rundown brownstones that segued off the Avenue.

The bus swayed to a stop beside Stuyvesant Park, still green in late August, with its collection of the middle income elderly, the sandpile set, and the bums who claimed the southern sector of the park as an extension of the Bowery. A three-layered confection, Seth thought, pleased with the image.

At Fourteenth Street two male drunks fawned over a female possessor of a bottle of cheap wine, and then the three were staggering into the park to share the bottle. The bus crossed Fourteenth Street, and it was home territory for Seth. The East Village.

The sidewalks were peopled below Fourteenth Street with the hippie types, the students, the long-time residents who might be Irish or Jewish or Italian. When the bus pulled to a stop just below Fifth, Seth stared compulsively at a pair on the corner as he disembarked. An old woman wearing a kerchief, despite the heat, scolded a fifteen year old girl with long, silken hair who was begging for change. The girl reminded him of Nadine. Damn, he'd wanted to find her before he left Chicago. He was unlocking the door to his pad when the phone began to ring.

Swearing at the necessity to cope with two locks, Seth finally strode into his minute living room, picked up the phone.

"Hello." Breathy from the hike up the stairs.

"Seth." His mother sounded relieved at hearing him

on the phone. "I've been so worried. Why didn't you call?"

"I'm fine, Mom," he dodged. "I meant to phone, but—" His voice trailed off.

"I'm expecting you for dinner tonight," Mom said firmly. God, he'd forgotten he'd promised to come over tonight. He was meeting Livvy late, but that wouldn't interfere with dinner. "Be at the house by seven. At the price of a good roast today I don't want to waste it."

"I'll be there on time," Seth promised. Thank God, Mom wasn't going to start the recriminations now. Damn, he should have phoned. "Shall I stop off at Cake Masters for something? A rum babka?" Mom was partial to rum cake.

"No," Felicia Coles said vigorously. "I've got Dad and myself on a diet. No desserts." She hesitated. "Seth, you're sure you're all right?"

"Absolutely," he soothed. They'd been watching the convention on TV, of course. They must have seen all the blood baths. "Not a scratch, Mom," he said more strongly. "See you at seven." Quickly, he hung up. Knowing he'd have to rehash Chicago later, as he had with the peace march in Washington. Right now, though, he was anxious to forestall the inevitable confrontation with his parents.

Off the phone, Seth walked into the bathroom, took off his clothes, and stretched. If he stayed in this pad another summer, he'd have to buy a secondhand air-conditioner. Unexpectedly, he chuckled. Livvy was great in bed, but Nadine would be special. He'd never wanted anyone the way he did that night, and she'd cut out.

He stepped into the stained, antique bathtub with

the cheap shower curtain, hovered beneath the ringed shower to adjust the unpredictable spray. There, it was okay. He stood beneath the lukewarm water, gearing himself for the sharp cold that he would initiate in a few moments. Days like this, when the heat was so oppressive, he appreciated Livvy's jazzy air-conditioned pad, even while he detested her right-wing parents who paid the tab.

Thinking about Livvy, he frowned. What the hell was happening to her, the way she was buying the radical scene? He didn't dig the violence bit. It did no good.

At seven twenty, Seth walked up from the entrails of the Seventy-Ninth Street subway. On the corner an army of black teenagers, bivouacked in a nearby welfare hotel, hovered in noisy restlessness, seeking free diversion for the evening. Cans of soda were being passed around among them. A white woman passed them with disdain, as though even this slight association might be harmful. A black girl noticed, made a derisive remark, and laughter ricocheted among them.

On the island that divides Broadway, the sprinkling of benches were thickly populated with senior citizens seeking to escape the heat of a cheap hotel room, or the loneliness of unshared, air-conditioned apartments. Across the street, on the west side of Broadway, a couple of homosexuals covertly inspected Seth with admiration, then dismissed him as he strode resolutely past.

As a child he'd relished living on Riverside Drive, overlooking the Hudson. He'd grown up with the luxury of the river view, with the bench-lined promenade for brisk walks. He had sorely missed the river in his move to the East Village. But now the Hudson was polluted, a constant reminder of what was happening to rivers and lakes all over the world.

At Riverside, he turned north, walked the short distance to his parents' building. Lucky that Mom and Dad were in a rent-controlled apartment, he thought guiltily as he waited for the elevator. With what it was costing to keep him in school, they couldn't afford a luxury rent, though this was bad enough. They talked, unhappily, about moving to Westchester when he finished school.

He couldn't imagine Mom and Dad in Westchester. They were real New Yorkers, who enjoyed the theater, the museums, the ballet, and the concerts. All through the years of his growing up, and with the late arrival of his sister, Audrey, they'd talked about the advantages of living in suburbia, and had abstained. But Mom taught in a junior high where she'd twice been physically maltreated by students. And these nights people were cautious about staying out past eleven. And still they didn't understand. They were living-room liberals.

The elevator-automatic for the past five years, chugged to a stop. The door slithered open. Seth moved inside. This had been a jazzy building once. The only thing jazzy now were the rents of those apartments which had been vacated often and thus carried escalated price tags.

Seth felt himself tensing as he rang the doorbell. Mom and Dad were so uptight about the whole current scene. For all their protestations about supporting McCarthy, for being against racism, they still lived back in the 1940s, when they were in college. The world never changed for them.

The door swung open, emitting savory aromas from

the kitchen.

"Hi." Audrey, thirteen, budding into adolescence, and presumably brilliant–grinned at him. "Mom was taking bets with Dad that you'd he late."

"Why should I be late?" He swatted her affectionately across the rump. She was going to be a beauty in two or three years. And hot, he thought uneasily, remembering incautious remarks. At thirteen she knew everything.

"How was Chicago?" she demanded casually, proud of her blossoming figure, undisguised by a bra. Her blue eyes, replicas of his, were avid. "I kept looking for you on TV."

"Seth?" His mother's voice was faintly sharp from anxiety. "I'm glad you're early. The roast is ready to go on the table." She lifted her face for his kiss, with a tiny, recurrent, feminine smile for his tallness. A small, weight-battling woman with short, dark hair and an infectious grin. "You know you can always call collect if you're broke."

"I'm sorry, Mom." Seth waved to his father, out in the recliner scanning the *New York Post*.

"How was Chicago?" Audrey pressed, and her mother shot her a reproving glance. Meaning, we won't talk until after dinner. Probably not until Audrey was en route to one of her social evenings.

"Everybody to the table," Felicia Coles ordered briskly. "Audrey, help me in the kitchen, and remember, I want you in the house before dark. I don't care how many girls walk you home."

The dinner conversation was determinedly maintained on an innocuous level. Mom and Dad refused to discuss Chicago in front of Audrey. That was a gas. Audrey was probably more hip on what was happening in this present-day world than his parents! While they sat over coffee, Audrey dashed off to meet the coterie of girls who had called up from the lobby.

"All right, Seth," Jim Coles said heavily. "What the hell really happened in Chicago?"

"You saw it!" Seth's face tightened, remembering. The whole ugly week, vivid. "Daley sent his pigs out for blood! You must have seen it on television. Half the world did!"

"We saw," his mother conceded tensely. "We stayed up most of the night watching. Night after night we watched! Seth, how did it get out of control that way?"

"The way this whole country is out of control," Seth shot back. "Thousands of kids went to Chicago with a dream, and for that they had their heads busted in. And all the time" he sighed tiredly, "all the time the convention was settled before the first kid hopped off a bus."

For a long while they rehashed the convention. His parents, like millions across the nation, were indignant, outraged. But they had to hear it from Seth before they could fully accept the ugliness of what they had seen on their TV screen.

"Oh, Seth, when I think you were in the middle of that!" His mother closed her eyes, shuddered.

"Seth, we know how you feel." His father cleared his throat nervously. "We're just as upset about Chicago as you are. The country's going through a rotten period, but we'll bounce back. We always do. But you've got your future to think about. Seth, no more getting involved this way." His voice acquired fresh vigor, a new sternness. "You've got to finish your schooling, get into your internship. That's where you're needed. You know the shortage of doctors in this country."

"Dad, I can't cut myself off from what's happening, shut my eyes!" Seth objected heatedly. "It's happening to me, too."

"Look, Seth, your first obligation is to yourself, your future." He ignored a warning glance from his wife. "And I don't want to see you mixed up with SDS crap either, all this demonstrating at the colleges. I don't want you running off to conventions and getting your head busted in. Now listen to me–" He waved down Seth's attempt to intercede. "We had our problems, too. It was no joyous life being Depression children, with every penny prayed over before it was spent, a hole in a shoe a near-disaster. Working like dogs to get grades high enough to make it into CCNY and Hunter. I spent three years of hell in the Pacific. But I came home and your mother and I got married and set out to make a life for ourselves. We were too busy fighting our way up to protest. You kids have everything handed to you on a silver platter, from the day you were born! You don't know what it means to fight!" A vein in his forehead throbbed angrily.

"Dad, you're still living back in 1945, when you got out of the army. You're still reaching out to touch the Depression, thrilled because you don't have to ask the price of meat at the butcher's. You've got a three-thousand-dollar car and air-conditioning and color TV, and you can send your son to medical school, " Seth grinned wryly. "With much budgeting, I admit. But, Dad, you're not seeing life as we see it."

"Seth, every generation rebels," his mother broke in. "It's the pattern of youth."

"This generation is different." Seth leaned forward earnestly. "Not just in this country. All over the world. We see new values. We don't want to be prisoners of a corporate system. What about the individual? With all that science has to offer, with all the wonders of technology, why must we live depersonalized lives? Society is dead. We want to bring it back to life again."

"Jim, tell him," Felicia Coles said with an air of urgency, and Seth tightened in awareness.

"Seth, we've talked it over seriously, your mother and I." Jim Coles' eyes were somber, his face tired. "We don't want to see you involved in any more student demonstrations. No more encounters with the cops. Screw the SDS, Seth!" His voice rose sharply. His wife frowned. "We want you to live a normal life when school reopens. No more of this nonsense, Seth, or you'll have to finance your medical education yourself."

"Seth, it's important you finish med school," his mother emphasized. Her eyes fearful. Education was the trust fund, the guarantee of the good life. "You've got three years to push through and you'll be interning. Every time there's another peace march, another demonstration, I'm sick. You could have your head bashed in, be maimed for life. Seth, we're not sweating to put you through school for you to wind up a basket case!"

Seth left his parents' apartment, headed earlier than anticipated, for the southbound IRT. He knew they were serious about withdrawing financial assistance. He realized this decision had been arrived at after much soul-searching. But it was the stinking regimentation again. Do as we say or else. Christ, he was twenty-two! Old enough to make his own decisions. Needing financial help, but not mentally incompetent. The old Establishment bit, "do as *we* say or else." Screw that

Scarsdale practice!

But there were the three years of med school ahead of him before he'd earn a dime. He couldn't swing it on his own. He had to play it their way. But that didn't mean he couldn't be mentally and emotionally involved.

The train roared into the station, heavily populated with the Saturday night diversion seekers. Seth found a seat, pulled a Vonnegut paperback from his jacket pocket, tried to read for the succession of local stops before he would disembark in the West Village.

He'd pick up Livvy and they'd cut out to a coffee house for the evening. In this heat, if Livvy's roommates weren't back in town, he'd sleep over in air-conditioned splendor.

Wearing an unexpectedly demure, quilted satin neck-to-floor robe, Livvy admitted him to her posh nineteenth-floor apartment. She complained regularly about the thunder of early morning truck traffic below, and ignored the magnificent Hudson view that sprawled in the distance.

"You took long enough to get here," Livvy bitched, but her eyes were passionate.

"I'm early," Seth reproached. "How do you feel?" The tests had all checked out negative, but Livvy had been in a rotten mood since they dismissed her from the hospital.

"I feel like making love," she said bluntly, and ran the zipper down the length of her robe. She was naked underneath. "No action in the hospital."

"Did you expect the interns to oblige?" he jibed, taking in the view. "Haven't you heard about how overworked they are?"

"You oblige." She smiled faintly.

Standing there with the quilted satin robe at her

feet, she lifted her arms above her head, stretched provocatively. Her woman's nipples hugely taut. The narrow, flat pelvis jutting toward him in invitation. He reached out for her, his body reacting on its own....

They went to a coffee house in high favor with the campus kids who'd flocked to Chicago. The Daktari. Seth was uptight because he didn't want to rehash that scene. Too close, too painful. But it was on everybody's mind, monopolizing the conversation in the coffee house.

"Next week," Livvy announced with relish, when the table hoppers had settled down in the semi-darkness and Seth and she were alone, "we're joining that group at Whitehall. You're burning your draft card, baby."

"The hell I am!" Seth shot back, stung by her decision making. Uneasily recalling his parents' bitter admonitions. That had not been an idle threat. When they lined up together against him, he knew it was for real.

"Some of the kids have this thing set up," Livvy pursued, ignoring his rejection. We'll demonstrate against the draft in front of Whitehall. It may be rough. I hear there's a bunch of longshoremen just standing by waiting for something to kick off. Real America-first types, the bastards." Her eyes flashed scornfully. "They're always hanging around, telling us to go back to Russia where we came from."

"I'm through demonstrating for a while," Seth said patiently. "To be exact, for the next three school years, until I finish med school. My folks laid it on the line—cut out or they kick me out on my ass. I can't screw up my education, Livvy."

"What the hell's the matter with you?" Livvy

shrieked. "I thought you were a man! What have you got between your legs? Frozen custard?"

"Look, I don't like it this way," Seth said honestly, "but I'm in a bind. I think it's important for me to finish med school."

"It's important for you to be involved now, not three years later!" Her voice rose dangerously.

"Cool it, baby." Seth gazed about in discomfort. The others were listening avidly to their private scene.

"I think you're full of shit," Livvy said furiously. "It's been a game to you, and now it's getting rough and you want out Well, baby, let me tell you, it's going to get a lot rougher before it's over. The kids have had it. You think Chicago was violent? Wait till you see what it's going to be like this year! We'll give violence back for violence!"

Seth pushed back his chair.

"Let's get out of here."

"You're acting," she said coldly, "like a damn scared-assed fag."

Outside the Saturday night hordes glutted the sidewalk, spilled over in the street, where the car traffic crawled. Tourist night in Greenwich Village, with the avid from the Bronx and Brooklyn, from Westchester and Connecticut, from Rockland County and Jersey pouring into the area. Seth held onto Livvy's arm to keep them from being separated. They skirted Washington Square, headed north toward Eighth Street, with its Saturday night carnival atmosphere.

"Let's stop off at Zum Zum for a burger," he suggested cajolingly. Livvy's silence made him uncomfortable.

"No," Livvy replied finally. "Walk me over to Pat Clayton's pad."

"What for?" He was startled. Pat Clayton was an obvious lesbian that Livvy had met through some women's lib meeting. For a while Livvy liked going to Pat's "Saturday Evenings" because the underground film people hung around and Livvy thought they were groovy.

"Pat told me she'd be home tonight." Livvy lifted her face to his, her eyes mocking. "This isn't one of her 'Saturday evenings.' She's alone." Livvy smiled, mocking. "She digs me. She's been after me all summer.

"What are you talking about?" Seth stared in distaste. "You're sore at me, so you're going to mess around with that bull dyke?"

Livvy's eyes were enigmatic.

"I want to see what it's like, baby. Maybe I can go ape without that male thing. What's wrong about doing it with another chick?" Livvy challenged. "At least, I won't get pregnant." She wouldn't get pregnant, anyway, and if she did, daddy would pay for an abortion.

Silently, Seth prodded her across the street. Tonight was the end of an era.

CHAPTER NINE

With an early season blizzard descending upon Chicago, the Casbah, where Nadine worked, closed hours earlier than scheduled. The tables had been barren of customers. The weather-casters had been exhorting all residents to hole up for the duration.

Nadine wrapped herself in the new winter coat she'd bought. A sense of guilt at this expenditure because this was six dollars she had earmarked for Christmas gifts for the kids back on the reservation. But the memory of anguish of last winter had propelled her into the neighborhood thrift shop in search of a bargain.

No place, Nadine thought with a shiver as she left the comfort of the Casbah for the blustery curtain of snow outdoors, was ever as cold as Chicago in winter. The few people on the streets walked with hunched shoulders faces, burrowed in collars, bodies bent forward hurrying to their destination. The weatherman predicted fourteen inches, and the drifts would be bad.

Her feet sodden, Nadine scurried frenziedly as she approached the entrance to her building. Inside, free of the wind, she paused for an instant to catch her breath. Nobody had expected this snow, when October wasn't yet past. With a shudder of distaste, she reached down to pull off one wet shoe, then the other, rubbed each sole in turn between her gloved hands. Upstairs, she'd make herself some hot coffee.

Approaching the landing on their floor, Nadine decided LaVerne must be out. The radio wasn't on. The first thing LaVerne did when she walked into the pad was to turn on the radio. She left it on, even when she went to sleep.

LaVerne would be in a neighborhood Indian bar despite the weather warnings, Nadine guessed. LaVerne constantly found some lonely Cherokee to buy her beers.

Nadine slid the key into the lock. Her hands, painful from the encounter with the near-zero temperature, we' awkward. It required several tries. She turned the knob opened the door, walked inside, stopped.

Laverne was home. She was naked in bed, her clothes a splash of color on the floor close by. Above her, beneath a blanket that formed a protective tent, hovered a board Cherokee. Nadine stared, her face hot, while the pair beneath the blanket, oblivious of her presence, rocked together.

Nadine returned to the chill hallway, quietly closed the door again, locked it, knocked loudly. She could visualize the shock of the pair on the bed at her unexpected arrival.

"Nadine?" LaVerne's voice husky.

"Yes."

"Wait a sec."

They weren't going to stop, Nadine realized, outraged. She felt a strange emptiness, too, because she stood out in a dark, dank hall, alone, while LaVerne and the Cherokee were working to a private frenzy on the bed. Her mind shuttled back to the night in the strange apartment near the park, when Seth fixed her cut. Involuntarily, her hand moved to her forehead. She could almost feel, again, the gentle touch of his fingers.

"One sec, Nadine," LaVerne called out again, her voice uneven.

And then the door opened and Nadine walked inside. The Cherokee was at the window, his back to her, zipping up his chinos.

"The Casbah shut up early because of the blizzard," Nadine explained, walking to the radiator with her wet shoes. Her eyes averted from the Cherokee.

"Hey, if it's that bad, I'd better cut out," he said to LaVerne with elaborate casualness. He reached for his jacket, pulled it on. "See you around, baby."

Nadine walked into the kitchenette, put up water for instant coffee. God, how she missed Jo! Everything about LaVerne annoyed her. Her sloppiness, bed never made up, clothes scattered all over, her sullenness, her drinking. This was the first time that she knew about LaVerne bringing a fellow up to the pad, but most nights she was at the coffee house. Maybe it was a regular occurrence.

While Nadine fixed herself coffee, LaVerne climbed into bed, flipped on the radio, fiddled around with the dial. "Wow, that beat is great!" LaVerne murmured with satisfaction, and settled down under the blankets.

By the time Nadine brought her coffee and a sandwich out into the other room, LaVerne was gently snoring.

Election night was cold and grim in Chicago. Somebody brought a TV into the coffee house so that the kids clustered there could listen to the returns. Nadine noticed the heaviness in the reactions about her as the returns began to come in. The taste of August still lingering, fetid in their mouths.

"The Dick or the Hump, what the hell's the difference?" a southerner high on grass intoned. "We've been sold out before we're old enough to vote."

"I'd like to castrate the son of a bitch who gunned down Bobby," a girl whispered. "Bobby should have made it."

"Gene and Bobby as a team," a university student said softly. "That was the stuff that dreams are made of."

"You buy that deal they talk about?" the southerner asked while the TV newscaster recited the latest rundown of votes in the Illinois area. "I mean, that the CIA had the brass to try to assassinate Castro ,and Castro got back by knocking off the two Kennedys?"

"Georgia, we won't know in our lifetime," the university student prophesied, "but the thought of the power the CIA wields makes me want to puke. They're practically autonomous, smack in the midst of a democracy."

Nadine moved silently among the tables, bitterness in her heart. With the two men who were running for the presidency, what did it matter to the Indians on the reservation who got into the White House? With McCarthy ,a man of such compassion, they bad a chance. Bobby went out to the reservations personally, talked eloquently about what he wanted to do for the fifth-class citizens and many believed him. But Nixon? Humphrey? Skepticism muted her interest in the election returns. What the hell did it matter? By the time she left the Casbah it was fairly clear that Nixon had squeaked through. All she wanted now was to go home.

Again, she climbed the stairs to an unfamiliar quiet from their apartment. She tensed in the memory of her last such arrival. But there was no ribbon of light beneath the door, she realized. Still, she knocked. No. Nobody home.

She slid the key into the lock, opened the door. The late-night chill of the room wrapped itself around her as she walked into the darkness, moved cautiously to the center of the room to fumble for the light pull.

Glancing about the room, she sensed something unusual. LaVerne's duffel bag, which held most of her wardrobe was missing from the area where it normally sat, where the two twin beds met at right angles. Alarm clutching at her throat, Nadine spun about to check LaVerne's decrepit but beloved record player. It was gone, along with the half-dozen LPs which comprised her record collection.

Nadine dropped to the edge of her bed, unbuttoned her coat. She didn't have to worry right away. They'd paid the rent for the rest of the month. The landlord was at the door with an outstretched hand right on the first. She must look around quickly for somebody to replace LaVerne, before the December rent became due.

This was a terrible month to find a replacement. This time of year the newcomers to Chicago were sparse. But she'd never be able to have a whole month's rent by December first, even if she lived on beans and potatoes. The electric was due, and the gas. Her shoes were practically worn through. She had to buy a new pair.

If she found an afternoon job, she might be able to swing the rent. Maybe Bob Frazer would help her, she decided with a first glint of optimism. But if she took an afternoon job, she wouldn't be able to go around to the theatrical agents about a possible singing spot. As soon as the weather got warm, she'd promised herself–and Jo–she'd start looking again. With a thicker skin this time.

The next afternoon Nadine tacked a notice onto the bulletin board at the Community Center. Whenever she could she worked with Bob, helping him with an Indian culture class, glad to be needed at the Center, glad to have Bob's friendship. She deeply missed Jo.

Days went past without any reply to her notice. As she'd suspected, this was a slow period for arrivals in the city. With desperation tugging at her, she asked Mama Stringfield to send over any girls who applied for space whom Mama couldn't accommodate. But Mama, this time of year, found herself with a vacant bunk.

The month moved inexorably to its close. Nadine denying herself painfully to save what she could toward the rent. With no dire emergencies arising, she might make it, she decided.

Bob Frazer invited her for Thanksgiving with his family. Nadine was visibly impressed by the middle income opulence of the Frazer apartment. Bob's wife, Joyce, in her early thirties and her third pregnancy, was stiffly polite to Nadine. She unbended somewhat when Nadine eagerly offered to take the children outdoors for a while prior to dinner.

Bonnie and Jean were ebullient, affectionate, clinging to Nadine, filling her with nostalgia for the younger brothers and sisters back on the reservation. When they returned, all of them exhilarated by the brisk outdoor romp, Bob was carefully bringing the succulent bird to the table.

"Oh, that looks gorgeous!"" Nadine exclaimed with admiration.

"Bob made it," Joyce reported with a faint smile. "He does every Thanksgiving and Christmas."

"When Joyce is this far along, she's in a bad state," Bob said gently, slipping an arm about his wife. "We have to spoil her."

They settled themselves about the table, the two little girls obviously delighted by Nadine's presence. Bob, in a jovial mood, carved the huge turkey, and served everybody. Nadine stared at the lavish portion he placed on her plate. When she was tiny they often had turkeys on the reservation. Before hunting and spray guns made them all but extinct. Back in the hogan today, her family would sit down to a Thanksgiving dinner of tortillas.

"Come on, everybody, eat hearty," Bob urged, enjoying the holiday.

Nadine struggled to feel at ease with Bob and his family. She ate with sincere gusto, vocal in her approval of the many dishes that crowded the table. The children helped her feel less self-conscious in the strange surroundings. Joyce spoke little. Nadine and Bob talked animatedly about the Steinbeck novels he had loaned her.

Late in the evening, she left the Frazer apartment with an unfamiliar, fleeting sense of well-being, and took a bus home. With a new distaste she walked into the squalid tenement that was home. Wondering if she would ever have an apartment like the Frazers'. Wondering if she would ever make it as a singer, if life would ever change for her.

The Saturday after Thanksgiving, while Nadine stood in the spill of the small spotlight at the Casbah and sang about August in Chicago, the police stormed in to stage a narcotics raid. Bedlam broke out instantly. The kids, verbal in their indignation, charged toward the exits.

A pair at the rear were surrounded, seized on charges of selling grass, and carted off to a squad car parked outside. Inside the coffee house, the owner and the employees, including Nadine, were rounded up and prodded into another squad car. Trembling, terrified, Nadine's eyes mutely questioned her boss as she sat beside him in the squad car, bound for the police station.

"Don't look like that, baby," he encouraged. "They won't hold us. They can't." But he was privately apprehensive.

At the station house they were briskly questioned, unexpectedly released, except for the pair who'd been caught carrying marijuana. But the coffee house would not reopen again. Their license was being revoked. Nadine was without a job.

Nadine was frantic. Jobs were hard to come by in the ghetto. The rent was due. No roommate yet. Mama would be disappointed that the two dollars weekly, which went to buy milk and fruit juice for the little ones, would be stopped.

Scared, fighting panic, she approached Bob at the Center. Instantly sensing her emotional state, Bob propelled her into his tiny cubicle of an office, sat her in the chair beside his desk. He listened compassionately to the story of the raid and the closing of the coffee house.

"I've been looking for work all day," she said unsteadily. "I can't find anything." Bob understood she didn't have the confidence to go down to the Loop to search for a job. She felt safe only here in the neighborhood.

"Would you have some kind of a job here at the Center?"

"I don't have a budget for nonprofessional help," he explained apologetically, but his eyes were squinting in concentration. "Nadine, for a few months, would you be interested in a job that didn't pay much more than board and room? Joyce is having a rough time. We could certainly use a mother's helper. You'd have to share a room with the kids," he warned. "We have a fold-away cot that could be set up in there. You'd have a place to live and–" he hesitated, juggling figures in his mind. "Plus twenty a week–that's about as far as we can go."

"I'd like that," Nadine accepted eagerly, even while she knew she'd miss the comparative privacy of her own apartment. The only thing she'd miss about it. "But do you think Joyce will want me?" Her eyes were somber, remembering that Joyce had been grudgingly polite at Thanksgiving.

"Joyce will be relieved to have help with the kids. They drive her up the wall right now. The last three months of pregnancy, she always has problems." Bob sighed tiredly. "She'll be great again, once the baby's born. With luck, a boy," he added whimsically.

"When do I start?" Nadine asked uncertainly.

It wouldn't be comfortable in the Frazer household. There was something disapproving in Joyce that turned her off. Yet what choice did she have? And working for the Frazers, knowing she had a place to sleep and eat, would give her time to go out to look for singing jobs. Bob would make sure Joyce gave her time off in the afternoons. All she'd need would be two or three hours each day. She'd be with the two little girls the rest of the time.

"You go home and pack up right now," Bob decided, smiled reassuringly. "Come back here and I'll drive you to the apartment."

Nadine settled warily into her new schedule. Joyce was plainly relieved at having someone on hand to keep the children off her back. She was having a difficult pregnancy. Still, she resented the presence of a stranger in an apartment hardly large enough to accommodate another, and Nadine was conscious of this resentment.

Nadine conscientiously fulfilled her duties about the house. She spent regular hours at the Community Center, rehearsing for the pre-Christmas revue to be held there. After Christmas, she promised herself, she'd start looking for singing jobs. She dreaded the necessity for making the rounds of the smaller agents who might just book someone with her lack of experience. Remembering her earlier forays. The only jobs offered her then had been as a topless go-go dancer.

Bob was jubilant about having a "star" for this season's revue—Nadine—Joyce annoyed by his frequent, good-humored ribbings about their "next big recording star."

Nadine shopped for Christmas presents at a discount store in the neighborhood. It would be the first time in their lives that her brothers and sisters would receive more than one inexpensive gift for Christmas. At a thrift shop she bought a warm coat for Mama, a sheep-lined jacket for her stepfather. With a sense of deep content she carried her awkward array of packages to the post office for shipment to the reservation.

Ten days before Christmas, late in the evening, Bob received a phone call from his parents' home in St. Louis. His father had a heart attack. Within two hours Bob was on his way to O'Hare.

Joyce was upset at Bob's absence, screamed at the children, clumsily dropped dishes, spoke sharply, without reason, to people who came to the door. Nadine tried to assume as much responsibility as possible, to make things easier for Joyce. They had no idea when Bob would return. His father was in the hospital, under an oxygen tent.

On the fourth night after putting the children to

bed Nadine, book in hand, walked into the living room. Joyce was frantically searching about. The TV blared noisily, totally ignored.

"Nadine," Joyce straightened up, frowning. "Have you seen my watch anywhere?"

"No." Absurdly, Nadine felt a flicker of alarm. Joyce had a hang-up about that watch. Her mother had given it to her as a birthday present, the last present she'd given Joyce before her death. "Did you check the bathroom?"

"It's not there." Joyce stared sharply at Nadine. "See if it's in the children's room."

"All right," Nadine forced a smile.

Nadine tiptoed back into the children's room, switched on the table lamp between the twin beds, temporarily removed it to rest on the floor so that the light wouldn't disturb the two little girls. She made a perfunctory search. Knowing she would find no watch. Joyce never set foot in that room, not since the day she'd moved into the apartment. She returned to the living room, where Joyce was turning the room into a shambles.

"It isn't in the kids' room," Nadine reported softly.

"It has to be somewhere in this house!" Joyce's eyes flashed with rage. "I haven't been out of here today."

"It's probably behind something," Feeling her face hot, Nadine began to move books about on the many shelves bracketed to the wall.

"It has to be here," Joyce reiterated fretfully, still groping about in corners.

"I'll go look around the kitchen," Nadine offered, conscious of the way Joyce's eyes refused to meet hers.

Nadine went out to the kitchen, frenziedly searched every inch of the room. She dropped to her haunches, slid exploratory fingers behind the refrigerator. Nothing but chunks of dust.

In the master bedroom Joyce was talking on the phone. She had probably given up looking for tonight, Nadine guessed with relief. The watch would show up somewhere tomorrow, when they weren't looking for it.

Nadine felt uneasy, unsure, when she went out into the living room again. Joyce had left the bedroom, sat tensely at one corner of the long, low modern sofa and stared stonily at the television screen.

"I've looked all over the kitchen...."

Nadine started at the sound of the doorbell. Joyce, her mouth in a tight white line, gestured her back and walked to the door.

"Mrs. Frazer?" A cop stood in the doorway, a smaller carbon copy by his side. Both young, fresh at the job.

"Yes!" Joyce cleared her throat nervously, stepped to one side to allow them to enter.

Nadine watched. The appearance of the police inevitably alarmed her. It was ghetto conditioning.

"You phoned in about a robbery," the taller cop said quietly, fishing a notebook from his back pocket. "We'll need some facts."

"Yes." Joyce's voice was unnaturally high. "My wrist watch—it's quite expensive—disappeared this evening. Someone had to take it. I wasn't out of the house."

"Lady, you call us about a watch you misplaced?" the shorter cop picked up tiredly. "You look around a bit—it'll show up."

"I tell you somebody stole it." Joyce's voice was strident. "I didn't misplace it."

Nadine stirred uncomfortably. The two cops were staring oddly at her.

"Hey, we know you," the taller one said suddenly.

"You were brought in for shoplifting!" The room was suddenly heavy with ugly overtones.

"No." Nadine stared, trembling. Jagged pieces of facts jumping into one nasty solid picture. Joyce had brought the fuzz here to arrest her! Joyce was sure she had stolen the watch.

"Come on, don't lie," the cop pursued brusquely. "We had you down at the station-house just recently. I know you!"

"It was nothing," Nadine whispered, white with terror. "I was at a coffee house, I was a waitress there. There was a drug raid," She stopped dead because Joyce was glaring at her in outrage. Bob hadn't mentioned the raid to her. "Somebody was selling grass, they said."

"Yeah, that was it." The cop snapped his fingers. "You were brought in during the bust. Go get your coat."

"What for?" Nadine stiffened defensively.

"On suspicion of robbery," he said tersely. "Mrs. Frazer, you'll have to come down and sign a complaint."

"I'm alone with my children," Joyce explained nervously, averting her gaze from Nadine. "I can't leave them alone tonight."

"Tomorrow," the cop stipulated. "Come down sometime tomorrow." He frowned because Nadine hadn't moved. "Okay, get your coat," he snapped. "We're taking you in."

Nadine turned supplicatingly to Joyce, who stared stonily ahead, ignoring her. Panic closing in about her, she hurried to the children's room, moving quietly inside so as not to disturb them, found her coat in the crowded closet

"I didn't take the watch, Joyce," Nadine insisted tensely, but Joyce refused to look at her. "I didn't."

"Let's go." The shorter cop reached for the door,

pulled it wide. "If she's got it on her, Mrs. Frazer, the matron will find it. Indians. They're all the same."

In the cold December night, with snow flurries beginning to drop from the sky, the cops herded Nadine into the blue-and-white squad car at the curb while a handful of passers-by gaped curiously. The car sped off, flasher whirling. Nadine huddled in one corner of the rear seat.

Numbly, Nadine allowed them to put her through the routine at the station-house. Answering questions in a whisper, her mind dizzy with the realization of what was happening to her.

"White?" the cop was asking her automatically, but already indicating this fact on the forms before him.

"Navajo," she retorted with pride.

"Half-breed," he amended, suppressing a yawn. It was late; he was anxious to go off duty.

A matron appeared to take her to another room to be searched. She balked only when the short, squat, thick-shouldered woman ordered her to strip.

"What for?" Nadine shot back indignantly. She wasn't wearing that many clothes that she could hide a watch on her.

"To see where you've got that watch stuck away," the matron retorted coldly. "Come on, down to the skin or I'll call the cops who brought you in to do it for you."

Her hands shaking, Nadine shucked away her clothes, feeling sick when she stood naked before the matron. Tall, slender, exquisitely fashioned. She saw the look of envy on the woman's face as she stared.

"Where did you hide that watch?" the matron demanded with deceptive softness. A hand suddenly darting between Nadine's thighs.

"Stop that!" Nadine backed away in

revolt at this intrusion.

"Checking," the matron said calmly. "Turn around."

"Bend over."

Tears stinging her eyes, Nadine gritted her teeth and obeyed.

"You're clean," the woman said finally. "No dope on you.

"I'm not here on dope charges," Nadine shot back, her eyes flashing. "The woman I work for said I took her watch, that's all there was. And I didn't take it."

"We got orders to check for dope," the woman said calmly. "Can't take any chances, with what we got holed up here."

Nadine was placed in a cell with three other girls. One, in narcotics withdrawal, lay writhing on the floor.

The other two—hookers—inspected Nadine, shrugged, and continued their private conversation. The girl in withdrawal was violently sick all night. The guards ignored her pleas for help. The two hookers swore loudly because the addict kept them awake. Nadine lay tense in a corner of her hard bunk. Frightened at the stark reality around her. Hating it. Hating the cop who had labeled Indians as "all the same." She ran her fingers through her dyed-black hair. Defiantly, she braided it.

CHAPTER TEN

Nadine was dozing. At dawn the pair of hookers had launched a noisy, hair-pulling battle and had been removed from the cell. The girl in withdrawal now lay on the floor, moaning in her sleep. Gradually, Nadine became aware of the insistent voice of the matron.

"Come on, girlie, you're getting out," the matron was repeating brusquely. "On your feet. You can get your beauty sleep someplace else."

Groggily, Nadine obeyed, followed her down the corridor between the cells. In a room at the end, Bob waited for her.

"Nadine, it was a terrible mistake," he said, his voice shaking. He put his hands on her shoulders, re-assuringly, then straightened up with a forced smile. "Come on, let's get out of here."

Bob kept a hand on her arm as he walked her to the cubicle where she collected her handbag and coat. Then he prodded her out into the bleak December morning.

"I've got the car here," he said gently, nodding to the curb. "But first let's go in down the street for some coffee. Did you have breakfast?"

Nadine shook her head quickly.

"I'm not hungry. But I'd like some coffee."

"We'll have breakfast together," he decided firmly, and swung left toward a coffee shop.

"Where did Joyce find the watch?" Nadine asked, with a compulsion to know.

"The kids must have been playing with it. I found it under Jean's pillow when she woke up this morning." He sighed heavily, his eyes apologetic as they rested on Nadine. "You know what a rotten state Joyce is in. Ordinarily, this never would have happened. And what the hell did the cop mean by bringing you in that way?" His voice rose in anger. "He should have known he had no right." He pushed the door of the coffee shop.

Nadine and Bob seated themselves at a booth in the rear. Bob ordered breakfast for them. The waitress sauntered off and Bob leaned forward, his eyes pained.

"Nadine, I can never make up for what happened last night," he said softly. "Did they give you a rough time?"

"They took me in because of the raid at the coffee house," she said with frustration. "That was the real reason! I hate this city!"

Bob stared at her, startled.

"Nadine, you want to go back to the reservation?"

"No!" she said violently.

"I stopped by and rented a furnished apartment for you," Bob said, watching her soberly. "You have to have a place to stay. It's kind of a fleabag. A one-and-a-half room apartment near the center. The rent's outrageous, for such a dive, but I took it for a week, until you can get reorganized." He gazed unhappily at the table. "I knew you wouldn't want to go back to the house again."

"No." Nadine's face suddenly stung with color.

"We'll have to start searching for a decent job for you," Bob continued with a show of reassurance that Nadine knew was merely window-dressing. "And a better place to live. Meanwhile, you're set for this week."

"Maybe I can find a job in another coffee house," Nadine said after a moment of concentration. She felt good in the coffee houses. She belonged. "If the cops don't make it rough for me," Nadine added, frowning.

"Nadine, they have nothing on you," Bob reminded sharply. "This was a ghastly mistake, I explained that. And you only worked in the coffee house. There was no formal charge against you."

"I know." Nadine forced a slight smile. It sounded so logical, when you put it into words. But the fuzz were down on her. Any little thing, they'd be after her, even if she had nothing to do with it. From the corner of her eye she saw the waitress bearing toward them with their tray of food. "How is your father, Bob?"

Bob sighed with relief.

"It was a mild attack. He'll be fine. He's scared enough now to take decent care of himself." Bob was silent while the waitress slid steaming platters of bacon and eggs before them, a plate of toast, coffee. "Thank God I was able to come back in time for the revue. Not every year I have a star like Nadine Scott." His voice was affectionate.

They finished eating and Bob piloted her out to the car waiting at the curb. Climbing into the front seat beside him, she saw her duffel bag-packed, no doubt, by Bob, and her guitar resting on the rear seat. No need for her to return to the apartment, even for a moment. She was grateful for that. She didn't want to come face to face with Joyce again. Joyce probably felt the same way. But the kids were going to ask questions, she surmised wistfully. They'd loved having her there.

Bob drove her the short distance to the shabby building where she was to stay for a week. Walking from the car with him, Nadine remembered how he hated these shoddy buildings. How hard he worked for an upgrading of the rundown housing in the area. How much he wanted to improve things for people who lived in the neighborhood.

"It's just one flight up," Bob said casually. "You won't have to go tearing up a lot of stairs."

At the landing Bob reached into his pocket, fished out a key, walked to a door at the rear. He opened it, walked into the drabness, flipped on the lights. The two windows faced an alley, allowing in meager daylight. She gritted her teeth.

The plaster was falling in several areas. A window pane was broken, makeshift repaired with a piece of plastic scotch-taped in place, hardly adequate to keep out the Lake Michigan wind. A faded slipcover masqueraded a sagging single bed as a couch. A vase of paper flowers sat on a coffee table whose legs had been a teething ring for a pup. A stained card table obviously served for eating purposes. The floor, scratched and stained, was incongruously adorned with a pair of minute scatter rugs. "It's not the greatest," Bob said sadly while Nadine silently inspected.

"I've lived in worse," Nadine acknowledged. She'd told Bob about the hogans on the reservation. "Thanks, Bob."

"Nadine you're entitled to two weeks' salary," he said, reaching into his pocket for his wallet.

"But you paid the rent for this place," she reminded.

"Just one week," he reminded grimly. "It's too expensive for you to stay, unless you landed a really good job." He was counting out bills. Ninety dollars.

"Bob, I get twenty a week," she reminded him.

"You won't be getting the board that's due you," he pointed out briskly. "Take it, Nadine." He shook his head unhappily. "I'm sorry things worked out this way. Scaring the hell out of you."

Nadine stared at the money Bob put into her hand.

"Bob, this town won't ever be right for me again," she said, striving for calm. "First the drug bust, now this. The fuzz will look for things to pin on me. Bob, you know that!" Her voice was edged with bitterness.

"What do you want to do, Nadine?" he asked gently.

"Go to New York." She held up the ninety dollars.

"This will buy me a bus ticket, hold me for a little while. The East Village is loaded with coffee houses. I've heard the kids talking. It's a whole new scene there. Oh, I'll stay and do the revue," she promised conscientiously. "I'll stay until Christmas because the rent's paid up. But then, Bob, then I'm cutting out for New York."

The revue—presented the night before Christmas Eve—was a huge success. The whole Community Center staff basked in satisfaction. Nadine was exhilarated by the enthusiastic response to her own performance.

It felt so good, out there in the spotlight, singing of things that were close to her. Singing her words. That was love, the closeness between those people out front and her. She wasn't alone when she sang. They were there, and she was a part of them.

The Center closed early on Christmas Eve. Nadine had spent most of the day helping to take down the stage set, store away the costumes and props. She glanced about in unexpected nostalgia. Perhaps she'd never see this place again. For a while it had been the one bright spot in her existence.

"Nadine." Bob, standing in the doorway of his office, beckoned her to join him. "I think you're doing the right thing in going to New York," he said encouragingly. "After that revue, I'm sure of it. You've got something to sell. You'll find your way in New York." He smiled, reached behind his desk for two gift-wrapped packages. One quite large, the other pocket-sized. "Something from the kids for Christmas," he explained with a smile. "They miss you like hell."

"I miss them, too," Nadine said quickly. Absurdly, tears stung her eyes for an instant. "I'm leaving tomorrow on the five PM bus," she reported. "Thanks for everything, Bob." Impulsively, she leaned forward to kiss him good-bye.

"Write, Nadine," he said. "Let me know how you're doing."

Nadine strode swiftly through the streets to the tawdry apartment. It was home for just one more day.

She slid off her coat, went to the window to bring in the TV dinner resting in the box outside. She crossed to the oven, lit it gingerly, fearful of gas leaks.

Last Christmas Eve Jo had been here. They'd eaten their spaghetti dinner in front of that silly little tree that Jo's boss at the luncheonette had let Jo bring it home and later they heard about that terrible storm out in the Southwest. Jo was doing all right at school, with the family she lived with, and in analysis.

Nadine opened the two Christmas-wrapped packages. The small package contained a transistor radio. Instantly, she set it on the table, fiddled with the dial with a sudden compulsion to fill the room with music. *"Silent night, holy night, All is calm, all is—"*

Not Christmas carols. Impatiently, she spun the dial to other stations, until "Aquarius, Aquarius" burst into the room, and she settled back to open the larger Christmas package.

Nadine smiled with a touch of whimsy as the psychedelic weekender emerged from the protective wrappings. Bob was replacing her duffel bag for the trip to

New York. Suddenly feeling light and adventurous, Nadine packed the weekender with her meager possessions. She hesitated a moment over the duffel bag. No, she couldn't discard it. She folded it up tightly, squeezed it into the weekender, The duffel bag was her link to home.

In the gray, bitter cold late afternoon, Nadine walked down a deserted Randolph Street to the Greyhound terminal. Inside, she was startled, pleased, to discover the bus station wearing an aura of festivity. There were still those who were en route to their homes, to festive gatherings, even at this late time, juggling Christmas-wrapped parcels of varying and awkward sizes.

Aboard the bus, Nadine looked for an empty window seat. An obese, smiling woman in a fake leopard coat and make-up that was too harsh for her years dropped heavily to the seat beside Nadine. Nadine searched in her bag for her book. Instinctively, she knew the woman would be garrulous. She didn't want to talk to a stranger on this Christmas Day, when she was going further from home rather than to it.

At recurrent intervals last night, this morning–her mind had been on the family. Mama, the children. Now, in the cozy warmth of the bus, Nadine felt wistful, nostalgic. Back home in the hogan, the children would be caught up in the spirit of Christmas. Mama would give the family an early supper so they could go to bed early. The weather was sharp, the fire in the center of the hogan adding little comfort. The children would nestle together beneath blankets, seeking warmth from one another, talking in soft, pleased whispers about the presents Nadine had sent them.

Despite Nadine's determination not to talk, she was drawn into conversation with the woman. Surprisingly, she discovered it a relief not to remain silent. The woman, living in a suburb of Chicago now, was a native New Yorker going home on impulse to visit a cluster of married sisters and brothers.

"New York's not the same no more." The woman sighed, shook her head with regret. "Blacks pushing their way into everything. Hippies squatting down in what used to be the Lower East Side. Now they give themselves a new name. The East Village," she said disdainfully. "Who'd you say you were going to, honey?" Her eyes were avid, curious.

"My married sister," Nadine lied after a split-second of indecision. "She has an apartment on Riverside Drive," Nadine fabricated with fresh assurance. That's where Seth Coles had said his folks lived.

"Not bad." The woman was apparently impressed. "It's nice to have a river view. Though what they've done to the Hudson, I hear, is a real disgrace. Time was, that river was one of the sights in New York."

Nadine curled up against the pillow and dozed irregularly through the night, finally being awakened by her neighbor when the bus pulled off the highway into the parking area before a diner. It was almost eight-thirty, Nadine noted on the diner exterior clock. In less than four and one half hours they were scheduled to roll into the bus terminal in New York.

With her neighbor Nadine trailed into the warm, window-steamed diner. The women passengers lined up for admittance to the small washroom. Inside, Nadine stared at her tired reflection in the mirror. The uncertainties that had plagued her these past few days congealed into a lump in the pit of her stomach.

Her neighbor, at her elbow, Nadine left the washroom, heading for the counter, conscious that the
money in her purse must last until she could find a
job.

"Toast and coffee," Nadine ordered austerely,
though the breakfast aromas about the diner emphasized her morning hunger.

"You kids," the woman chided. "Never eat right.
Always starving yourselves to stay skinny."

Back on the bus, Nadine drifted off to sleep again.
Until she felt an insistent tugging at her arm.

"Honey, wake up. Take a look at the city! We're
going into Lincoln Tunnel in a couple of minutes."
Nadine reluctantly opened her eyes as the bus lum-
bered around the sharp curves on the descent to the
tunnel toll booths. Winter sunlight bathed the skyline
of Manhattan with gold. Below, Nadine spied the tall
smokestacks of an ocean-going liner.

"That's the Empire State over there," her neighbor pointed out with proprietary pride. "When I see
that, I always know I'm home."

The bus continued the steep descent, amid light
truck and car traffic, past the toll booth into the subterranean route into the city. Nadine sat up, feeling a
chaotic blend of excitement, anticipation, and alarm.
She was going into a whole new scene. A city even larger
than Chicago. Everyone here a stranger. Except Seth
Coles.

CHAPTER ELEVEN

Nadine moved down the escalator at Port Authority terminal, into the milling midday crowd, weekender tightly gripped in one hand, guitar cradled in the other arm. Her eyes anxiously scanned the faces. Plenty of kids here. Like the kids in Chicago, who'd sprawled on the grass beside her in Lincoln Park. Like the kids in the coffee house who leaned forward with earnest, intent eyes every time she sang.

Moving slowly through the horde of humanity, Nadine focused on her immediate destination. She remembered avenues, streets, from reading the *Village Voice*. St. Marks Place, Second Avenue—that was where the kids hung out.

"Excuse me," she said diffidently to a man behind the newsstand. "How do I get to St. Marks Place from here?"

"You want to go by subway or bus?" He grinned at her with friendly interest. "Take you two buses," he warned. "No transfers in Fun City."

"Bus," Nadine said quickly. She wasn't yet ready to cope with New York subways.

She listened attentively while the man directed her, thanked him warmly, and moved toward the Eighth Avenue doorway. Behind her an irate customer was complaining at being kept waiting.

Nadine walked north to Forty-Second Street, climbed aboard a cross-town bus, stared avidly at the movie house marquees with their blue movie offerings, the garishness of Times Square, the giant-sized ads. Bryant Park on the right, the imposing rise of the Filth Avenue library. Her eyes anxiously watched the signs at each avenue because she was supposed to change buses at Second.

There it was, Nadine noticed with relief, struggling to her feet, striving to stay erect with both hands too occupied to grasp a pole. She got out, skirted around to the Second Avenue bus stop. A bus was coming. She joined the line, climbed aboard, made her way to a seat at the rear. Watching the streets.

At Eighth Street she emerged from the bus. Instantly feeling herself at home as her eyes scanned the area. St. Marks Place. She was here! The faces about her young. The shop on the corner, a boutique, lifting her spirits. This was where it was at. Here she would find a place to spend the night. Here she would find a job.

Nadine walked slowly south, feeling herself part of the scene. She strolled into a luncheonette—a hangout for the kids—ordered a doughnut and coffee, inspected the others around her. Oh, Jo would dig this scene!

One of the two waitresses, a black girl with an Afro hairstyle, fantastic earrings and doll-like features, served her briskly. Her dark eyes rested speculatively on Nadine, on the guitar she cradled so protectively.

"You new in town?" the girl asked casually.

"Yes."

"You play that thing?"

"Yes. I used to sing in a coffee house in Chicago." Nadine smiled wistfully. "Until we were busted." The black girl would know she slung trays along with the singing.

"You got somewhere to stay?"

"No."

"Hey, Cindy?" the waitress yelled, and beckoned to a tall, thin girl in poncho and chinos. "Got room at your place for one more?"

"We've always got room for one more." Cindy's face was friendly. "When did you blow into town?"

They talked casually while Nadine finished her doughnut and coffee. Then the two girls slid from their stools and went out into the bustle of Second Avenue. They walked across East Fifth, past First, past Avenue A.

This was a slum, Nadine's mind catalogued as they strode past the fire-escape-fronted tenements, here and there a small store, a storefront neighborhood club, a house whose owners made a perky effort to reclaim it from anonymity. Yet this was not Chicago slums. The kids were here.

A whole army of kids, with their way-out clothes and their long hair and their dreams, along with the Puerto Ricans who occupied houses with ghetto density as though this closeness was a protection, and all-black houses, and those miscellaneously tenanted by Irish and Jews and Italians. It was new and, beautiful, and Nadine was glad she was here.

"We've got about eleven now," Cindy reported as they approached a shabby building whose window sills had all been recently painted a brilliant blue. "Stay here as long as you like."

"What about jobs?" Nadine asked softly.

"You don't have to work," Cindy reproached gently. "Not until you want to. Somebody always gives us money for food, and when we need the rent money, somebody always gets a job for a few days. Like Alicia," Cindy went on, and Nadine glanced at her inquiringly. "That beautiful girl at the luncheonette, with the Afro. She lives with her husband downstairs. She's always snitching food from the luncheonette for us." She gestured vaguely. "We get by."

"I have to have a job," Nadine said firmly. "I could work in a coffee house."

"I'll take you around tomorrow," Cindy promised, while they climbed the badly lit stairs that wore the familiar tenement smells. At a fourth-floor rear door, Cindy paused, dipped into the front of her shirt, fished out a key suspended from a chain about her neck.

"We have to lock up now," she said apologetically. "Since that girl was murdered last month, just down the block."

Cindy unlocked the door, walked into the kitchen.

What was that odd scent? A girl stood before the broiler of the gas stove, lining up slices of toast and cheese for grilling. She glanced at Cindy and Nadine, smiled.

"Craig brought home two pounds of cheese. Would you like some grilled?"

"No," Cindy said, turned inquiringly to Nadine.

"Thank you, no." Grass, Nadine pinned down the scent, with incense burning in another part of the pad.

"You can put your valise in one of the bedrooms," Cindy said, walking across the tiny living room to the narrow foyer that separated the two bedrooms.

Nadine started, not expecting to all but stumble over the pair making it on a blanket on the floor. The girl, no more than fifteen, lay on her back, her eyes shut tight, her face ecstatic while she whispered to the bearded youth above her. His hands fondled the naked, adolescent breasts that showed between her parted blouse.

Cindy ignored the pair on the floor, as she ignored the couple stretched across the living-room cot, smoking grass, caught up in their own private world. In one tiny bedroom a startlingly obese girl with a face like a

Botticelli angel snored gently. In the other bedroom, a boy about nineteen leaned over a relic of a typewriter, oblivious of their arrival.

"You can put your gear in the corner there," Cindy said. "Then let's go back to the Avenue. Maybe somebody knows something about a job or there may be something in one of the papers."

Nadine was at the crash pad for five days before she landed a job at The Pit. Ostensibly, she was a waitress. If there was a lag in free entertainment, she filled in. Here she felt comfortable. But she was uneasy in the free atmosphere of the crash pad.

"Look, don't worry about all the sex and all the pot," Cindy urged. "Everybody has a right to do their thing." She was thoughtful for a moment. "Nobody's on hard drugs, they're too sharp for that. And if they like screwing, who gets hurt!"

"It doesn't bother me," Nadine lied. "I'm glad I have a pad." But if she could get a paid singing job, she could afford to rent a room somewhere. At the coffee house she worked for tips, most of which she was putting into the community kitty because that was the thing to do.

"You'll cut out soon," Cindy predicted calmly. "Nobody stays too long in a crash pad." She shrugged this aside with a philosophical smile. "I dig the kids popping in and out." Only for Cindy, who always managed to meet the rent, was this a permanent pad.

"I'm going up to Times Square," Nadine said, uneasy about invading a strange area. "To see this agent Dick told me about." Dick, who entertained gratuitously at every opportunity, talked knowingly about the coffee house being a jazzy "showcase." A place where you could sell yourself to agents. Dick Powers had been singing there for a while. He kept saying he was going to make it right up there with Joplin and Cash.

"Sure," Cindy nodded knowingly. "Get some guy to come down to see your work."

Nadine nervously pulled out the scrap of paper she'd clipped from the current issue of Show Business.

"How do I get to this address on one carfare?" she asked anxiously, extending the excerpt.

"Subway," Cindy said briskly. "Walk over past Astor Place to Broadway and Eighth, take the BMT local up to Times Square." She paused. "You got any bread, over your carfare?"

"No," Nadine looked up inquiringly. "I may have tips tonight." But Thursday was slow, she knew. Over the weekend the tips were more plentiful because the straight kids, and the curious twenties and thirties, came in search of fresh excitement. They brought their middle-class money and their middle-class tipping habits with them.

"If you can, buy some milk," Cindy suggested gently. "We've been out since yesterday morning."

"I'll bring milk," Nadine promised. From the small store that was open till four AM.

She wouldn't have mustered up the courage to make this trip uptown, even with Dick's prodding, if there hadn't been that encouragement last Friday night. At a lull, with the small coffee house jammed with kids, Jock had sent her out onto the floor. Jock, her boss, was a tall, brawny white man with a poetic soul and a lack of bigotry which Nadine cherished. When she'd told Jock that she was Indian, he'd immediately launched into a learned dissertation on Indian culture.

She'd sung the new song she'd been struggling over for months. About what it was like to he an Indian in the late twentieth century. When she'd finished, she'd been scared for a moment by the absolute silence, but then the applause started up and it was ear-splitting. On both Saturday and Sunday nights she hadn't been able to sing again. She was the only waitress who showed up and it was a rat race to serve the customers. Weeknights were slow. Only when there was a solid house did Jock ask entertainers to perform. He considered it an insult to ask them to get up before half-a-dozen customers. She would be happy to sing for two.

Nadine walked down to the subway, already aware of a tightness in her throat at the prospect of walking into an office and trying to sell herself. She'd never been up to Times Square. The East Village was her scene. But if she wanted to make money, money to get her out of the crash pad, her best chance lay in landing singing jobs. Dick said you could pick twenty dollars a night, going out to sing.

"You lie, baby," Dick had said with that faint superiority of the "in" character. "You tell them you sang at the Blue Moon in Omaha, Nebraska, or the Silver Slipper down in Columbus, Georgia–you tell them how sensational you are."

Out on Broadway, she walked slowly up the street, unimpressed with the garish displays of the stores, too uptight about the task ahead to soak up impressions. A skinny blonde with an ostentatious platinum wig inspected her handmade Navajo boots with fleeting interest. A hooker, Nadine recognized, the blonde was transacting business at the curb.

She walked into the minute lobby, heavily occupied by a cluster of elevator-waiters who wore a common glow of confidence. *Show Business* and *Variety* nonchalantly held in one hand or extruding from a jacket pocket. Girls with false eyelashes and way-out phony fur coats. Fellows exchanging glib information about who was casting what around town. But they weren't auditioning for Broadway musicals here. This was the habitat of those at the lowest rung of the show-business ladder.

Nadine stood with her back against the wall, painfully trying not to be intimidated. The eighth floor. She was going to see Barney Soloff on the eighth floor. He hired lots of singers for small night clubs and resort hotels.

Once you cracked the ice, the others came easy, Dick said.

Half of the occupants of the elevator disgorged from the stuffy car on the sixth floor. The others, except for a delivery boy from the Gaiety Delicatessen who carried a brown paper bag, shoved importantly out of the elevator at the eighth floor. Nadine trailed behind them.

The hallway was paint-hungry, wearing an aura of defeat. Barney Soloff's waiting room was no better. A peeling, imitation-leather sofa sat against one wall, with an array of autographed photographs filling every available inch above the sofa. The opposite wall offered two past-their-prime club chairs and additional photographs. A black girl with an Afro and an enormous scrapbook sat on the sofa. An elderly man clutching a valise sat impassively in one chair. Instantly the available seating was commandeered. Self-conscious, Nadine stood by the door.

A few minutes later the door to the inner office flew open. An overblown redhead with a wig case dangling from one arm sauntered out, followed by a short, squat man smoking a cigar.

"Okay, who's next?" he demanded imperiously. "Have your photos and resumés ready."

Startled, Nadine watched the concerted rush to bring forth photos, mimeoed sheets from envelopes, attaché cases, or scrapbooks. What was a resumé? Dick hadn't said anything about that–about photos.

The girl with the Afro rose, tall and elegant in a severely simple beige coat, and walked toward the inner office. Nadine waited till the door closed behind Barney Soloff and the girl, then hurried through the outer door into the hallway again.

She walked slowly down Fifth Avenue, inspecting the shop windows, trying to erase from her mind her flight from the agent's office. Wondering what she would say to Dick and Cindy.

It was almost dark when she arrived at the coffee house, deserted except for an intense, interracial couple at a table at one side. They were arguing about Jimi Hendrix. The squat, lit candle between them lent a bizarre glow to their faces.

"I tell you, baby, that cat is out of sight," the bearded black student was insisting. "When he went over to London, he was lucky to earn thirty bucks a week. Now he pulls in thirty thousand a night. He did that one night last summer at the Hollywood Bowl."

"Slow night," Jock warned Nadine in the kitchen, where he sprawled in a chair reading Norman Mailer. "Nobody's coming out, the way the temperature's sliding down."

"Tomorrow's Friday. We'll be jammed." She crossed eagerly to the range to pour herself coffee from one of the ever-present silexes. She sipped the strong black liquid with a low sound of pleasure, simultaneously dropping bread into the toaster. Jock knew they were always hungry when they came to work.

Tonight's patrons were clearing out early. But just

before closing time three fellows sauntered in, blowing against the sharp drop in temperature. Deep in campus conversation, they settled themselves about a table. Nadine sauntered over to take their orders.

Not until she was practically at their table, with the candlelight full on their faces, did she recognize the tall, dark-haired new arrival who sat against the wall. He glanced up, broke off a heated remark to one of his companions as recognition washed over him.

"Nadine," Seth Coles said with quiet pleasure. "How long have you been in New York?"

"Since Christmas Day." Excited, happy, shy, not really believing she was talking to Seth Coles again.

"What time do you get off?" His eyes held hers.

"We close in thirty minutes." Her hands trembling as she gripped order pad and pencil.

"I'll wait for you," he said, and suddenly grinned "Don't you dare cut out through the back." The other two were avidly eavesdropping. "Nadine and I met in Chicago," he explained. "During the big bust."

Seth was alone, standing near the door, when she emerged from the rear in her coat.

"The temperature's trying to set some kind of record tonight," he warned. "Put on your gloves, something over your hair."

She pulled the gloves out of her pocket, obediently. "I don't need anything over my hair."

"Take this," he ordered with mock sternness, pulling the scarf from around his neck. "Kooky kid, you want to make business for the doctors?" He was staring intently at her face now. "No scar," he noted complacently. "I figured it would heal without a scar."

"Good doctor," she said. Trembling inside.

He pulled the door open. They walked out into the sharp night cold. She felt tense, uncertain.

"My pad's five minutes from here," he said, putting a hand at her elbow. "Let's go up there. It's too cold to walk around."

Nadine hesitated.

"All right."

They walked swiftly, Seth talking with calculated animation about the off-off-Broadway production he'd seen the night before. Talking because he was as tense and as uncertain as she.

"Do you live on Fifth?" Nadine's voice was unfamiliarly breathless.

"Yes, right down here. I told you it wasn't far," he reminded.

"I'm staying at a crash pad just a block the other way," she said unevenly and he frowned in disapproval. "I'm going to start looking for a place next week," she said rapidly. "When I get ahead on money."

"Crash pads can be messy," he said somberly. "You never know when trouble's going to start up."

A stray mongrel wandered over, sniffed at Seth, shoved his nose beneath Seth's hand in a wanton demand for affection.

"Here we are," Seth announced, giving the dog a final scratch beneath his jaw and nodding toward the low stoop of the building where he lived. "This fleabag "

Together Seth and Nadine entered the dark, sour-scented hallway, started up the stairs, Seth's hand reaching for hers as they climbed upward. At the second floor an unshaven drunk fumbled with his key while a cat meowed anxiously inside. "Gimme a hand, fella?" the drunk asked Seth with an ingratiating smile and held out the key. "I'm kinda incapacitated."

"Sure." Good-humoredly Seth took the key, slid it into the lock, and opened the door.

A fat black-and-orange cat pushed into view while his intoxicated owner made a near-disastrous bow and showed off the tall can of salmon which had nestled in the corner of his arm.

"Dinner, Misty," the drunk crooned. "Comin' right up."

"Wow, how much further?" Nadine laughed breathlessly, halting for a second at the fourth-floor landing.

"Just one more." Seth dropped an arm about her waist, prodded her upward with a smile. "Come on, baby. One more flight."

She waited, absurdly trembling, before the door to Seth's pad while he manipulated the pair of locks. He motioned for her to remain at the door while he walked into the darkness to grope for the light pull. He found it, flooded the kitchen with brightness.

"You're cold," he said gently, drawing her into the room.

"A little," Nadine conceded.

"I'll put up coffee for us." Seth moved into the minuscule living room to switch on the lamp beside the double Hollywood bed, sedately covered with a paisley cotton throw. "Instant," he warned humorously.

"Is there any other kind?" Nadine tossed back. Wanting, painfully, to sound sophisticated.

She slid off her coat, stood there in the heat-hungry room hugging her arms about her slenderness. The flannel-lined sweatshirt and much-washed chinos no match for the cold that infiltrated the warped windows. A cold unrelieved by heat at this hour.

"I'll put on the electric heater. Sit down. You'll be

warm in a few minutes."

Seth drew a rectangular electric heater from its corner hiding place, plugged it in, turned it up. Nadine leaned forward appreciatively, almost immediately feeling a welcome rush of heat.

"We'll make sandwiches," Seth announced with relish. "I'm always hungry. But let's have a round of coffee first."

Nadine curled up on a corner of the wide Hollywood bed, straining toward the heater. Heart pounding. Painfully, exquisitely, conscious of the glances Seth shot in her direction as he spooned instant coffee into a pair of mugs, brought down sugar, waited for the water to boil.

"How do you take yours?" Seth asked when the teapot began to whistle.

"Black, no sugar," she said.

Seth poured water into the two mugs, brought them over to the Hollywood bed, and set them on a much-scratched oak table beside her.

"Warm enough now?"

"Yes." She smiled, reached for a mug of coffee.

"Sure?" he pursued. "You can have a blanket."

"No, I'm fine," she insisted unsteadily. "The coffee's great."

"Little kook," he reproached softly. "Why did you cut out that way in Chicago?"

"What happened to your friend?" Her eyes avoided his. "Was she badly hurt?"

"She was okay," he said, frowning. "Livvy always looks for trouble. She wanted me to phone her folks back in New York." He leaned toward her. "By the time I got down to the street you were nowhere in sight. I didn't know where to look for you. You said you had no phone."

"I thought I'd never see you again," she whispered.

"I never stopped thinking about you," he said, reaching for her, his mouth coming down to hers. Her arms closed in about his shoulders, a sudden, painful urgency in her.

"Wait, baby," Seth whispered huskily.

He reached beneath the Hollywood bed to bring forth a brilliant plaid blanket to protect them against the night cold of the tenement flat. Beneath the blanket Seth groped for her. She waited, tears stinging her eyes, while he shucked away her chinos, the tights she wore against the winter weather.

"Cold?" he asked again, solicitously, because she shivered.

"No," she denied quickly, her hands tightening at his shoulders.

Seth's mouth sought hers again. His hands moved on her narrow thighs. She shivered with a new excitement, moved beneath him in response. More physically awake than ever in her eighteen years.

"Okay, baby?" The warmth of his body, the weight of him, poignantly welcome.

"Yes," she whispered, clinging. "Yes."

They moved together with mounting intensity. Her body taking over, blotting out thoughts, joy in her that she was giving him pleasure.

"Oh, Seth! Seth."

Beneath the covers she dressed again. Feeling warm, relaxed, exhilarated. Seth knew she'd never made it with anybody before. She was glad she hadn't. Tonight could only happen once. With Seth it was right.

Seth, whistling, moved about the kitchen, making

sandwiches. Guiltily, Nadine glanced at the clock on the table. Tomorrow was a school day.

"I'd better cut out soon," she said apologetically when Seth came into the room with a plate of sandwiches. "You have classes tomorrow."

He grinned, reached to brush her face gently with his fingertips.

"What's the difference? Tonight had to happen. I'll be up in time to make my first class. I'll set the alarm. You sleep late." She started. "You don't have to be at the coffee house until evening, do you?"

She shook her head quickly. But her eyes were uncertain.

"Baby, I don't want you going back to that crash pad. Move in with me. Tonight. Tomorrow we'll go over together for your gear. I have no roommate, there's plenty of room here for two." His eyes caressed her. "Nadine, I'd worry about you if you were living over there."

"All right," she acquiesced.

"If you disturb me nights when I'm studying," be jibed tenderly, "I'll clobber you." His eyes shone with satisfaction. He reached out to cover one of her hands with his.

CHAPTER TWELVE

Nadine settled into her new existence with a joy that sometimes terrified her. She hurried home each evening from the coffee house to find Seth waiting for her. They never tired of touching, holding, loving.

In the mornings Seth reluctantly crept out from beneath the mound of blankets, away from the comfort of Nadine's body, the room ugly with cold, only a faint grunt of heat rising in the ancient radiators.

Seth refused to allow Nadine to get out of bed to serve him breakfast. Coffee and toast for him, which he prepared himself, and with a flourish brought coffee to Nadine in bed. Later, between classes, he firmly promised each day, he would grab a decent breakfast. With Seth rushing out of the pad to classes, Nadine would doze off again until perhaps noon.

By the time Seth returned, the place would be immaculate. A small roast, bargain-shopped, would be in the oven, or a stew bubbling atop the range. Nadine contributed towards their groceries because Seth existed on a stringent budget.

Nadine relished being part of this potpourri of a neighborhood, enjoyed the forays into the supermarkets, a gourmet delight to her. After all this time away from the reservation, it was still a wonder to her to be able to put meat upon the table nightly.

On Friday and Saturday nights, Seth usually brought a couple or two over to hear Nadine sing. Afterward, they went to somebody's pad to rap and drink beer. Seth was particularly vocal these days about the problems of doctors in the ghetto hospitals.

She was developing a following, becoming a definite—though still unpaid—part of the entertainment. Seth good-humoredly kidded her about not trying for out-side singing jobs. But for Nadine it was enough to be with Seth, to sing at the coffee house. Right now it was enough.

At the end of her third week of living with Seth, the phone rang at an hour when she knew Seth must be in class. She stood there, hesitant, discomforted, while the phone jangled insistently.

Oh, this was silly. Seth expected her to answer the phone. Suppose it was something important?

"Hello." She tried to sound casual.

There was a faint pause. For an instant, Nadine thought there was no one on the line.

"Is Seth there?" a woman's voice asked with con-trolled politeness. An older woman. Seth's mother, Nadine guessed instinctively. A pleasant cultivated voice. She taught school.

"I'm sorry, he's–he's at school," Nadine stammered, her face hot. "May I take a message?"

"Tell him he's an uncle," Seth's mother said casu-ally, but Nadine felt the tension. "His sister, Linda, had a son three hours ago."

"I'll leave a note," Nadine promised with warmth. Hoping to sound like a transient. Someone who bor-rowed the apartment to study.

"Thank you." Then a click disassociated her from Mrs. Coles.

Later, preparing dinner, Nadine discovered herself listening anxiously for the sound of Seth's feet on the creaky stairs. She relished cooking for Seth, finding pleasure in his appreciation of the meals she placed before him. Willing herself to believe this closeness between them would go on forever.

She straightened up from the oven where she stood basting the supermarket special-of-the-week chicken which was turning a golden brown. Seth, bounding up the stairs. A glow on her face, she hurried to the door to welcome him.

"Something smells great." He dropped an arm about her shoulders, kissed her lightly.

"Roast chicken," she reported. "Oh, you had a phone call. Guess what? You're an uncle!"

"Hey, what do you know?" He grinned, but his eyes were questioning. "Mom called, huh?" She nodded, watching him. "Boy or girl?"

"Boy," Nadine told him. His mother hadn't introduced herself, but there'd been no need.

"I'll call up later and congratulate grandma," he decided, moving into the kitchen with Nadine. "How about some coffee? I have to meet a couple of interns from the hospital for a quick conference."

"Be back in an hour," Nadine warned with mock sternness, "or my chicken will be a wreck." How serious he was about this conference. She knew how much this hassle with the ghetto hospital meant to Seth. The staff doctors were putting up such a frenzied battle to improve care.

"I'll be back," he promised, moving into the living room while Nadine poured coffee into a tall mug for him, "in an hour."

"Why so somber?" Seth chided gently, accepting the mug of coffee. How beautiful, she thought, the way he sensed her moods.

"I was thinking about your folks," she said candidly. "The way they're uptight because you're working with the hospital group."

"They don't know I'm working with the group," Seth reminded, his eyes troubled. "Of course, I know they're deeply in sympathy with the whole scene; we discussed it at dinner last week. But I can't take a chance on saying I'm involved."

"Duck, if you see any TV cameras closing in," she jibed tenderly. "There's bound to be plenty of newspaper coverage, the way the doctors are talking out. Don't get your face splashed across the front of the *New York Post*."

Seth sighed heavily, shook his head with a lack of comprehension

"They're so mentally committed to this kind of thing. They were livid about Chicago. But they're so adamant about cutting off my money supply if I get into a clash with the fuzz. Let's face it." He forced a smile. "I don't make it through medical school without them behind me. I can't let anything get in the way of my degree."

"You're not involved in clashes with the fuzz," Nadine protested. "You're trying to help a bunch of doctors do a better job for people who need them desperately!" Her eyes flashed as she recalled the last meeting she'd attended with Seth. She'd come home with the framework of a new song, words falling into place in her mind.

"Honey, when I get my degree, I can run my life the way I want." Seth's face was taut with determination. "I'll manage to pay them back. I can do without the fancy trappings of the fancy practice. Maybe I'll set up practice on a reservation," he teased, and for a moment Nadine was startled at the possibility of such a move. Seth chuckled, drained his coffee cup, leaned forward to kiss her lightly. "See you in an hour, baby."

Nadine made the salad dressing, set the table.

At loose ends, she went into the living room, picked up the guitar, cradled it lovingly. Tomorrow evening, every Thursday evening, Seth would be going to his family for dinner. He'd adopted this habit to appease his mother. Nadine told herself it was absurd, but she felt painfully cut out of Seth's life, those brief hours each week when he went off to that world she didn't know. His parents' world. His kid sister Audrey's world.

Seth talked about his parents, about Audrey, and his married sister Linda with a vividness that made them real to her. But what would they think, if they knew he was shacked up with a girl who was half-Navajo?

A sharp rap sounded at the door. Not Seth–she would have recognized his footsteps coming up. Nobody came here during the day. Sometimes, in the evenings friends of Seth's, friends of theirs, dropped in. "Who is it?" Seth ordered her never to open the door to anyone she didn't know. Too many junkies in the neighborhood.

"Livvy." The girl outside sounded startled. "Doesn't Seth Coles live here any more?"

"Yes, he does." Involuntarily, Nadine unlatched the door, with a compulsion to see this girl. Livvy. That was the name of the girl who phoned Seth that night in Chicago.

For a moment the two girls inspected each other.

"Hi," Livvy said coolly. "I just dropped by to say hello, I was in the neighborhood." She hesitated, her eyes seemingly amused. "You Seth's new girl?"

"Yes." Color warmed her face. She hated the inference that Seth slept with a long line-up of girls. "He'll be back soon. Would you like to wait?"

Unexpectedly, Livvy laughed.

"I think Seth would flip if I did. I'll see him around one of these days." She smiled, taking detailed inventory of Nadine, then spun about and headed down the stairs again.

Nadine swiftly shut the door again, wanting to blot

out the amused face of the strikingly attractive girl who once was part of Seth's life. Feeling herself dishearteningly inadequate, unsophisticated, in comparison.

The chicken was done, a gleaming mahogany masterpiece. Nadine manipulated the pan from the oven, lifting the chicken onto an elegant platter Seth had rescued from the garbage last week. She straightened up, a smile touching her mouth at the sound of a key in the door. Seth was home.

"You had a visitor," she announced flippantly, but her expressive eyes were watching him. "Livvy."

Seth lifted his eyebrows in astonishment.

"Well, what do you know?" he drawled. "What did Livvy want here?"

"She said she was in the neighborhood, she just dropped by." Nadine managed a calculated note of amusement. "What about her, Seth? Did she mean a lot to you once?"

Seth shrugged, smiled faintly.

"Livvy was part of my radical-youth period."

"What am I?" she demanded, suddenly angry. To what period did she belong?

"You," Seth said with infinite tenderness, reaching for her, "are the girl I'd choose to be with on a desert island. You're the girl who makes life beautiful."

"Oh, Seth." But he didn't say, the girl he wanted to live with forever. Because forever meant marriage. "Seth–"

The chicken sat on the table, hot and delectable, but Seth was moving her backward with calculated caution, out of the kitchen into the adjoining living room. To the double Hollywood bed where they lay so often in love.

"Seth, dinner's ready," she whispered reproachfully.

"Screw dinner," he said, and they both laughed.

She felt the edge of the bed hit the back of her knees. How groovy, the way Seth would want to make love this way, with no warning at all. She shut her eyes tightly, releasing herself.

Seth lowered her across the bed, left her to cross to the windows to pull down the spidery, dark green shades against any prying eyes. Then he returned to her, his breathing already quickening with excitement.

"Baby, thank heaven I found you again. I was only half-alive without you." Gently, he was shucking away the chinos that were practically her uniform. His hands were cold, but she didn't care.

It was more than just a shack-up, what she had with Seth. This part was great, sure, but there was all the rest of the time. She was happy, just sitting close to Seth and reading a book while he studied. She found joy in waking in the morning, close enough to press her face against his shoulder. She was so proud of his brightness, his earnestness, his determination to become a good doctor.

"Oh, baby, baby," Seth whispered hotly. "How did I ever live without you?"

The days blended into weeks, the weeks into months. May was the most marvelous month in the world, Nadine decided. On brilliantly sunny weekends, they explored Central Park, rode the Staten Island Ferry, went to the Bronx Zoo. One Saturday, splurging, they took the Circle Day Line tour around New York, and it was as exciting to Nadine as a trip to Europe might have been to Seth. On days that were drab, chilly, they visited museums. The Metropolitan, the Museum of Modern Art, the Guggenheim and the Whitney. When his parents bought a new TV, they fell heir to the old, in need of minor repairs, and became late-late show buffs, as Seth had been before his old set conked out.

Seth was set for a summer job in a Village bookstore when May segued into June. Nadine was conscious of a new restlessness in her with the approach of summer. She had hungered, with the first sign of spring, to take herself uptown, to make the rounds of the showbiz agents who might send her out on signing jobs. But if she started taking nights off, she'd lose out at the coffee house. The money she earned was essential.

Each week she sent money home to her mother. A pitifully small amount, yet she knew how much it meant in a family where every dollar seemed a small fortune. Despite Seth's early, unrealistic objections, she contributed substantially to their food budget, bought the small treats that dotted their lives. Each week a dollar or two was tucked away in the bottom of the weekender Bob Frazer had given her last Christmas and each week, when she opened that weekender, Nadine felt faintly guilty. Bob had such faith in her ability as an entertainer. He expected such fabulous things of her. She hadn't even dropped him a postcard. What was there to say? The only singing she did was at the coffee house.

Early in June, Seth's mother phoned the house again.

"Please tell Seth we'll expect him for dinner tonight," Felicia Coles was saying casually. "His older sister flew in unexpectedly with the baby, since her husband had to come in for a sales conference. Dinner'll be the usual time," she wound up briskly.

"I'll tell him," Nadine promised politely, defensively. "Thank you."

The soft click at the other end told her Seth's

mother had cut her off from that other, distant world. With a need for activity, Nadine reached for her purse, took down from its wall hook the light poncho Mama had made and sent to her last week. Usually, she waited for Seth to go with her to the supermarket when she bought meat for the week. This was their big food investment, she liked his reassurance that she was choosing properly. Today, she wanted to be away from the apartment. Away from the phone.

Nadine strolled pleasurefully in the brisk June afternoon, just enough coolness in the air to make it comfortable. Wearing the poncho was like reaching out to home. She touched the hem with tenderness.

On the sidewalk a pair of late-teen mothers, each with carriage in tow, chattered animatedly about baby appetites. The two in the carriages were probably a year old, Nadine guessed, smiling warmly at their friendliness. Their mothers were probably no older than she.

Linda's baby was an infant, Nadine thought wistfully. Seth's nephew. If Seth and she were married, he would be her nephew, too. Her mind flashed back to the hospital where Jo had given birth. She remembered her first sight of the baby, the tiny, red-faced morsel with flailing hands, who was Jo's son. Jo had been so upset, though she tried to hide it, those first few nights after her mother took the baby back to the reservation.

But she would never send her baby to Mama. A maternal tenderness, of which she never suspected herself capable, closed in about her. How unbearably sweet, to carry Seth's child within her. To hold Seth's child in her arms. But Seth had two more years of college after this, and then came his internship and his residency. Seth couldn't be tied down with a child.

The sound of the key in the door jarred Nadine into reality. Seth was home. For a little while he'd be with her. And when she came home from the coffee house tonight, he'd be here. His mother couldn't take that away from them.

"You had a phone call," she reported brightly, when he'd kissed her, nuzzled comfortably against her for a moment. "Linda's in town with the baby. Your mother wants you to come up there for dinner."

"With the baby?" Seth lifted his eyebrows in astonishment.

"Linda's husband came in for some business meeting," Nadine recalled. "I gather she flew in on impulse."

"I hate to cut out tonight," he apologized. "But Linda would be hurt."

"Sure." Nadine forced a smile. Of course, he had to go up to see his sister. Mentally, she could accept this. Emotionally, she rebelled. "Shower and change," she jibed. "Don't take the smell of Fifth Street up to Riverside Drive with you."

In a few minutes they sat down together at the small kitchen table while Seth reminisced about Linda. He looked forward to seeing her, Nadine realized with a small sense of loss, wishing to share everything that mattered to him.

"I'd better cut out," he said reluctantly, when Nadine had finished her hamburger and salad and he had downed two cups of coffee. "I'll be home before you will." He grinned. "And we can sleep late tomorrow. It's great not to have to get up till eight-thirty."

Seth didn't have to be at the bookstore till nine forty-five. He'd landed the job a few days ago, quite unexpectedly. The salary wasn't much, but it allowed him to let his folks off the hook for the summer. Seth felt good about that It bugged him to be taking so much from them.

She'd hoped that they might be wildly extravagant and buy two tickets for that rock festival in northern New Jersey this weekend. Seth said some of the kids from med school were going, they could probably hitch a ride. But they'd decided to be practical. Instead of the festival, they'd go to the next concert at Fillmore East.

On Thursday, Seth was late coming home from the bookstore. They'd have barely half an hour together, Nadine thought fretfully, before he'd have to cut out for the uptown subway. His mother expected him for dinner again, even though he'd been there Tuesday. Linda and her family were taking a late plane back to the Midwest tonight.

Nadine opened the door before Seth could reach for his key.

"You got stuck," she greeted him sympathetically.

"Yeah." He grinned wryly. "A customer who was buying out half the store wanted assistance. She thought I was such a nice boy," he drawled.

"Tell her hands off," Nadine said with mock peremptoriness. "You belong to me."

"Hot outside, you know." He drew her close. "Like me, hot inside." He ran a hand down her back to the delicate curve of her rump.

"You have to be at your mother's." Her liquid brown eyes holding his, wanting him to dismiss the date uptown. To take her to the bed which had known so much love. "Is there time?" she whispered, because he was turned on, too. She felt the first faint hardening of him against her.

"Later, baby," he promised, reluctantly putting distance between them. "Mom will flip if I don't show.

And I probably won't see Linda again for a year.

"Your folks' place must be lovely," Nadine said wistfully. "You said you can see the river from the front windows–"

"It's jazzy compared to this," Seth conceded. "But nobody, except the fuzz, dares to walk down to the river these days. Not even in broad daylight. Too many muggings. When I was little, before Mom put in the air-conditioners, we'd walk down to the river on sweltering nights. It'd be loaded with people."

"Tell me about the furniture, Seth," she coaxed, moving about the kitchen as she prepared a small salad. Her frank was under the broiler, Seth's coffee perking. "You say your mother has such a talent for decorating." She'd love to fix up their pad, but they didn't have money for such luxuries. She was delighted with the leather-inlaid coffee table, barely scratched, which they'd picked up on the street the other night. They walked past just as the man was putting it at the curb. "Come on, Seth, tell me," she prodded.

"Honey, I wish I could take you with me," he said gently, reading through her Thursday night front. "But they'd absolutely flip."

"Because you're shacked up with an Indian!" Nadine flared, her face hot.

"Nadine, my folks wouldn't care if you were red, white, or purple. They're just uptight at the thought of my getting serious about any girl. They want me clear of emotional entanglements until I'm fully launched as a physician. They know what I've got ahead of me."

"Oh God, Seth, and you talk so much about being your own man!" Nadine swung away from him, pretending to be intent on the task of removing her frank from the broiler.

Seth stared at her, looking troubled.

"Nadine, I can't get a medical degree on my own. I must have my parents behind me financially." He reached for the percolator, poured himself a mug of coffee.

"That's all you care about!" Suddenly Nadine was trembling. "Your damned degree! Right now that's the most important thing in your life."

"Baby, it has to be," he insisted urgently. "I can't afford to goof up. This is it. I won't get a second crack at going through medical school." He reached for her hand, but she managed to evade him. "Nadine, it has nothing to do with us, but I can't risk taking you home with me. For now, we have to play it my parents' way." He forced a grin. "Seth on the straight and narrow, no emotional entanglements, aiming straight for the degree. Baby, you know about the generation gap. They don't dig our scene."

Two more years of medical school, Nadine considered with anguish. Then his internship. He couldn't support a wife on an intern's salary, when be was determined to start paying back his folks the minute he was out of medical school. It was an obsession with Seth. He'd vowed to start paying them back out of his first salary check.

She occupied only a small corner of Seth's life.

School and his parents crowded her out. Later, if they remained together, it would be the hospital and his parents. She belonged nowhere. Not on the reservation. Not in Seth's white world.

CHAPTER THIRTEEN

Nadine stood motionless for seconds, staring at the door. Listening to the staccato rhythm of Seth's feet going down the stairs. She couldn't be a small corner of Seth's life. That wasn't enough.

She gazed about the paint-hungry but immaculate kitchen with fresh eyes, as though to absorb every inch within her memory. Those mugs on the shelf—Seth surprised her with them after she'd fallen in love with them in a shop window on Third Avenue. The bulletin board—she'd set that up for Seth's notes, and he'd been so pleased. The kooky cartoons about doctors which she'd collected for Seth—they formed a panel beside their kitchen table, and she'd framed the panel with strips of leather. No more would she move about this kitchen, listening for the sounds of his arrival.

Tears stinging her eyes, she moved about the minuscule rooms, collecting her belongings. Few and swiftly packed. With weekender in one hand, duffel bag slung across her shoulder, guitar in her free arm, Nadine left the fifth-floor flat. On the third floor, Mrs. O'Malley yelled sharply at a pair of squabbling youngsters in her kitchen. Downstairs, the stoop was empty at this hour, for which Nadine was grateful.

She walked swiftly west, in this first hot spell of the summer. Three months ago the street would have been night-garbed at this hour. Now it might have been mid-afternoon.

Nadine had remembered the hotels where poor people went. Kids who flowed into town and were unable to locate crash pads. Welfare clients.

She'd listened often to Seth and his clan talk earnestly about the bad conditions of the welfare hotels. But, at least, they were cheap. Compared to the rest of New York's living quarters they were cheap.

She smiled self-consciously at a pair emerging from the laundromat, a couple whom Seth and she encountered regularly around the neighborhood, with whom they talked casually. The other two waved, inspected Nadine with overt curiosity. The gear she awkwardly carried advertised a split with Seth.

Nadine walked with a sense of urgency, impatient to put the neighborhood behind her, to be engulfed in anonymity. She'd phoned the coffee house, reported that she was leaving town suddenly. They hadn't asked questions. The turnover was heavy. She'd remained longer than most girls.

Perspiration caused the colorful cotton print she wore to cling between her shoulder blades, glistened at her hairline. Nostalgia tugged at her as she put distance between herself and what, for a poignantly beautiful little while, had been home. She had deluded herself into believing she belonged there.

At the corner before the tall, dirt-laden hotel, whose neon sign identified it unmistakably, Nadine halted with a sense of discomfort. The area before the entrance was glutted with humanity. Adults, noisy teenagers, scampering children, babies in carriages and strollers. Mostly blacks.

A transistor blared out a recent Jimi Hendrix recording. At the curb an ice-cream man dug into his cart to serve eager, small customers. A blonde girl clung to a tall, skinny teenager with ruddy sideburns and an unkempt beard. They were avidly absorbing the scene. Strangers.

The blonde spied her, smiled, said something to her companion. Heartened by the presence of the pair, Nadine shoved her way through the mob into the shabby lobby, where a trio of elderly white women sat in desultory conversation, holding tightly to the handles of their utilitarian purses.

Nadine was startled at the price of a night's lodging, but paid for one night, signed herself in as Joanne Ross, in case Seth inquired at the desk.

The clerk inspected her with more than businesslike interest, which Nadine found disconcerting. She smiled politely, accepted the key he handed her, dutifully repeated the room number, and hurried toward the elevator. Lock her door, Nadine reminded herself, though surely her attitude had been sufficiently discouraging to ward off any night visiting.

The couple she'd noticed on the sidewalk were walking into the lobby now. They went up to the desk to inquire about the room. The clerk smirked, took their money, handed over a key. By the time the elevator finally grunted its way down to the lobby, the couple were beside her.

"You play that?" the blonde asked with a liquid velvet southern accent.

"Yes." Nadine felt a strange relief in this communication. "I sing. My own material, mostly."

"You going to the festival tomorrow?" the fellow inquired with interest. "We drove up all the way from Alabama to be there."

"I wish I could," Nadine said wistfully. "Twenty dollars a ticket is way out of sight for me."

"Honey, you don't buy tickets," the girl scoffed in high good humor. "You come in close enough to hear, that's all." She grinned in satisfaction.

"Didn't they say something about calling it off?" Nadine squinted in thought. "Something about the township thinks it's going to cause trouble, with so many kids showing up."

"It'll come off," the blonde prophesied ebulliently. "With everybody showing, it just has to!"

The elevator door rumbled open.

"Look, we drove up in David's car," the blonde said "If you want to drive up to the festival with us, there's plenty of room."

"To the festival?" Without having to pay for a ticket, according to these two. Excitement spiraled in her. Actually to be there at a rock festival!

"Kathy and I are packing some grub and beer and starting up first thing in the morning," David said with a slow anticipatory smile. "You're welcome to go with us. And don't worry about that twenty-buck ticket," he reassured "There'll be more crashers than payers."

"I'd love to go," Nadine accepted with a dazzling smile.

"Leave an eight o'clock call at the desk," Kathy instructed. "We'll meet you downstairs at eight-fifteen sharp. We can stop for breakfast on the road."

"Eight-fifteen in the lobby," David emphasized because the elevator was stopping at Nadine's floor. "See you then. Hey, what's your name?" he yelled after her, but the elevator slid closed before she could reply.

Nadine unlocked the door to her room, walked inside, and sought the light pull. A fair-sized, walk-in closet, she thought distastefully. The overhead light was a dismal forty watts. She reached for the lamp on the narrow chest. Another twenty-five watts. She glanced about, at the lumpy, narrow bed, the makeshift closet set up in one corner, the stained wash basin.

With a need to bring air into the room, she crossed to the one window, pulled up the shade, stared in shock at the square of wire which covered the window. Like a jail! Then she saw the notice attached to the window frame: "DO NOT THROW GARBAGE OUT THE WINDOW." That explained the wire across the window. Suppose there was a fire? Nadine shivered.

The window moved a scant six inches beneath her persistent tugging, refused to budge further. The air was muggy, fetid, but it would have to do for tonight. She crossed to the wash basin, turned on the cold-water faucet. She washed her face, stretched out on that uninviting bed, to think about tomorrow. Not about tonight, when Seth would return to the pad and find her gone. That part of her life was over. With Seth she was going nowhere.

At eight-fifteen sharp, yawning because sleep had been elusive, dreams punctuated with memories of Seth, Nadine handed in her key at the desk. The three old ladies, in their staid cottons, their sensible shoes and shiny straw hats, who had sat in the lobby when she arrived last night were seated there again. Relics of another era in the hotel's history. Nadine smiled faintly.

It was almost as though they were a permanent feature of the lobby.

She hovered uneasily at the desk, watching the elevator's painful descent to the lobby. Conscious that she was the cynosure of the old ladies' interest. Relief rolled over her when the elevator door slid open and Kathy and David strolled into the lobby.

"We heard an announcement on the news. They claim the festival's definitely off," Kathy reported, her enthusiasm unmarred. "We don't care, we're going there, anyway. We've come fourteen hundred miles for this scene. The kids won't stop."

David went to the desk to hand in their key, and then joined the two girls with a broad smile.

"Let's go pick up the car and get started," he said, positioning himself between them. "I just hope that tired old heap makes it."

"Oh, David, cut it out," Kathy scolded. "It came up here without a grunt, didn't it? It'll take us up there and back home, the same way."

They strode out into the early morning sunlight, turned south for two blocks to pick up the 1964 Valiant, dusty, with red clay stains. David stowed their gear and the three settled themselves on the front seat.

They cut across town, headed north up Eighth Avenue toward the Lincoln Tunnel. Traffic was sluggish, subways and buses disgorging their rush-hour hordes. David swore, simultaneously angry and unnerved by the audacity of city drivers. But at the tunnel they discovered they were driving against incoming traffic, moving speedily into the subterranean tube while the incoming cars, trucks, buses inched along like arthritic old ladies.

They moved past the toll station. Onto the curves that led to the highway. Nadine remembered, with a sudden quickening of her pulse, the lumbering Greyhound bus that had brought her along this route into the city. How long ago that seemed!

"David, I'm starving," Kathy complained. "Let's stop off and eat somewhere. A joint," she warned, swinging to Nadine with an impish grin. "We're way low on cash."

"Me, too." Nadine smiled faintly.

The three of them scanned the highway for something modest, turned in at a pancake house after a quick conference. They'd have pancakes and coffee, then watch for a supermarket to buy enough food to last for the three days they planned to remain at the festival.

A mile beyond the pancake house they spied a huge, sprawling supermarket, and cut off the highway to park. Inside, they shopped in high spirits. Bread, sandwich makings that wouldn't spoil in the heat, a bagful of fruit, doughnuts. With their food in tow they returned to the car.

"So the old cows up there think they're canceling this bash," David chortled. "We'll have a 'people' festival, groove on our own!"

"'They're dirty-minded old creeps." Kathy's eyes blazed with fresh indignation. "They said we're all 'lewd and dope addicts'. What nerve!"

"They're scared, old people," David said impatiently. "They won't accept the 'now scene'."

"Any chance that some of the rock groups will show?" Nadine asked wistfully. She tingled at the prospect of hearing them in person, out in the open, under the skies. All the big ones!

"The local kooks got court orders canceling the concert," David said. "Rock artists' agents won't let 'em show. But we'll make our own sound, baby, you wait and see," he promised with a surge of optimism.

Traffic was routine on routes three and forty-six. Then they cut north, and the traffic acquired a fresh, vital color. Young people in predominance, Nadine noted, excitement taking hold of her. Traffic was heavier up here--kids en route to the festival.

At the side of the road hitchhikers began to show. David pulled up to take on two fellows and a girl, who'd held up a sign indicating their destination was the festival. The air was suddenly rich with anticipation This was a pilgrimage, a pilgrimage of the young.

By the time they arrived within fifteen miles of their destination, according to the map spread across Kathy's lap and which she laboriously perused, traffic was congested, crawling along.

"Wow, they're all headed for the festival!" David crowed. "Did you ever see so many kids in your life?"

"Never," Nadine said softly, caught up in the spirit that pervaded them all. She was part of something marvelous, a happening unlike anything she'd ever encountered in her life. Joy surged through her, lit up her face. Thousands of kids, with one destination.

Many of the cars were old. Several became overheated, caused tie-ups. Further up, somebody labored to change a flat, with half-a-dozen willing helpers milling about. These were good kids, Nadine thought exultantly, glad she was part of this.

Every car was jammed to capacity with youthful humanity. Transistors blared, hamburgers and paper-containered malts in evidence. In one car a folk-rock group--heavy on enthusiasm, light in talent—provided their own entertainment. Nadine frowned in annoyance when a barrage of soda cans went sailing from a car before them. David sounded off in rage at this lack of concern for other people.

"Let's stop off at the next stand for a cool drink," one of their hitchhikers urged. "I'll treat. God knows what facilities they'll have at the festival with the locals against it."

The roadside stand where they stopped was doing a fantastic business. The fellows behind the counter grinning as they served, obviously in sympathy with this mass invasion.

"You go on and do your thing up there," one youth counseled in good humor. "Maybe they canceled the festival, but they can't stop you if you want to gather and groove together, can they? Sheriff Hogan's got two kids of his own. He says nothing bad is going to happen unless agitators come in to start it up."

Uneasily, Nadine remembered Seth's reservations about the festival. Seth had been concerned that the Weatherman faction of the SDS might try to start up a disturbance.

Nadine's clique piled into the car again, inched along the tree-lined country roads that led to the two-hundred-eighty-acre farm that was the site of the festival. What would have been a ten-minute drive under normal conditions consumed almost an hour and a half.

The word spread quickly. The kids had begun to arrive the night before. Maybe ten thousand were already there, with the owners, openly sympathetic, making weak pleas for their departure, under pressure from the fuzz.

"My God," Kathy whispered as the unbelievable expanse of parked cars came within their view. "It looks like General Motors with diarrhea."

They cut off the road to park where they could, collected their gear, and moved with the masses ahead of them toward the area where a wooden bandstand had been hopefully erected.

"No amplifiers," one of the fellows they'd picked up on the road remarked. "That's going to be a bastard."

"See the ice-cream truck over there." David pointed to the wagon dispensing pops. "You can hook up the amplifiers to their battery. It'll be a snap." His eyes scanned the scenery. He pointed to another truck, offering heroes and canned soda. "There's another. We'll have amplifiers," he predicted happily.

Faces wore an aura of anticipation, even though word was spreading that the sprawling green acres of the farm were going to be sealed off to new invaders. Word had just filtered through that local authorities were turning back food trucks. Yet despite this seal-off of cars, Nadine, as did the others, noted the continuing invasion on foot, with no attempts by the local fuzz to stop them. So the kids would park a few miles down and hike.

"Let's settle here," Kathy decided, choosing an open spread of grass not far from the pond where earlier arrivals already sloshed about in the water. Everywhere hordes of youngsters were settling in for the duration. With air-mattresses, bedrolls, blankets, tents.

Already, the scent of marijuana permeated the air, making Nadine uneasy. All drugs, even pot, reminded her of Eddie. She was conscious, too, of the overt commerce in drugs. Thirty feet from where she sprawled on the grass hashish was being openly sold.

"Good black hashish for three-fifty," a hawker called out exuberantly.

"Buy one tab of acid and get a free tab of smack," a competitive pusher invited.

"The cops are not going to run us off, are they?" The girl they'd picked up was also uncomfortable.

"What can they do?" Nadine questioned calmly. "There must be twenty thousand of us, and twenty of them. They wouldn't dare start a drug bust under conditions like this," she said with quiet assurance.

Nadine lay on her back, content for now to lie in the sun, surrounded by her own. Nobody asked if she were red, white, or purple here. Here she belonged. With these kids like herself. At the pond a bunch were shucking to skin and jumping into the water. It all seemed so natural, nothing wrong. Like the open love-making. It was beautiful, Nadine thought, with a surge of pleasure and wished, wistfully, that Seth were here to share the experience with her.

As the day waned, with the sun a dramatic red in the background, an impromptu performance began. And as David had prophesied, amplifiers were powered by the batteries from the ice-cream and the hero trucks, doing a sell-out business on the grounds. The kids closed in as well as they could, with David adroitly maneuvering his clan close to the stage.

Nadine sat on the grass, her arms wrapped about her, as the entertainers took their places on the wooden platform. Unknown groups of varying talents, but the kids joyously receptive to all offerings. At a lull in the program, she impulsively reached for her guitar, plucked a few chords.

"Come on, Nadine," David insisted spiritedly, leaping to his feet, tugging at her arms. "Go on up there. Give!" Trembling, Nadine allowed David to prod her up onto the wooden platform, before the sea of young faces. In the dusk, she held the guitar in her arms, closed her eyes, began to sing. Remembering how it was on the reservation. Remembering what it was like to be a fifth-class citizen. Telling it all, distinctly, hauntingly, poignantly. The cry of three hundred years of anguish at the hands of the white man.

Her voice faded away. The last twang of the guitar echoed in the distance. Nadine hovered there for an instant, her eyes shut tightly. Mentally back on the reservation. Seeing Mama's face. Aching for the comfort of Mama's arms. And then, with shattering suddenness, the thunder of the applause assaulted her ears. She opened her eyes, shaken. Overwhelmed by the thousands of hands clapping their approval.

"More, more!" the cry went up, and was taken from one to another.

For forty minutes Nadine stood before the rapt crowd of her peers, and wailed out the words she'd formed into song. Remembering the dirt-floored hogan, the lack of food, the cold, the anguish of the Indian boarding school, the constant, degrading discrimination. Remembering in painful detail the suicide rate, the mortality rate, the average Indian died at forty-three, the average salary for the Indian, thirty dollars a week when even in black Watts the average was sixty-four dollars. Crying out against the accepted movie vision of the Indian, "the only good Indian is a dead Indian." Recounting the historic wrongs done to her people, the four hundred treaties, dating back to the one signed by George Washington, which have never been kept by the United States Government.

She mourned for the Indian boys who died in World War II and in Korea, and Vietnam, the war particularly meaningful to her listeners, and reminded them of the report by a U. S. Army lieutenant, who testified about the Sand Creek Massacre of 1864: "I also heard of numerous instances in which our men had cut out the private parts of females, and wore them in their hats while riding in the ranks."

She sang about Bobby Kennedy, and the student at Blackfoot, Idaho, High School who said, "When Robert Kennedy came, that was the only day they ever showed any respect for the Indian, just on that one day, and after that, they couldn't care less." Nadine cried out for 600,000 forgotten Americans, and the eyes of the young were wet.

She stood there, tall, and straight. For a while she was washed clean of bitterness. She was the cry of every minority group in the nation. The blacks, the Jews, the Spanish-Americans, the Mexican Americans—the Indians.

Nadine, tired but exhilarated, sat cross-legged on the grass and bit hungrily into her sandwich. David and Kathy had disappeared, temporarily, behind a clump of bushes a hundred yards away.

"You were great." The deep, mellow, casual male voice lifted Nadine's gaze to its owner's face.

"Thank you." He wasn't one of the kids. Somewhere in the thirties, Nadine guessed. Hair a bit long. He needed a shave.

"I'd like to talk to you." His hazel eyes holding hers.

"Sure." She smiled tentatively. On impulse she liked this tall, broad-shouldered, rather handsome man, who was too heavy for his age. A magnetic quality about him, which Nadine suspected was pushed on and off upon demand.

He dropped down to the grass beside her, surprisingly graceful for a man of his weight.

"I'm Jason Friedlander," he introduced himself. "Not one of the kids, I'm pushing thirty-six." His smile was wry. "I came here looking for something. I think you're it. Now cool it, honey," he said quickly because she instinctively tensed. "This is not a pitch– I'm not interested in sleeping with you. I'm looking for a performer to develop, a singer who'll make a bundle for both of us, with the angles I know. I spent a year in Korea, went to dramatic school under the GI bill, didn't have the brass to make acting rounds, switched to promotion. I was married for a while, and divorced. Before the divorce I was on my way up. I skidded back with the crackup of my marriage. Now I'm ready to climb again. I can take us both a long way. What do you think?" His eyes were gravely challenging.

"What do we do?" Nadine hedged.

"You put yourself into my hands. Professionally," he added with a grin. "You trust me, every inch of the way. I've got some small cash to get us started.

You've got it, Nadine." He'd remembered her name. "The spark. Now let me work with you." His voice was low, unhurried, yet she felt the excitement in him, and found herself responding. "I can take you up to the top."

"Okay," Nadine said quietly. "Tell me what to do."

CHAPTER FOURTEEN

Nadine and Jason walked through the dusk-coated fields, with the sounds of the festival behind them. The last group of the evening, probably, on the wooden platform, a wistful imitation of The Rolling Stones. Beyond them cows grazed in a fenced-in area. The first early star of the evening showed in the sky.

"It's not much further," Jason said consolingly, with Nadine's weekender and duffel bag in hand. "I wanted to park where I could get out without too much difficulty."

"I'm used to walking," Nadine said with a faint smile, experiencing first doubts about her impulsive decision to leave the festival with him.

"There," Jason pointed complacently to a sedate blue Mercedes with ready access to the road. "My sister's car," he explained. "Cindy and Dick and the kids are in Europe for six months. I have their car and their apartment on loan." They settled themselves on the front seat, with Nadine's gear in back. Before starting up the car, Jason turned to her. "Nadine, I want to level with you. I think we can make a lot of money together, or I wouldn't be bothering this way. I've been looking for somebody I could build into a top moneymaker, been looking for eight months. I'll take thirty percent of what you earn as your personal manager. And I'm going to work my ass off to make that thirty percent. We'll put all this in writing. Is it a deal?"

"Yes," Nadine said firmly. Feeling herself coated with unreality. Yet it all made sense, if Jason

Friedlander could bring off this dream. Right now, he was earning thirty percent of nothing with her.

"We've got a hell of a lot of work ahead of us, but it'll be worth it." He started up the car, reached for the radio, fiddled with the dial until he found a news program. The focal point in the newscast was the festival.

"A bunch of good kids up there," he said with satisfaction. "The kooks were the gawkers on the outside."

"I'm glad I came," Nadine said softly. This was what Bob Frazer had wanted for her, Nadine decided with exhilaration.

Jason chuckled, "I'm glad we both came. Fate, with a little help from me." He turned to her in the darkness of the car. "Where do you live?"

"I don't have anywhere to go." Nadine admitted, suddenly tense again.

"You can stay at my sister's apartment," Jason said calmly. "There're two bedrooms. That way we don't worry about rent." Again, he chuckled. "And don't get all uptight. This is no pitch—we're business partners."

"I know," she said quickly, striving to sound sincere. "My sister has this great co-op on Gramercy Park," Jason explained. "She's a bug on antiques, and her husband doesn't want to rent out because God knows what she'll come back to, so I'm, in reality, apartment sitting."

Nadine sat beside Jason, momentarily disconcerted by the revelation of her new address. Gramercy Park, a fair walking distance from the East Village. But Seth never walked above St. Mark's, she reminded herself. Any destination uptown entailed the Astor Place subway or the BMT at Broadway and Eighth. There might just as well be an ocean between Seth and her, Nadine placated herself. No danger of walking into him in that area.

"Your mother was Navajo?" Jason was digressing from impersonal conversation, which automatically made Nadine wary.

"Yes." In the darkness Nadine frowned. Bracing herself for the inevitable next question.

"And your father?" Friendly curiosity in his voice.

"My mother never talked about him," Nadine said tightly. "My stepfather is Navajo."

"You could pass for white," he said casually.

"I don't want to pass for white!" she flashed back. For a discomforting moment the atmosphere in the car was thick with hostility. Then Jason took his right hand from the wheel to touch Nadine reassuringly on the shoulder.

"That was a bitchy thing for me to say. I didn't mean it the way it sounded. You wouldn't be true to yourself if you wanted to pass for white," he conceded quietly. "But you can't deny the white part of you, either." Beside him, Nadine balled one hand into a fist. What was the white part of her? Any time she'd tried to ask, Mama had cut her off. Someday she'd find out. She'd hate that white man who walked out on Mama. "The way you sing, Nadine," Jason continued. "*What* you sing will he particularly appealing to an audience who knows the truth. That a white fellow came along and loved your mother."

"I want no part of him," Nadine resisted with a rare display of violence. "I'm Indian. I even dyed my hair to make me look more Indian." Seth had never seen her as a blonde. It had made no difference to him.

"What color was your hair before you dyed it?" Jason asked, with an interest that further antagonized her.

"Blonde," she shot back defiantly. She moved away from him, hugging the door on her side.

"Okay, you go blonde again," he decided with a touch of excitement lacing his voice. "Blonde hair won't make you any less Navajo, but it's gorgeously unexpected. A blonde Indian flattering as hell, too, with those dark eyes of yours. Nadine, you go blonde," he reiterated forcefully. "It's a great angle. Audiences will dig the combo."

"They're coming to hear me sing," she said bitterly. "We hope."

"Come on," he rebuked gently. "You know we have to 'window-dress'. This is big business, Nadine. Music is where the money is."

Nadine sat in tense silence, hunched against the door, hardly hearing Jason expand on his plans for her. Inwardly rebuking herself for coming with Jason this way. She'd get back to New York and she'd cut out. They'd made no real arrangements between them. It was all rapping.

"Nadine, stop putting up fences between us," Jason reproached quietly, and Nadine was startled that he was tuned in to her misgivings. "I'm thinking of the performance. I'm not trying to deny your Indian background, that's your *schtick*, baby. That's what's going to make Nadine Scott a superstar."

"I don't want to be a blonde," Nadine repeated stubbornly.

"We'll talk about that later," Jason soothed.

"And don't get me wrong, kid, I know as much about prejudice as you do. I'm Jewish. Maybe I haven't been kicked in the gut the way you have, living on a reservation. But I've been there." His voice was rich with remembrance. "I grew up in a small town not too far from the festival. No more than seventy miles out of New York City, but there were only four Jewish families in the whole shitty town. On the surface, among the so-called elite, we were accepted. Assimilated. But to the average family we were 'the Jews'. And when a sixteen-year-old slut got herself pregnant, she yelled, 'that Jew kid raped me.' My brother, who'd never even kissed a girl in his life, was thrown into jail. Everybody in town knew she screwed anything in pants, for money or for free. If my father hadn't hocked his store to hire the fanciest Jew lawyer from New York, those sons of bitches would have thrown that 'Christ-killer kid' into jail for rape."

"Three hundred years, Jason," Nadine said bitterly. "Three hundred years they've been keeping us down."

"Five thousand years plus, and we're still fighting," Jason said quietly. "Now let's get it clearly understood. Both you and I know what prejudice is about. Let's spread the word around, loud and clear. And collect a basketful of bread while we do."

Nadine was delighted with the antique-filled co-op high above Gramercy Park. She enjoyed standing by her bedroom window at night, in the pleasurable air-conditioning, and gazing down at the lushly green park with its wrought-iron fence, its lights, the sprinkling of dog-walkers on the outside, no matter what the hour.

Jason, with an instinct for what was exactly right, made her rehearse endlessly. Nadine respected his insistence on perfection. This was a good time, she told herself, except for the truant moments when Seth invaded her thoughts. She knew he was working in the bookstore in the Village. In fifteen minutes she could walk over there and see him. But that was over. Dead. Finished.

Jason took her to a beauty salon where her hair was restored to its normal blondness, to a hair stylist who charged fifty dollars to change her part from the side to the middle and to clip a few strands of hair on either side of her face. A make-up artist showed her how to play up her eyes with cosmetics. Another hundred dollars on a tan-colored suede outfit, the skirt and jacket fringed at the hem.

Jason brought in a coach to work with her at a horrendous fee. He took her around to the agents, the small ones with grubby offices and low-paying jobs because he said she needed to learn to sing before crowds larger than coffee-house audiences. He drove her, in his sister's highly polished dark blue Mercedes, to the plush borscht-circuit hotels with their miles of glass, where she sang on midweek evenings for a pittance plus a pre-performance kosher dinner which Jason enjoyed and she barely touched because she could never bring herself to eat before she sang.

On weekend nights Jason managed to book her in bungalow colonies, which sprawled about a lake or swimming pool. Sometimes she was well received. Some of the middle class, middle-aged audiences were unresponsive. Once there was a mass exodus, which left Nadine shaken. Jason cut the song, which told about the white men's atrocities to Indian women.

But occasionally audiences swarmed backstage to compliment her, to invite her to remain with Jason for an after-show party. These were the liberals, impressed by message as well as performance.

In the fall, Jason struggled to obtain bookings at colleges. Nadine was impressed with the suddenly elevated fees, until she realized the traveling expenses they would incur with these dates.

Early in October Nadine played her first college booking at a school close to New York. En route the Mercedes had a flat, and they arrived at the last moment, with the vast auditorium already filling with students. Nadine was elated but a little nervous at the sight of the signs out front, advertising her appearance, her photographs on either side of the box office.

"Come on, this way," Jason said briskly, taking her arm.

They sped to the side entrance, where a waiting committee welcomed them with obvious relief, though Jason had phoned, briefed them on the flat, and promised to he on hand by curtain time.

"We've got a groovy crowd," a senior in charge of the program said exuberantly. "With a student group to open. We'll get them on while you dress."

In her dressing room, Nadine could hear the opening announcement, as she speedily applied make-up while the student group performed. They weren't bad, she acknowledged with respect, and listened to the spontaneous applause as they finished.

"Nadine?" Jason at the door, calm as usual,

on the outside.

"I'm coming."

Her hands were ice-cold as they gripped her guitar. Jason smiled reassuringly at her.

"Okay, baby, sock it to 'em," he ordered briskly.

Nadine walked out into the startling brilliance of the stage. Faces on the first rows were visible in the spill of light. She pulled the stool up before the microphone, sat down, smiled uncertainly at those hundreds of student faces out front. Her throat momentarily tight, her eyes cast down at the guitar, she plucked at the strings.

Before Nadine finished the first song, she knew the audience was hers. She could feel the tremendous communication between them and her, the way she'd felt it at the coffee houses, at the festival. She gave all there was to give, and they knew this. The applause at the end of the first song was thunderous.

Nadine sang her entire program, then repeated requests until she was exhausted, and Jason insisted, his face glowing with exhilaration, that the concert was over. He guided Nadine from the wings, while the students out front roared their approval. His arm about her, he propelled her to the dressing room, and firmly shut the door. Already enthusiastic students were swarming backstage. Later, she'd go out and talk to them. This moment belonged to them alone.

"Baby, you were great," he said with quiet satisfaction.

"Oh, Jason, Jason."

She flung herself into his arms, her face against his shoulder. Thinking of Mama back on the reservation. Thinking of Seth. Joanna. Eddie. Bob Frazer. All of them woven into the fabric of this moment. All the agony, the loneliness, the fears suddenly worthwhile.

Nadine and Jason bopped about the country for college engagements. New dates popped up with encouraging frequency because reports of earlier appearances were getting around. Jason permitted no let-up in the work schedule. He was priming Nadine for a record session.

"Baby, to make it big, you need a record, to get up there on the charts. No amount of personal appearances can compare with deejay plays and slots in the jukeboxes."

Jason industriously pursued the A&R men at the major labels, bombarding them with brochures from Nadine's campus successes. She was in top demand on the college circuit, her fees spiraling. Record men listened with interest to Jason's eloquent sales pitches, but adopted a wait-and-see approach.

Desperately, Jason began to woo the smaller labels, though he was leery of the promotion a fly-by-night operator could afford to put behind a record.

"Give me a fair record with a major promotion behind it," Jason said honestly, "and it'll out-sell a great record with shitty promotion. What we want is a great record with great promotion."

In his frenzy to put Nadine on a disk, he booked her, accepting a lower than normal fee, at a campus close enough for an A&R man to make the trip.

In a heavy early December snowfall that reminded Nadine distastefully of the long winters in Chicago, Jason and she set out in the Mercedes for the college campus, leaving early to avoid any complications about arriving in time in case the roads were bad. They cut across town toward the West Side ramp, with the flakes charging down huge as silver dollars, quickly forming a ground cover.

"Ted Brooks said he'd be sure to drive out tonight," Jason reminded briskly. He was the only A&R man who'd nibbled at the bid to come up to see Nadine. "Revelation isn't the greatest company in the field, but we'll sign for only four sides if they make an offer. It's a jumping-off point, baby. And I met this chick, Claire Kenyon, who's just started up her own music promotion agency. A sharp one–she ought to make it. For a few bucks she'll get us some plugs."

"Jason, you expect Ted Brooks to drive up in this?" Nadine stared unhappily at the steady onslaught of snow.

"I called just before we left," Jason reported somberly. "I gave him the train schedule. He can cab from the station– it's a ten-minute trip. No sweat about that. Revelation is all uptight about building up a new vocalist for their label. They can't do better than Nadine Scott."

"It costs so much to go into a session," Nadine reminded with a wry smile. "A company as small as Revelation probably prays over every dollar they spend."

To a record company, even a small one, how much did her success mean? Its importance was ignominiously ebbing away in her mind. Even though Jason kept insisting it was the kids who were the big record buyers. The kids who made a singer.

They drove up the Sawmill, with the snow a

heavy curtain around them. They missed a turnoff and Jason swore at the extra mileage. Still, he'd cautiously allowed them plenty of time. They'd arrive well ahead of schedule, even in this rotten weather.

The usual committee was waiting to welcome them. Hot coffee and sandwiches were whisked into the dressing room, The aura of excitement that always preceded a concert wrapped itself pleasingly about Nadine. Jason went out front three times to check on the arrival of the A&R man from Revelation. She was in the wings, waiting to go on, when Jason returned from his last foray.

"Maybe Brooks missed the train," Jason suggested tiredly. "There was another thirty-five minutes later. Maybe he'll show on that one."

The audience reception was, as usual, warm, enthusiastic, uninhibited. These kids cared, Nadine told herself with jubilation, as she listened to their response. They wanted to hear what she had to tell them. Someday, she'd bring Mama to a concert to hear her.

Nadine thought with satisfaction about the warm winter coats she'd sent for all the children, for her mother and stepfather. Not from a thrift shop this time. New. While her fees were escalating, money was still not plentiful because traveling expenses ate away at what came in. Early in March Jason's sister, who'd delayed her return sixty days, would be returning from Europe with her family. Jason was trying to put money aside for rent security when they'd have to move. They'd been forced to spend money for repairs on the car. Jason bought snow tires. Did Mama think she was being miserly, in the face of this success? She'd have to explain....

After the concert, after the customary stampede backstage because the kids were vocal in their enthusiasm and wanted to meet her, Nadine turned to Jason with somberly questioning eyes.

"The bastard didn't show," he said tiredly. "The seats I left at the box office were never picked up. Damn it to hell!"

"Can we make it back to New York in this?" Nadine asked after a moment of heavy silence. She crossed to the window to gaze out at the unrelenting snow.

"We'll make it back," Jason promised grimly. "I'm going over there to Revelation in the morning, to chew off Ted Brooks' ear. The only reason we took the date at this stinking low fee was to have a chance for him to see you in action. The lousy son of a bitch," Jason swore softly. "The stinking bastard!"

CHAPTER FIFTEEN

Christmas was approaching. Jason had no concerts booked until early in January. Nadine worked long hours daily on fresh material because Jason was doggedly confident he'd come up with a recording date, and she must be prepared. Work, too, was an escape from reality.

Christmas was an especially anguished period for Nadine. She'd shopped extravagantly for a battery-operated television set to send home for a family present, feeling briefly close to the hogan. But now she felt the aching emptiness of a holiday away from home, away from Seth.

She walked the streets with a wistful realization that he might he minutes away. More than at any time since she'd walked out on Seth she felt a need to be with him. To see him. She shopped in small boutiques on St. Marks Place for beads, a belt, a blouse, because this was Seth's turf and she might, just might, run into him here.

If she saw Seth, she'd play it cool. Not let on about the nights she lay sleepless, thinking about him, wishing he were in bed beside her. Hungry for the sound of his voice. If she could see that quick, earnest smile of his, just reach out and touch him for a moment,

Christmas Eve, Jason was taking her to a musicians' bash on the East Side.

"Look your jazziest, baby," Jason called through the closed door while she dressed. "There should he some music-business characters floating around there that could do you good."

"Okay, Jason." Her eyes somberly regarded her reflection in the bathroom mirror. She dreaded going to this bash, but Jason had this hang-up about her being seen around town. She felt so uncomfortable at cocktail parties!

Jason grinned in approval when she walked out of the bathroom. She wore a starkly simple black shift with a rich display of her Navajo jewelry and a headband about her burnished gold hair.

"Groovy," he said complacently. "Now let's cut out."

Downstairs they walked east to where Jason had parked the Mercedes, climbed inside the car. Christmas Eve traffic was light. A night to stay home, Nadine thought nostalgically. Even if home was a hogan with only a fire in the center of the room against the winter cold. In a hogan there could be love.

"Look, I've been doing a lot of thinking about how we get you on a record," Jason was saying ebulliently as he shot up Third Avenue, making every light. "I've been yakking with a pair of recording engineers. These guys have a little spare cash around. Maybe we could cut four sides cooperatively."

"Jason, a session costs a lot of money," she protested. But Jason had a way of making things happen.

"I know, baby." He refused to abandon his enthusiasm. "The studio, the musicians, and union scale runs high–plus arrangements for the men to back you up. Then comes the whole pressing plant bit. We have to run at least a thousand pressings to get the ball rolling." He squinted thoughtfully. "Relax, Nadine, let me work on this."

The party was in a small, self-consciously mod-furnished apartment on East Fifty-Second. The lay-out was identical to thousands of one-bedroom apart-ments in new, so-called luxury buildings. As soon as Jason and she walked into the foyer, Nadine caught the scent of pot. Every inch of space occupied with convivial guests. Not everybody went home for Christmas Eve.

"There's Chet," Jason said, a hand at her elbow. The tone of his voice said Chet was a major reason for being here.

Nadine was glad that it wasn't necessary for her to contribute much to the conversation. When it came to discussing music, though, she was startled at her own eloquence. Jason seemed surprised to see her open up when a hot discussion on Vietnam erupted.

Still, it was a relief to Nadine when Jason, tuned in to her aversion to the growingly overt drug scene about them, collected her coat from the pile in the bedroom and piloted her to the door. No need to say farewell to their host. He was stoned.

"I talked to the three guys I want to back you up," Jason reported smugly as they walked down the carpeted hall to the elevators. "I told them straight, 'fellows, we're bust', but they'll work for scale if they can fit it into their schedule."

"That's just part of it, Jason," Nadine warned. "What about the studio and the arrangement, and all the other jazz?"

"Nadine, we've got to swing it." Jason's face wore a glow of determination. "I'll corner those engineers I told you about, with the spare cash. This is the time." A vein pounded in his temple. "I've got this barometer in me that says now's the time to put you on a platter. I won't rest until I'm personally carrying those masters over to the plating plant, and I know we're on our way to popping off Nadine Scott pressings. You're a name on the campus circuit, baby, but that doesn't mean a damn out there where the big money is. Somehow, we've got to get you on four sides, push like hell. I'm seeing Claire tomorrow." Jason looked uneasy. "I hate leaving you alone on Christmas."

"I'll watch TV," Nadine said quickly. It disturbed Jason sometimes that she had no friends. "Tomorrow night I'll phone Jo out in California." When the after-nine rates were in effect. Jason knew about Jo— she had a song in her repertoire about the hospital incident. Would Jo be there at the professor's house where she lived, or at some swinging campus bash?

"Let's open up one of Cindy's bottles of champagne when we get home," Jason suggested when they were out in the street and heading for the car. "Cindy and Dick won't mind."

They circled two square blocks four times before they found a parking spot in the area of the house. They walked toward the co-op in the cold Christmas Eve, aware of the holiday mood. Traffic light tonight, only an occasional cab in sight. Christmas lights in windows here and there. At Gramercy Park they paused to admire the Christmas tree.

Upstairs, Nadine and Jason settled themselves before the wood-burning fireplace, sipping what Jason assured her was vintage champagne, and raked among the coals of their past. Talking less with each other than to each other.

"I really fell apart when that broad told me she

wanted out," Jason said dryly. "I wasn't making it fast enough for her, and all the time I didn't realize how I hated that rat race, being part of an organization. I wanted to be my own man, doing my own thing. Like now."

Nadine gazed at the birch logs crackling in the fireplace and thought about Seth.

Jason and she talked and drank champagne and grew warm-faced before the fire, until Jason gently removed the champagne glass from her hand and ordered her off to bed.

"Merry Christmas, Nadine," he said softly, and kissed her lightly on the cheek.

For a moment, close to Jason that way, she wished he would do more than kiss her on the cheek. She wished he would make love to her, every way. For one terrifying moment, they clung together, an electric charge zigzagging between them. And then Jason moved away, startled. His eyes veiled.

"Merry Christmas, Jason." Shakily, she turned away and stumbled toward her room. It wouldn't happen again. Neither Jason nor she would let it happen. What a traitor the body could be to the mind! She needed to be loved—

Jason slept till early afternoon on Christmas day, emerging from his room with a sheepish grin.

"Wow, I got smashed last night," he admitted with a chuckle, showing signs of interest in the bacon sizzling in the frying pan on the kitchen stove.

"I got up, went back to sleep," Nadine was reaching into the refrigerator for eggs. "Do you have time to eat breakfast with me? There's plenty of bacon."

"Great. I don't pick up Claire until four.

Fix me whatever you're having." He squinted at the percolator. "Coffee ready?"

"Just," Nadine decided, switching off the jet. "Here, " She reached for a tall mug, poured for him.

"I hate leaving you alone on Christmas day," Jason said apologetically.

"Don't be a kook," she brushed this aside. "I've got an idea kicking around in my head. This'll be a good time to work at it."

Nadine and Jason had breakfast, then watched a TV special that featured a folk-rock star. Then Jason cut out. Nadine tried to concentrate on the new lyrics. The words were elusive.

She crossed to the brass firewood box. Empty. No wood fire today. Restlessness surged through her. For a moment she toyed with the idea of putting on her coat and going downstairs for coffee. Just to be with people. She moved about the apartment, at loose ends, waiting for the evening when she'd take a chance on calling Jo. She'd written and said she might.

Dusk descended early this shortest day of the year. Nadine stood at the window, gazing down at the park. At the elegant houses that encircled this small oasis in the midst of the city. From the apartment below came the poignant swell of a chorus singing a Christmas carol.

"All is calm, all is bright—"

An intolerable loneliness swept over Nadine as she stood at the window in the antique-filled living room. The grooviest Christmas in her life, she chastised herself silently—when did she ever have it so great? But she stood here alone by the window, staring out at all those other windows—behind which people were not alone—and wished she were home.

She swung away from the window. Her heart aching with remembrance. She shut her eyes tightly, wrapped up in feeling. Almost believing Seth would come to her, touch her. Her mouth remembering his. Her body remembering his hands. His gentleness, his strength, his passion.

She glanced impatiently at the clock. She couldn't call Jo for hours yet without paying the regular charge. Money wasn't so free that she'd ignore the bargain rates. She turned on the television.

At nine sharp she put through the call to Jo, her pulse racing at the sweet expectation of hearing Jo's voice.

"Hello," A friendly, woman's voice. Not Jo's.

"Hello. May I please speak to Jo? I'm calling from New York." Nadine's voice strained, anxious, eager.

"Of course." How nice the woman sounded. "One moment."

Pleasure wrapped itself around her while she talked with Jo, with an eye on the clock. Relating, jubilantly, Jason's plans for her, Listening to Jo's news about the group of Indians with whom she was working. Jo vibrant, intense, pleased with life now.

"Why in hell don't you come out here?" Jo demanded. "You could pick up a coffee-house job with no sweat, I know lots of people. And Nadine, you could work with us."

Us meaning the group of Indians who were militantly organizing to back up the Indian college students who'd invaded Alcatraz a few weeks earlier, to claim it by citing an 1868 treaty allowing the Sioux possession of unused federal lands.

"I can't," Nadine hedged guiltily. "I've got these

singing dates lined up,"

"Screw the singing dates," Jo said with quiet intensity. "This is where the real action is!"

Jo considered her selfish, Nadine thought unhappily. She ought to be like Jo, dedicated to their problems. Indian problems. But she couldn't stop the singing.

The two girls parted on a self-conscious note, disparate interests drawing them apart. But it wasn't as though she were turning her back on her own people, Nadine reassured herself uncomfortably. Most of her repertoire centered on what was happening to the Indians. Did Jo think she was using her Indianism?

Nadine gazed somberly at the clock. She'd be alone here for hours. She wasn't blaming Jason for leaving her alone on Christmas night. But she didn't want to be alone. She didn't want to think. She could call Seth. She could dial his number, then pretend it was a wrong number and hang up.

Trembling, she went to the phone, searching her memory for Seth's number. Kooky! But she'd never called from the outside. It was always Seth, calling her.

Oh, she was out of her mind! But compulsively, she reached for the phone. Dialed. Her heart pounding, she listened to the ring at the other end. Visualizing the pad in sharp detail. One, two, three. Don't hang up yet. Maybe he's in the shower. You can kill yourself getting out of that tub in a hurry. Nine, ten, eleven, twelve. He's not at home.

As though the phone was suddenly burning, Nadine set the receiver down on the cradle, stared at it. Seth was out at some swinging bash.

Maybe he was shacked up somewhere with a chick. With Livvy.

Late in January, with the check from the last campus date warm in his wallet, Jason brought two young recording engineers home for dinner. Nadine broiled steaks for them, the way Jason had taught her, baked a pumpkin pie for dessert, the way Mama had taught her. Norm and Fred listened to Nadine go through choice selections from her college repertoire, while Jason kept an impassive mask as he watched for their reactions.

"Great," Norm agreed uninhibitedly. "She turns me on!"

"You can't put her on a record with just a guitar," Fred reminded pessimistically.

"Sure, we need a group behind her," Jason conceded, and leaned forward with a glint in his eyes. "I've got just the guys, the greatest. You name the stars, they cut with them. They'll work for scale and a piece of the royalties."

"We can borrow the studio at night," Norm admitted with a grin, turning to Fred for corroboration. "So we're up there working on tapes—who's going to follow up?"

"One thing we have to consider," Fred turned warily to Nadine for an instant. "All this Indian scene is groovy, it's 'now', but one side ought to be something that relates to the kids, regardless of color. Something they can all identify with." He swung to Nadine again with an apologetic smile. "You dig me, Nadine?"

"Sure," Nadine said quickly because Jason's eyes were urgent on her. "I can write fresh material." She forced a smile while rebellion zoomed in her. Jason refused to meet her eyes now.

"Look, we can't jump right in," Fred hedged seriously. "How much bread will we need for this deal?"

"I've got the budget all worked out," Jason reassured, strongly confident. "You know what 802 scale is for the session, that's our big bite. We'll keep it down to two sides instead of the regular four, so there's no danger at all of our running overtime."

Fred grimaced eloquently.

"Yeah, overtime could be murder. We ran over eight hours on a date yesterday. You can imagine the tab."

"We'll need masters, mothers, and stampers for two sides only," Jason continued. "That's small money. We press only a thousand records, that's enough for the deejays, promotion people, to put in on consignment in a few local shops where there's heavy sales. We sell a distributor on handling the record, and we will with the promotion we'll get behind it, and he'll back us at the pressing plant. Look, for peanuts, when you split it three ways, we've got a chance to make a bundle."

"Get a sheet of paper and a pencil," Norm ordered briskly, and Nadine jumped to comply.

Nadine sat curled up in a chair by the fireplace while the men worked out the exact cost of the session. The leader of the group to back up Nadine would do the arrangements on spec. Claire Kenyon would work with Jason on promotion on the strength of handling Nadine if she clicked.

Jason walked with Fred and Norm to the elevator, then charged back into the apartment when they were descending, swooping up Nadine with jubilation.

"Baby, we're on the way to the big scene!"

"What do we use for money?" Nadine stared at him uneasily.

"The check from the concert." Jason grinned, patted his hip pocket complacently. "Plus the nest egg."

"Jason, we've got an enormous telephone bill coming," she reminded nervously. Jason was constantly on the phone, though that was business. "Suppose something happens to the car?"

"We've got the cash I've been putting aside for security when we have to cut out of here," Jason reminded. For two apartments, Nadine remembered uneasily. "Nadine, you have to play your hunches. This is our time." He squinted in thought. "Fred was right, about making sure one side is something relevant to all the kids. Something that could happen to any girl your age. Only it happened to you."

"Chicago," Nadine pinpointed, her mind ferreting for material. Chicago was Seth, too, that one charged night. "The convention."

"That's been done to death." Jason shook his head. "Something new, baby. Think hard. Some little thing, some small incident that says a lot to those kids out there who buy records."

"Jail," Nadine said quietly, and smiled because Jason appeared startled. There were some things about her Jason still didn't know. "What the fuzz in Chicago did to me when that witch I was working for thought I stole her watch." She gazed somberly into space. She was back in that Chicago jail, the bull dyke matron leering at her. "Bend over–"

"Work," Jason said quietly. "It'll be great."

The session was scheduled for ten at night, when Norm and Fred would be completely free at the studio. Nadine had worked long and earnestly at the new song, alternating between despair and elation. It had to he right. The second side would be one that was a favorite with the college audiences—about Eddie's death in the hall toilet of a Chicago tenement. Nadine insisted on this, overriding Jason's doubts about another record with a drug background.

At quarter of ten, equipped with containers growing soggy with hot coffee, Nadine and Jason walked into the night-empty lobby of the small building, signed the book as indicated by the elevator operator, then rode up to the modest, fifth-floor studio.

"It's not WOR recording," Jason said whimsically, "but for a small group the studio's sensational"

Nadine's hands were cold, clammy with a fresh kind of fear as she clutched her guitar. They had so much riding on this session.

"I wish I'd had a chance to rehearse with the fellows," Nadine said wistfully, for the fourth time, while they approached the studio door.

"You don't worry about them, baby," Jason soothed. "We'll have a few run-throughs of each number, and that'll be good enough. Forget they're there. It's up to them to complement you."

Jason pulled open the door to the small reception room, lights muted at this hour. Norm was in the control booth, Fred in the studio setting up. Nadine noted the instruments sitting in the corner of the studio. It was suddenly very real.

"The fellows were up," Fred pointed to the instruments. "They went down for a quick beer."

"Have your coffee, Nadine," Jason urged

casually, knowing she was uptight. "I brought some up for you guys, too." He was taking containers out of the brown paper bag, fishing out packets of sugar and stirrers. "Hope everybody takes it black."

The four of them settled down, briefly, to coffee. Nadine swigged down most of hers, then set the container down on a stool to pick up the guitar, finding comfort in familiarity.

"Okay," Fred said briskly, after a few minutes. "Let's try some voice levels, Nadine."

At a minute before ten, the three musicians who were to back her up were striding into the studio. High-spirited, with a special interest in this session because they had more at stake than usual. There was the incentive of a royalty.

The air was suddenly crackling with electricity. Jason's eyes moved compulsively to the clock. They had three hours in which to cut the two sides, or they would be facing financial disaster for this venture. Overtime would eliminate their bankroll. Knowing Jason's concern, conscious of Fred's uneasy glances at the clock, Nadine felt panicky, uncertain.

Jason stood inside the booth, appearing reassuringly cheerful, optimistic now. He lifted a hand, watching the second hands on the clock to time a test run.

"Okay, run it."

Nadine shut her eyes, concentrated on the words. Eddie's song. She was at a college campus, singing to the kids out there, feeling the terrific communication with them.

They wrapped up the first number on the third try. Everybody was jubilant. The second side—which would be the "A" side—presented problems.

They reran a dozen times, with Jason still not satisfied.

"Jason, it's good," Fred acknowledged uneasily, his eyes traveling anxiously to the clock.

"It's got to be great!" Jason shot back, and Nadine nodded. Jason had an instinct about such things. "Sound effects," he suddenly pinned down the missing element. "We need the music out and effects in there behind her voice, to build up the tension, give it drama."

"Yes!" Excitement charged through Nadine. Instantly, Nadine knew what Jason meant. "It has to live!"

"Jason, we're late," Fred protested, his eyes on the clock again.

"Hell, man, it's got to he right!" Jason exploded, but his face showed concern.

"Hey, Jason," the drummer called out, aware of the conflict. "Forget about the overtime. It's a three-hour session, see?" And the other two musicians nodded.

Fred and Norm raided the sound-effects files, came up with what Jason wanted. The studio ricocheted with excitement. One of the musicians, intrigued at being used in this capacity, acted out three seconds of the girl in withdrawal on the cell floor. It was raw, effective. Only twenty minutes past the session, the second side was wrapped up.

"Let's go over to the Stage Deli for corned-beef sandwiches and coffee," Jason suggested jubilantly. "If this doesn't hit the charts, I'll walk naked from Times Square to Columbus Circle!'"

But Nadine was quiet, introspective, as they left the building and walked out into the late-evening cold. Nobody ever knew about a record until it was out there with the deejays, with luck, in the jukeboxes.

Jason said they'd have the pressings in two weeks....

CHAPTER SIXTEEN

Nadine sat curled up in a chair across from Claire Kenyon's desk in the small, two-room music-promotion office high above Broadway.

Claire was involved in a lengthy, high-pressure telephone conversation with a TV production man.

Nadine watched Claire's attractive, volatile face, the striking green eyes, with friendly interest. Jason said Claire was en route to Hollywood stardom when a bad car accident interrupted her career. The accident was followed by a bad marriage.

Claire–she might be anywhere between thirty and thirty-five, Nadine guessed–spoke quite openly about the four years of analysis it took to put that marriage behind her. It was a kind of link between Jason and her, that both had pulled out of marriages hurting.

Nadine hadn't expected to like Claire. She'd built up a resistance to meeting her. Yet when Jason took her to Claire's apartment for dinner one night, so they could meet in informal circumstances, she'd liked the tall redhead on sight.

"Jason ought to be back soon with the pressings," Claire comforted, finally ending the phone conversation. "He buzzed from the pressing plant half an hour ago and it's right across the George Washington Bridge."

"Do you think we'll get some deejay plays?" Nadine asked, anxious for encouragement. "That's what starts a record selling, isn't it, Claire?"

"The answer is 'yes' to both questions," Claire said warmly. "I've got several important spots where

I'm sure I'll get plays–I've brought them guest shots they've wanted bad. Also, I'm starting this deejay column for one of the fan magazines, and the word's around." She smiled confidently. "I happen to think you're great, Nadine. I wouldn't break my head for you on spec this way if I didn't think so. Even with Jason managing you," she concluded with candor.

Nadine swung about with expectancy at the sound of the reception-room door opening. Claire, svelte and smartly dressed, rose quickly to her feet.

"I need a derrick to carry this crap," Jason complained good-humoredly as he strode across the reception room into the doorway with a corrugated carton in tow. "Here's a hundred. I've got another four hundred in the car trunk. I can pick up the other five hundred tomorrow."

"Open up a box, let's hear it," Claire ordered, crossing to the playback equipment built into one wall of her office. "The stampers were okay, weren't they? No clicks?" They'd bargain-shopped for pressings at a plant where such niceties could be ignored if they needed stampers to keep the presses rolling.

"I stood there personally while they pulled off the test pressings, to make sure the stampers were okay." Jason was struggling to open the small, inner box which contained twenty-five records. "Nothing's going wrong on this deal."

The three of them sat back, Nadine's face charged with excitement, while Claire's faultless playback equipment poured forth the poignantly agitated lyrics.

"It's the most mature material you've ever written," Jason said with satisfaction when the record was over. "You hit them right in the gut."

"I'll take the pressings around personally," Claire decided thoughtfully. "Maybe I can shove in a few potent, private words."

"I'll try to stock a few of the Broadway shops on consignment." Jason fished two boxes of twenty-five each from the carton. "Then I can run to the distributors and say, God, look how they're moving in the stores, and here we are with no distributor and no capital to run inventory."

"Jason, I'd bankroll another couple thousand pressings," Claire said slowly. "If that will keep you rolling."

"You are a big-hearted doll, but if this record clicks the way I expect, we'll need ten thousand bucks in a hurry to divide up between maybe a dozen pressing plants so we can get records moving into the stores while the platter is at its peak."

"Right." Claire nodded wryly. "I was thinking naively of playing small store. This is big business."

"Claire, do you think you can plant Nadine on some deejay show to talk up the record?"

"It'll take some doing," Claire warned. "I need a hook. Let's play it by ear, see what develops."

At Jason's prodding, Nadine concentrated on new material, to be prepared if the record clicked and a company came along with a contract offer. Jason dashed around town trying to push five hundred records into key stores on consignment. Claire alloted every free moment into promotion. They waited impatiently for the first air plays, hoping for a substantial response. Knowing what this could mean. And then the totally unexpected happened....

Nadine was at the apartment working when Claire called, late in the afternoon. From the tone of Claire's voice, Nadine knew immediately that something had gone wrong.

"Honey, is Jason there?"

"No, he had an appointment with a jukebox man on Tenth Avenue. Is something wrong?"

"Some complications," Claire hedged. "Look, why don't you run up here? Leave a note for Jason, in case be comes there. Tell him to come straight up here. Don't worry about dinner—I'll call downstairs to the deli."

Thirty-five minutes later Nadine was charging breathlessly into Claire's office, almost colliding headlong with Claire's part-time secretary who was leaving for the day.

"Claire's expecting you," the secretary said with a warm glow of sympathy. "Go on inside."

"Hi!" Claire forced a smile at Nadine's appearance.

"What's wrong, Claire?" All the way uptown Nadine had wracked her brain, trying to figure out what could have gone wrong.

"Sit down, baby," Claire prodded gently. "This is really wild." She took a deep breath. "The record's been banned for air plays."

"Why?" Nadine was ice-cold. "Because of what I said about the Chicago fuzz? That bit about the matron? It happened! To me!" She was trembling now.

"Look, I know it did," Claire soothed. "But somebody must have put the pressure on to stop the plays. I nearly keeled over when the word got through to me. I never expected it, Nadine."

"What do we do now?" Nadine's face was drained

of color. All that money down the drain. All that hope. Everybody knew it was the radio spins that sent a disk up to the charts.

"We sit down here and pick one another's brains," Claire said briskly. "Nadine, this is not the end of the trail. Oh, Jason buzzed me—he's on the way over.   He's got a couple of Broadway stores spinning the 'A' side on their loudspeakers. If you want to hear yourself on Broadway," she said with wry amusement, "walk past later." She leaned forward to pick up the telephone. "I'll buzz the deli for sandwiches. We'll need food to make the think-tank scene."

Seth sat at the yellow formica-topped table in his mother's kitchen, obediently eating the roast-beef sandwich she had placed before him, and tried not to appear shocked by what she was relating with such agitation.

"Seth, what did we do wrong?" his mother demanded, lacing and unlacing her hands on the table, ignoring the cup of coffee growing cold before her. "Why should a kid like Audrey turn to drugs? She's not living in the ghetto. She's not from a broken family. Her parents aren't jet setters, we care about what happens to her. Why do the police have to call us, and your father has to go running to the stationhouse, because our daughter has been dragged in on a drug raid? She was there, Seth—she can't lie her way out of this!"

"Mom, it's all over," Seth said gently. Mom knew that. "Look at all the dope up in the suburbs, on the campus—these aren't deprived kids."

"Deprived kids I can understand!" A vein

throbbed in Felicia Coles' forehead. "But a girl like Audrey. Why?"

"Mom, you said it wasn't hard drugs. Just pot."

"Just pot," his mother mimicked, and Nadine's face suddenly flashed across his mind. Nadine hated drugs, too, even pot. "It's against the law, Seth," his mother went on, her voice shaking with frustration. "You kids have respect for nothing."

"Mom, a lot of kids find it impossible to respect some laws," he reminded. Including himself. "Don't light into Audrey when they come home. You'll just alienate her."

"What do I do, welcome her with open arms? We're delighted to bail you out of jail!" His mother rose abruptly from the table, took her cup to dump the contents into the sink, relit the percolator. "I have to worry every time she's out of my sight. When do I start checking her arms for needle marks?"

"Mom, Audrey's not going on hard drugs," he said with a show of confidence. "A lot of kids try pot. A lot of adults try it," he added forcefully. "Plenty of people think it ought to be legalized."

"Come on, Seth, don't give me that garbage about marijuana being no worse than alcohol. We've got too damn many alcoholics in this country. Do we have to add more addicts to that problem by legalizing drugs?"

"They're coming," Seth listened to the sounds in the hall. "Mom, don't light into her," he urged earnestly. "You'll just drive her away."

But his mother was already at the door, pulling it wide.

"Audrey, what the hell is the matter with you?" Felicia Coles demanded, while her husband hastily closed the door. "What do you mean, doing this to us?"

Seth sighed, flinching before the recriminations his mother threw at Audrey, even while he knew they were born of fear and frustration. Mom, who could be so calm and rational at that high-trouble area school where she taught, fell apart when confronted with this situation at home. Mom and Dad didn't know what it was like, actually, out of their middle-class isolation tank.

Despite his mother's reproach, and her obvious hurt because he had moved in doggedly to Audrey's defense, Seth prepared to take an early leave. Audrey, who had shot him grateful glances for his support, was now seething behind the privacy of her bedroom door.

"Mom, I've got to cut out," he said uncomfortably. "I have an early class tomorrow, and some work to get done tonight."

"You think we're too hard on her," his mother said, searching his face. "The trouble today is that parents have been too easy all along. We've made a terrible mistake with this generation. We had nothing, we wanted our kids to have everything. Now nothing has value. It's all too easy."

"Audrey'll be okay," Seth insisted quietly. "She's scared now, because of the bust. Just don't ride her."

"Everybody has to be a psychiatrist," his father said bitterly. "It's the new scene."

Seth left the apartment, walked across to Broadway to take the IRT local downtown. The train was jammed. There'd been some delay in service earlier. He wedged himself with distaste into standing space near a pole, his mind revolving about Audrey.

Poor kid, she'd looked scared to death when she'd walked into the apartment with Dad.

At the Fiftieth Street station there was a delay in service again. With the doors remaining open, Seth impulsively pushed his way out of the foul-aired train, onto the platform, and up the stairs into the late-evening activity of Broadway. Here the night air was crisp, dry, invigorating, unusually free of pollution. He'd go in for coffee, then cut across to Lexington, take the bus the rest of the way downtown.

Seth had a burger and coffee, decided to stroll south to a paperback store before heading for the bus. Approaching a record shop, he stopped short, startled. Nadine. That voice had to be Nadine's!

He stood immobile, listening to the words. Remembering Nadine, her head on his shoulder, talking about the ugly encounter in the Chicago jail. There it was, on a record. God, he'd been distraught when she'd walked out that way. He'd searched the area like a madman, coming up with nothing. No trace.

He'd been upset, scared for Nadine on her own. She was so vulnerable. But Nadine was doing all right. The store was plugging her record, that meant she had a potential hit.

He aborted his instinctive move to stride into the store, buy the record, check the label, try to track her down. No. Nadine didn't need him.

Walking into the corridor of his building, Seth almost stumbled over the girl huddled on the lower steps.

"Well, you finally got home," Livvy drawled. "I've been waiting here almost an hour."

"Hi!" It had been a long time since Livvy.

A long time since anybody, he realized, because his body was truantly remembering the good times with Livvy. She was on her feet now, moving in to him with that kitten-like thrust he knew. Strange, the way he'd run into that recording of Nadine's a little while ago, and now Livvy here on his doorstep. But it was Nadine he wanted to take to bed. Uncomfortably, he remembered the last encounter with Livvy, when she was running off to that bull dyke. "What's doing these days?"

"I heard you'd split with the chick. And baby," she whispered, nuzzling up against him, "nobody makes love like you."

"Maybe I should hang out a sign," he jibed.

"You'd be the most successful call-boy in town."

"What happened?" he mocked. His body reacting independently of his mind. "The bull dyke stopped turning you on?"

"That was for kicks. Once. Okay, a few times," she acknowledged sullenly. "Come on, let's get up to the pad before I shove you on your back and climb aboard right here."

Together, with matching impatience, they mounted the stairs. while Seth fumbled with the key, Livvy, an arm draped about his shoulders, shoved her free hand down beneath his belt.

"Baby, cut it out," he ordered thickly.

Seth reached to pull on the kitchen light. Livvy was already throwing off her clothes. Seth moved to the bed. Right now all that concerned him was burying himself in Livvy.

"Wait, sweetie," Livvy protested, slithering out from beneath him, her hand between his thighs. "Let's do this right after all this time."

With Livvy it always had to be a major production, he remembered in annoyance. She must always be the aggressive one. That always bugged him. But he stretched out on his back, knees flexed, bracing himself for the hot mouth that bore down on him. His hands moving forward to close in about the incredibly large nipples set in the small, high breasts. Wow, this was a passionate chick!

"Hold it, Livvy. Hold it!" he exhorted, his body going berserk. Enough of her way.

He gripped her roughly by the shoulders, swung her over on her back, driving toward her with haste. Hearing her excited laughter, the accelerated breathing. Her triumph because she turned him on this way. Tonight with Livvy was enough. Tonight he was so damned horny he could have screwed a sheep!

Afterward, Livvy sat on the floor, the bed a backrest for her, and talked intensely about the Weathermen group.

"Seth, they're right!" Her hazel eyes bristled with rage. "Didn't Chicago teach you anything? It's us against them, and you don't pussyfoot with naive demonstrations. You bomb! You make them see you're not afraid, you mean action! Baby, that's the only way."

"I'll never believe that," Seth reiterated. "Violence begets violence."

When Seth awoke in the morning, Livvy had left. Swearing at the early morning cold, he went into the bathroom to run a hot shower. He wanted to get the taste of last night out of his mouth.

If only it had been Nadine last night.

But Nadine had moved beyond his reach. She was in that hectic show-biz world, and she would make it big. Seth was certain of that. For the next seven years, he was no place, plodding his way through his last year of med school, the internship and the residency, before he could even make an attempt to set himself up in practice. Seven years was a lifetime. And Nadine would be a lifetime removed from him.

CHAPTER SEVENTEEN

Nadine stifled a yawn as she sat curled up in one of the comfortable, black-leather-upholstered lounge chairs that flanked Claire's walnut desk. She'd found sleep an elusive monster last night, except for brief, dream-wracked intervals. The banning of air plays on the record had been a traumatic shock.

Claire, behind her desk, leaned absorbedly over her telephone book, slowly turning pages, perusing names. Hoping to come across a name that had been missed so far. A name which might stir up fresh hope at this point.

"Jason ought to be here soon," Claire glanced up, smiled compassionately. Aware of Nadine's depression. "He called from some office over on Tenth Avenue."

"Jason's here," he called out briskly from the reception room. "How'd you make out this afternoon?" he demanded of Claire as he strode into the office.

"I batted zero," she said dejectedly. "I can't get her on any deejay program because of the ban."

"What about the B side?" Jason persisted, pulling off his coat. Nadine watched him compulsively. Jason's determined optimism mildly assuaged her own despair at the current impasse. Jason was omniscient. "Can't you get some plays on that?"

"They don't want to touch the record," Claire pointed out. "The ban on the A side gave them the jitters."

"Damn it, even the B side is great!" Jason exploded.

"But to know they have to listen," Claire flashed

back. Unexpectedly, Jason grinned, lifted his feet to rest on the edge of Claire's desk.

"I came up with a minor break-through. This jukebox operator over on Tenth Avenue is putting the record into a few boxes for a trial run."

"Oh, Jason!" Nadine's eyes shone.

"Wait," Jason cautioned. "We're still a long way from anywhere."

"You know," Claire said quietly, squinting into space, we ought to be able to use this banning bit. Look what it does to a book or a movie when they're banned."

"Records don't sell via newspaper ads," Jason reminded grimly. "If we had the money to spend on an ad campaign, which we don't." He shook his head tiredly. "It keeps bugging me. We have this gimmick with the ban and we don't know how to use it! Damn it!" He slammed one fist on the arm of the chair.

"Wait a sec—" The electric quality in Claire's voice commanded their attention. "Maybe we're trying the wrong angle. TV instead of radio. A TV appearance for Nadine."

"Come on, Claire," Jason scoffed. "Who's going to put on an unknown?"

"Todd Madden might," Claire said, her eyes bright. "He's big for minority groups. He got his head bashed in at the Democratic Convention. He was roughed up by local fuzz at that civil-rights demonstration down South With Nadine's Indian background, plus the banning of her record, he's the show-biz personality most likely to rally around."

"Can you get to Madden?" Jason swung his feet to the floor, leaned forward intently.

Claire smiled brilliantly.

"Darling, I can get to anybody." Her green eyes acquired a glint of caution. "The problem will be to sell him."

Eight days later Nadine sat in a TV studio with Jason, awaiting the taping with Todd Madden, listening tensely to the sounds of the gathering audience in the theater.

"Don't be uptight," Jason soothed quietly. "Todd'll take you through the interview with no sweat."

"I know." She forced a smile. "He's great." While she was in the dressing room making up, Todd had dropped in to discuss what they would talk about. Jason and Claire, of course, had plotted this out with her before. She was on the show to plug her record.

She stiffened to attention when Todd introduced his first guest. She had no reason to be uptight, she chastised herself, she was used to appearing before large audiences. This was just another concert. The interview would be very short, Jason kept reminding, she was here to sing.

The program would be telecast a week from now. Would Seth watch? Sometimes he'd cut from studying for an interview show. He liked Todd's relaxed style. She'd sent Mama an airmail about the show, the family would gather in the hogan next week and wait to see her. Mama would be so excited, though she wouldn't let on.

Jason was chatting casually now with the other guest about Todd's high rating while Nadine kept her eyes glued to the monitor, trying to focus on the exchange between Todd and his guest. And then more swiftly than she'd anticipated, after the requisite number of commercials, Todd was introducing her, and a coordinator was indicating she was to stand by.

Jason glowed triumphantly as Todd mentioned the banned record, winked with satisfaction at Nadine. This mention of the record could trigger a rush to the record shops.

"Okay, Miss Scott," the coordinator said briskly.

Nadine picked up her guitar and, as rehearsed, left the studio to take her place on the stage before the set-up microphone. She closed her eyes and began to sing "How Eddie Died in Chicago." It was a favorite with campus audiences. Todd had been enthusiastically approving when she'd sung it for him earlier.

Nadine finished the song, stood before the microphone immobile for a moment. As always caught up in the emotion of the lyrics. She was faintly startled by the intensity of the studio-audience response. Unexpectedly, tears filled her eyes.

Todd strode over to kiss her, took her by the hand and brought her to a chair. Even the interview was painless, Nadine conceded inwardly as she talked with Todd about life on the reservation, about Chicago, about the record.

A week later Nadine, Jason and Claire gathered together in Claire's inner office to watch the telecast.

"I told Todd we'd be catching the program here in the office," Claire said. Nadine caught the loaded exchange between Claire and Jason. Claire expected some report from Todd.

The delivery boy from the deli arrived with corned-beef sandwiches and tea, just as Todd was introducing his first guest. They sat in silence, absorbed in the performance on the screen. Claire was too involved even to complain as usual about the crassness of tea in paper containers. When she appeared on screen, Nadine fidgeted restlessly, stole uneasy glances at both Jason and Claire, who appeared pleased with what they saw.

The moment Nadine's segment was over Jason flipped off the program.

"Baby, you were sensational!" He leapt to his feet, too turned on to remain seated. "If that appearance doesn't start the ball rolling, nothing will."

"Wait," Claire cautioned, but she, too, glowed.

Jason began a self-righteous tirade against the network for banning the record, pacing the small area of the office.

"Jason, they may have done us a favor," Claire finally intervened. "We never would have picked up nationwide coverage like this without that hook."

The phone rang. Instantly the air was electric. Nadine gazed tensely from Jason to Claire, who was diving for the receiver. This was the call for which they'd been waiting.

"Claire Kenyon." Her warm musical voice sounding almost normal.

Claire crossed her left middle and index finger and held them aloft while she listened. Her face turned on like the Empire State tower between dusk and midnight. Nadine's face was hot, her throat tight.

"Oh, Todd, that's gorgeous! Of course, Nadine will be thrilled. Thanks so much for everything, Todd."

"Well?" Jason strode forward urgently while Claire put the receiver down.

"The switchboards have been jammed at the network," Claire reported jubilantly. "Everybody wants to know where they can buy Nadine Scott's record! Kids, we've pulled this off!"

On the strength of the response to Nadine's appearance on the air—abetted by column items astutely placed by Claire—Jason quickly lined up a small record label that was willing to turn over all presses contracted to them to roll off the Nadine Scott record. They were guaranteed national distribution. Without a single air play the record was zooming.

With incredible speed Nadine's fees for new college dates spiraled. Claire went out all on promotion, booking Nadine, again on the strength of the Todd Madden appearance, on half-a-dozen radio and TV talk shows. To their mutual delight Jason hooked her for a TV guest shot.

Every moment of each day was jammed with planned activities, Nadine recurrently unnerved because interviewers, intrigued with her parentage, inevitably asked about her father. In the bios which Claire shipped around, Claire simply said that Nadine was born of a Navajo mother and a white father.

With disconcerting frequency, Nadine's thoughts revolved about her father. Mama had always refused to talk about him. But now she was grown, Nadine told herself defiantly, she had a right to know. What did he look like? What did he think? What was he doing with his life?

In April, with her record high on the charts, Jason signed her with a major recording company, with a contract which could net her a quarter of a million dollars, less Jason's share, in the next three years. Less than a year ago she had sung at a rock festival for nothing.

Jason promptly went into court, since she was still a minor, to arrange for a solid chunk of her earnings to he directed into a trust fund. His sister returned from Europe, and Nadine and Jason moved into two studio apartments in the same building, on West End Avenue, minutes from where Seth's family lived. Each time Nadine walked the streets of the neighborhood, she searched the faces of passers-by, half-expecting to encounter Seth. She never did.

In May, almost three years since she had walked off the reservation in the midst of Eddie's funeral, Nadine was booked on a campus two hundred miles from the reservation, filling in at the last moment for a cancellation.

"You can fly home for a day," Jason said quietly, seeing her face light up when he gave her the locale of this date. "We can arrange for a charter flight. Your next date is forty-eight hours later in Ohio."

"Oh, Jason, that would be great!"

As usual, Nadine's program ran long past schedule, with students eager to talk with her afterward, to express their own feelings about the problems of their generation. Many of them were vocally sympathetic toward the Indians, both on the reservations and in the ghettos. While never completely at ease in these personal encounters, Nadine always emerged with a sense of exhilaration, of being part of something good.

"We'll eat and you hit the sack early," Jason said sternly, when they left the auditorium. "You've got a ten o'clock flight out of here."

Nadine made no complaints when Jason deposited her at her hotel door, though usually they sat around rapping for hours after a concert. Tomorrow night she'd be sleeping at the hogan. Mama didn't know she was coming. What a surprise this would be!

Nadine knew sleep would be sporadic tonight. She crawled into bed with a transistor at her finger-tips, hoping music would help. It was close to dawn when she finally drifted off into troubled slumber. At nine the switchboard operator woke her. Before the second call, she was on her feet.

Jason drove with her to the airport, helped her lug the assortment of packages that were to go with her to the hogan. They'd stopped off for breakfast, but she'd been too excited to eat.

"Cloudy now but it's going to clear," he encouraged, scanning the sky. "And relax, baby," he coaxed, while he helped her settle down in the small plane, "or you'll explode before you arrive. Oh, here's a newspaper to read en route." He kissed her on the cheek and hopped down. "I'll meet you here tomorrow at one; we fly out at one forty-five. Don't flip and forget the time."

"I won't miss the flight, Jason," Nadine promised. Twenty-four hours with Mama and the family.

Nadine sat back in her seat. She was going home! After three years she was going home. Did she look any different? Would mama be disappointed? Mama had been so excited about seeing her on TV. Would the kids remember her? Jody, yes, she decided; Jody was twelve when she left. But the others?

Tenderly, she touched the poncho that lay across her lap. The poncho that Mama had sent to her from the reservation, made by Mama's hands, and which she inevitably wore, even in the heat of summer, when she was to sing publicly because it was part of

Mama being there with her.

By the time the plane set down at the small airport outside of town, the gray May morning had erupted into a blaze of sunlight. She left the plane, inspecting the familiar line-up of Piper cubs that dotted the field. Folks with any money at all out here owned a Piper cub.

There was no taxi waiting at the airport. She had to phone for one. Five minutes later a late-model Olds rolled up before the hangar. Nadine hurried forward, then stopped dead at the unmasked disapproval of the man behind the wheel. The glare of distrust.

Her face tightened. She was hurtled backward into the past. Back here nothing had changed. The driver looked at her, mentally tabbed her. Half-breed. Here everybody was conscious of the Indians. Here the younger generation would be horrified at garbing themselves in the Indian attire city kids found appealing. Here she was just another Indian off the reservation.

Impatiently, Nadine reached into her hand-stitched suede bag, made for her by her stepfather, as a tacit admission of forgiveness for running away, pulled out bills and handed them to the driver.

"The reservation," she ordered coldly, and gave him specific instructions, for one ugly moment expecting him to refuse.

"I'll take you to the trading post," he compromised, stuffing the bills into his pocket. "I ain't breaking an axle on them roads."

A handful of people loitering before the trading post stared curiously as Nadine stepped from the car. Nadine smiled faintly, gathered together her bundles, and began the hike to the hogan in thonged, leather sandals that would soon be coated with dust.

She walked with long, even strides, tense but elated. Oh, how sweet the air was here! How broad, how blue the sky! Her arms ached as she walked, but pleasure flooded her as she drank in the vastness on all sides.

She walked briskly, encountering no one until the cluster of hogans rose into view. Drawing closer she saw a small boy playing before their hogan. Teddy. He had been just three when she left. Six now. Would he remember her?

"Teddy," she called out, flushed with excitement "Teddy!"

The small boy turned somber eyes on her. Curious, faintly uneasy. He seemed on the point of running inside the hogan as she hurried toward him, but curiosity won out.

"Teddy," she said tenderly, dropping to her haunches before him, gently scooping him close. "Teddy, don't you remember Nadine?"

She held him away from her, inspecting the small, serious face. Saw recognition dawn in the dark eyes.

"Mama, Mama!" he shrieked and darted into the hogan. "Come see who's here!" He didn't remember her, Nadine realized, he recognized her from the TV appearance.

Mama came hurrying out, disbelieving, wary of the newcomer.

"Nadine–" The word was wrenched from her throat. "My baby, my baby."

While Teddy darted about rounding up the other children, Mama rocked Nadine in her arms. How old

Mama looked, Nadine thought with shock. How old was she? Thirty-six. Claire would be thirty-six in August, but she might have been fifteen years younger than Mama.

"Come inside, my daughter," Mama said, shaking with happiness. "Come see what we do with the money you send us."

The hogan, as always, was immaculate. But now the walls were lined with three sets of bunk beds. A foldaway cot sat against one wall. In the middle of the room, on a handmade wooden table, sat the portable TV Nadine had shipped out with such care.

"We see you on the television set, Nadine," Mama said with pride. "You didn't forget your people. You are one of us."

All day Nadine sat in the hogan with Mama and talked.

In the evening she ate with the family, their menu now enlarged via Nadine's regular checks. At the foot of one of the bunk beds Nadine noticed the book on nutrition which she had sent to Mama.

At night Nadine slept in one of the bunk beds, Teddy sharing with his older brother for the night.

Eight in one room, as it had been before she ran away.

The whole village knew that Nadine was home. Nobody disturbed them out of respect for the briefness of her visit. Tears stung Nadine's eyes at Mama's happiness.

Mama had never expected to see her again.

In the morning Nadine's stepfather went off to his meager-paying job in town. The children cavorted outside, delighted with the gifts Nadine had brought. Nadine was curled up at the foot of the bunk bed where she'd slept and waited for Mama to bring strong fresh coffee for the two of them.

"Mama," she said quietly, when her mother was seated beside her. Forcing herself to remain casual. "Please tell me about my father. I have to know." The minute she knew she was coming home she'd determined to face Mama with this.

"Nadine, there is nothing to tell," her mother rejected evasively. But Nadine's eyes forced her to continue.

"I met him at boarding school, and—and it happened." Her eyes were cast down. "Later, in spite of my shame, your stepfather married me."

"Mama, I must know about him," Nadine said urgently. "Who he is. I want nothing from him, Mama, I swear. Just to see him for myself."

"It happened far away," her mother said, her voice barely audible. "I was sent away to live with a family and go to high school. His name was Cliff Arnold. He was the only one in the class who was nice to me. I liked him so much. We'd sneak out and meet, and he'd bring me things. We talked about running away together after graduation. But I—I got pregnant. The lady I lived with guessed. She said terrible things, and packed me up and sent me home."

"What about him?" Nadine pressed. "Didn't he know where you were? Didn't he try to find you?"

"He was seventeen." Her mother's eyes were downcast. "We knew his folks would never let him marry me. A squaw from the reservation. He never even knew about you. What was the use of telling him?"

Cliff Arnold. Nadine filed the name away in her memory. Her father's name was Cliff Arnold. Oh, she had things to say to him!

On the plane en route to her next engagement Nadine told Jason about her father. "I want to find him, Jason," she said, her voice deep with intensity. "I have to see him. That's all, just see him."

"It'll cost," Jason warned. "Detectives come high."

"I don't care what it costs!" Nadine's eyes were overbright. "Jason, am I allowed enough money from the fund to pay for detectives?"

"You think it's worth it, baby?" he probed. "You could be buying yourself a lot of hurt."

"I have to do this, Jason," she insisted. "I must."

"Okay," Jason agreed gently. "We'll have funds released to find your old man."

With the meager information supplied by her mother, Nadine and Jason consulted a private-detective agency. Within a week she was informed that Cliff Arnold had moved away from the town where he'd lived at the time she was conceived, but the detective agency was optimistic about the follow-up. Nadine walked around with a savage joy because soon she would be able to confront her father. Jason was uneasy.

"This is a hang-up with me, Jason," Nadine pointed out while they drove to a campus concert date. "I have to see my father. I have to look him squarely in the eye and say to myself, 'you son of a bitch, you walked out on Mama and me!' Not to him," Nadine said quickly. "Just to myself, to wash him out of my life." She managed a shaky laugh. "Like Claire says, its cheaper than going into analysis."

"Okay, baby," Jason accepted this warily, and grinned. "You know, you're really sharpening up, hanging around Claire and me."

"It's been a fantastic year," she reminded, still brushed with wonder that so much had happened. "I feel at least ten years older."

"For both of us it's been a fantastic year." Jason braked for a red light. "I'm thinking about marriage again, Nadine. I never thought I would."

"Claire's terrific," Nadine said honestly, yet punctured by a sense of loss at the thought of Jason's marrying Claire. She herself had absolutely no social life, which worried Jason. For her, work was everything. Not that fellows didn't make pitches. She tightened up, pushed them away. She was scared. Claire said every fellow you met in New York had one destination in mind. Bed. It scared her because sometimes she met somebody who turned her on— for that. She didn't want to make it with somebody who wasn't important to her. Jason was important, though not in that way. Sometimes she wondered about Jason and her. There were times when all he had to do was touch her, and she'd be ready. "Jason, I think Claire will be great for you," Nadine reiterated with determined forcefulness. Claire was candid about wanting to marry Jason.

"What a difference between Claire and my ex-wife," Jason said with dry humor. "She was beautiful, brittle, financially demanding and sexually frugal. She wanted the house in suburbia and she got it, but the marriage splintered. Claire gives," he said with satisfaction. "She's more woman in one night than my wife was in all the years of our marriage."

"Claire will be good for you," Nadine said,

leaning forward to touch his arm affectionately. "Marry her, Jason."

Early in July the detective agency phoned Nadine. They'd located Cliff Arnold. He was living in a prosperous suburb of a middle-sized Midwestern city. A college town. He was married and had three children. Two boys, eight and six, a girl five. Trembling, Nadine wrote down all the information, though the man on the phone assured her they were forwarding a full written report.

Off the phone, Nadine sat stiffly erect, her eyes fastened compulsively to the sheet of paper in her hand. Her hand shaking. Cliff Arnold was a chemical engineer. His wife, active in cultural affairs, the man on the phone reported, was her stepmother. His three children were her half-brothers and her half-sister. She'd never thought about that until this moment. Another family that was hers.

The doorbell rang. Nadine started. She'd forgotten, with the impact of this phone call, about the reporter who was coming over to interview her for the music column of some women's magazine. Frowning, she hurried to the door. Jason had promised he'd be here, too. She felt more confident with him at hand. Her hand reaching for the knob, she glanced at her watch. Oh, the reporter wasn't due for half an hour.

She pulled the door wide. Jason hovered there, a shaker of cocktails cradled in one arm, a trio of glasses clutched in his free hand.

"Hi, I come prepared for the press," he said lightly. Knowing she would be uptight about the interview.

"Jason, the detective agency located him," she

said breathlessly while Jason deposited his bar supplies. "Here—" She extended the paper, watched him read her hastily scrawled notes. "Jason, sign me up for a concert in that town. There's a college there, it ought to be easy. Even if we have to take much less money than usual. Jason," she pleaded urgently, "please do this for me."

CHAPTER EIGHTEEN

Grumbling but sympathetic, Jason booked Nadine for an early October concert in the suburban area where her father lived with his family, at a fee which hurt his pride. A concert sponsored by a suburban cultural group, not a college.

October would have been anguishedly distant to Nadine through the long, hot summer. But she was busy with a record session, personal appearances, a major rock festival date scheduled for mid-August, interviews with magazine people. Jason and Claire, quietly married over the July 4 weekend, made a point of including Nadine in their lives.

Weekends the three of them sprawled on the white sand at Fire Island and soaked up sun, isolating themselves from everyone else because this brief oasis of solitude was essential to sustain them through the hectic week in Manhattan. After all the years of living with the desert, Nadine passionately loved the ocean, relished the Monday morning ferry rides back to the mainland, with the salt spray in her face. In and out of air-conditioned offices, studios, apartments, Nadine hated the humidity of the New York summer streets.

Late one August afternoon, several days before the highly publicized rock festival, she cabbed to Second Avenue, walked across Fifth Street to Seth's apartment. Her mind tried to fasten on some casual, sophisticated remark to throw at Seth when he opened the door to her. If he was there.

Trembling, she walked into the fetid hallway of Seth's building, began to climb the stairs. A calico

cat she remembered came darting down the hallway, halted, waiting to have his head scratched,
meowing his gratitude.

Faintly breathless, from a blend of exertion and
expectation, Nadine approached the landing on
Seth's floor. Her eyes moved eagerly to his door, and
desolation swept over her. A huge black-power poster
stared at her.

Seth must have moved. She hadn't bothered to
check the names on the mailboxes. The bells, of
course, hadn't worked for years.

Despite the poster, Nadine approached the door,
knocked self consciously. A tall, pencil-slim girl in
orange chinos and an exaggerated Afro hairdo
opened the door several inches.

Yeah?" The girl inspected Nadine with insolent
curiosity.

"Does Seth Coles live here?" Nadine was uncomfortable because the girl stared with such persistence.

"Not in this pad," the girl said emphatically. "Say,
aren't you Nadine Scott?" Respect in her eyes now.

"No," Nadine denied swiftly, and forced a smile.
"A lot of people think I look like her."

Nadine spun about, hurried down the stairs. Re-
alizing, all at once, how far she'd come from the East
Village. She wasn't part of the neighborhood any
more. Jason was talking about a possible date at
Fillmore East. She was Nadine Scott, folk rock star.

At the rock festival, as Jason had prophesied,
Nadine was a smash. *Variety* headlined the festival
and her appearance there. Back in New York again
Nadine sat down with Jason to figure out finances.
She was determined to buy a house for Mama and

the family in the small town near the reservation. Jason went with her to the attorney who handled her trust fund. Buying the house could be arranged with no legal hassle.

To Nadine's astonishment Mama rejected this.

"I know you mean well, Nadine," Mama wrote, *"but we belong here on the reservation. We could never live in that world outside. You are good to us, my daughter. It is enough this way, what you do for us."*

Nadine sat in the comfort of her New York apartment, on a sweltering early September day, and talked with Claire about Mama's letter.

"Claire, Mama doesn't want the house," she reiterated with bewilderment. "She wants to stay there on the reservation. You don't know what it's like, nobody knows who hasn't lived in a hogan." Her eyes glowed in painful memory.

"Maybe your mother's right," Claire said gently.

"About not wanting to leave the reservation. Sometimes it's an awful wrench to leave familiar surroundings." She squinted in thought. "Maybe you can bring a house to her, Nadine." Nadine glanced up quickly. "What about a mobile home? You can order that right here in town, have it delivered right to the reservation. None of that business of having to wait for a house to be built."

"Oh, Claire!" Nadine glowed. "That's it!" She could just see Mama's face, her stepfather's and the children's, when the mobile home was towed out to their land.

"Get out the classified," Claire ordered briskly. "Let's see what we can do."

The next morning Claire and Nadine drove in a

rented car out to New Jersey to look at mobile homes. Nadine inspected every model with childlike absorption, finally chose the most luxurious. With Claire behind the wheel again on the return trip to the city, Nadine leaned back, caught up in a fantasy of Mama's reaction when the mobile home, completely furnished, would be delivered.

"I wish they could have running water and electricity and a telephone," Nadine said wistfully. "Nobody has those things in the whole village, only the trading post."

"Why don't we try and find out what it would cost to bring those in?" Claire suggested.

"Claire, it must cost a fortune." Nadine was startled, but hope stirred in her. "How do we find out?"

"Ma Bell," Claire pointed out humorously. "I'll get on the phone with the utility companies and see what we can dig up.

"But right now," she said firmly, gazing into her rearview mirror for road clearance, "let's cut over to Howard Johnson's and have some lunch."

Within two days Claire had come up with the information that running water was available at a total cost of sixty dollars for pipes and labor. For thirty years the water pipeline had been there. Nobody in the village could afford to lay out the cash to bring water into the hogans.

"I know one family," Nadine recalled somberly, "who have a bathtub in the hogan. They found it thrown out somewhere and brought it home to hold the firewood."

A few days later, with characteristic efficiency, Claire arranged for a telephone and electricity to be provided when the mobile home arrived. It would be costly, but Nadine was thrilled with these small miracles.

The mobile home was delivered. In her small, cramped handwriting Mama wrote about the family's delight with this minor masterpiece. The mobile home was the focal point of interest on the reservation.

Nadine found recurrent satisfaction in the improvement of her family's living conditions. Yet as the date approached for the concert in the suburban town where her father lived, she was increasingly uptight. Four days before the concert Jason had an appointment with a TV packager about a spot for her on a spectacular starring Hollywood luminary Alan Faith. She struggled to show her enthusiasm.

She waited in her apartment for Jason to come and tell her the results of the meeting with the packager. She had a mild headache and her stomach was queasy. She stretched out on the sofa, her mind focusing ominously on the coming concert.

She was dozing when the doorbell jolted her into wakefulness.

Hurriedly, she left the sofa to cross to the door. Jason stood there, wearing an exuberant smile.

"Baby, it's set," he reported jubilantly. "You're doing the Alan Faith spectacular. We fly out to the Coast in mid-December. They didn't bat an eyelash when I told them what we were asking."

"Jason, that's sensational!" She tried valiantly to display excitement, but her headache was worse. She wished she hadn't eaten lunch.

"You feeling okay?" Jason inspected her with

sudden concern.

"I've got a headache," Nadine conceded. "I feel kind of rotten." She pantomimed the insignificance of this.

"You've picked up a bug, baby. This is no time for you to get sick!" He reached over to touch her face. "You're running a temperature."

"I'll be all right tomorrow," she insisted quickly. She had to be, with the concert only four days away.

"You get yourself into bed," Jason ordered sternly. "I'm calling Claire to come over and stay with you. Also, she's got this lady doctor friend who'll make a house call if she asks."

"I don't need a doctor."

"You want to play that concert Thursday night you do what I say," Jason ordered with mock gruffness, already dialing Claire's office. "Get into pajamas and into bed."

Nadine's virus ran an energy-robbing forty-eight-hour course. Jason—solicitous about her health—threatened to cancel out the concert. Nadine insisted she was well enough to sing. She'd waited so long for this confrontation with her father.

Still slightly shaky from her bout with the virus, Nadine boarded a morning flight with Jason on Thursday. It was a short haul, bringing them into the city at noon. During the entire flight she sat hunched tensely in her seat, eyes fastened to the window. Seeing nothing. Trying in her mind to picture her father. It was finally happening. She was going to see him.

The plane hit the runway right on schedule. Jason spied their welcoming committee—three women waiting to take them to luncheon and to settle them into a hotel to rest up for the concert.

"We'll have an early dinner at the hotel," Jason reminded Nadine as they walked toward the committee. "They're sending a car to pick us up for the drive to the high-school auditorium."

The committee, composed of three young, smartly turned out suburban matrons, spilled over with friendliness and enthusiasm about the concert.

"I'm Kathy Evans," the tallest, executive-type member of the group introduced herself briskly. "This is Laura Comstock and Betsy Arnold." Kathy Evans gestured with a broad smile to her companions. "Now let's get you to the hotel and to luncheon."

Nadine was trembling. Conscious of the faint, reassuring pressure of Jason's hand at her elbow. He knew she'd reacted to the name. Betsy Arnold. Her stepmother. This slim, elegant, young woman who was talking so animatedly about the scheduled concert. She remembered the detective's report. "*Mrs. Arnold is active in local cultural affairs.*"

Nadine forced herself to appear politely attentive to the conversation as they settled themselves in the car for the drive to the hotel. Aware that Jason was turning on his impressive charm to detract attention from her. Giving her time to regain control.

At the hotel their bags were sent upstairs and they joined the three women in the hotel dining room for lunch. In convivial spirits the party ordered, and the conversation settled on the evening's concert. At irregular intervals Nadine contributed to the table talk, but was relieved when the waiter arrived to place a fruit cup bedded in ice before her and she could pretend to be absorbed in eating.

Involuntarily, she glanced at Betsy Arnold, with disbelief that this could be her father's wife. She thought of her mother, who was old before her time, while she gazed upon her stepmother, who was young past her time. The whole ugliness that had haunted her all the years of her life rose up in sinister mockery. The affluent, spoiled whites on one side of the scale, and the Indians steeped in poverty and degradation on the other. When would it balance out?

"We were so delighted you could come here," Betsy Arnold smiled warmly at Nadine. "We never expected to be able to afford you," she admitted with candor. "Until Mr. Friedlander contacted us and began negotiations. Everybody's so excited."

"Nadine's appearing here at a sharply cut fee," Jason explained casually. "She had to be in the area, anyway, so we decided to fit in a concert."

"Cliff said it had to be something like that," Betsy said effervescently. Nadine's eyes dropped to her plate. "He was so pleased we'd been able to book someone with such marvelous appeal for the kids. Cliff isn't exactly the chamber-music type himself," she jibed affectionately.

Nadine wished the luncheon would end. She didn't want to sit here at this table exchanging small talk with her father's wife. Betsy Arnold was so young, so pretty, so friendly. She'd expected an older woman, cold, impersonal.

"You're not eating," Betsy exclaimed reproachfully, focusing her attention on Nadine as though she were a child.

"I'm not terribly hungry," Nadine stammered.

"She's just recovering from a virus," Jason

explained. "You know what that does to the appetite."

Nadine was relieved when they left the table. They said their farewells to the welcoming committee and headed for the hotel elevators.

"Baby, play it cool," Jason urged while they waited for an elevator. "You're here. You're sure to see your father at the concert tonight." He smiled whimsically. "Committee wives inevitably bring their husbands backstage." He paused, frowning in thought. "Nadine, they're nice people."

"What about me?" Nadine demanded in an impassioned whisper, though they were alone before the elevators. "What about my mother?"

"Don't jump like that," Jason reproached. "I just don't want to see you hurt." His eyes told her he regretted their coming.

"I want to see my father," Nadine said tightly. "All my life I've promised myself that. And tomorrow, before we leave for the airport, I want to drive around the part of town where he lives. I want to keep circling till I see the kids."

"Nadine, the kids will he in school!"

"Then let's take a later flight, Jason." Her two brothers and her sister. As close to her as Jody and Teddy and the others. Her second family. "Jason." Her eyes were pleading with him. "We can rent a car, can't we? Change our flight?"

"Okay, Nadine." He sighed heavily, reached out to squeeze her hand. "Will do."

The switchboard operator buzzed to announce the car was waiting. Nadine and Jason, with her guitar and weekender in tow, headed downstairs.

The chauffeur seated them in the car, slid behind the wheel to head out for suburbia. The rush-hour traffic had run its course. The car sped swiftly through the early evening.

Out of the city into the suburban area with its rows on rows of well-kept, affluent homes. Nadine stared at the passing houses with anguished intensity. Which one belonged to her father?

"That must be the high school up ahead," Jason guessed, leaning forward slightly.

The high school was an impressively long, low modern building that evidently had caused many a taxpayer to complain about its cost. One wing, Nadine guessed it to be the auditorium, was brilliantly lighted, as was the expansive parking area adjacent.

Kathy Evans was at the door, waiting to receive them. "We can get to the dressing room through the side here," she said with a brisk smile, leading Jason and Nadine away from the lobby. Nadine felt the familiar pre-concert excitement welling in her.

At the door of the spacious, lavishly appointed dressing room, Nadine and Jason made the perfunctory, flattering remarks about the accommodations. A pretty teenager called avidly to Kathy Evans about the tardiness of the ushers, simultaneously shooting a worshipful gaze at Nadine.

"Excuse me," Kathy said apologetically. "Just some last-minute details to be smoothed over. If you need anything, just ask anyone you see back here to chase after me."

Kathy Evans hurried away. Nadine and Jason went inside the dressing room. Jason set the weekender across a chair.

"Not the usual audience tonight," Jason reminded her. "A mixture of every age group. It's a challenge, baby."

"Maybe you were right," she said nervously, "when you said we ought to have a group behind me when we play non-campus dates." It would be awful if she bombed out tonight. Especially tonight. She'd fought against having a group behind her. She didn't often fight Jason—he was boss.

"You were right, Nadine, about playing it alone. Just the guitar and you out there. That's right." He took a deep breath, his eyes somber as she brought out makeup, spread out costumes. "Look, this is just another concert. You'll have a lot of parents out there, who're hungry to know what's going on with the younger generation. You're bringing them some answers. They may not dig everything you say, but they sure as hell want to hear it."

"I'm okay," she said softly. "Stop worrying, Jason."

"Sure." He smiled warmly. "Get ready. I'm going out to case the joint."

On the stage, in the spotlight, she pushed everything out of her mind except the performance. When she concluded, the applause was thunderous. This audience was too polite to demand repeated encores, as campus audiences invariably did; but she was drawn into one well-received encore.

She left the stage elated, exhausted, strung up. Jason, beaming, guided her to the dressing room, diplomatically avoiding the kids who were suddenly appearing backstage. He shut the door behind Nadine, stayed outside to talk to the backstage callers while she removed her makeup.

"Baby, they're throwing some bash for you in the lounge," Jason reported. "They're waiting for you."

Nadine's eyes widened.

"For me?"

Jason grinned.

"For you."

Jason propelled her to the lounge where a lavish buffet was set up in one corner. Across the room a coffee urn and cups were arranged on a colorfully decorated splashed table, with Betsy Arnold and a pretty fifteen-year-old in attendance.

"Jason, let's have coffee." Nadine's voice was unnaturally high. Betsy Arnold was here. Somewhere in this room was her father. "I'm dying for something to drink." Compulsively, her eyes grazed the convivial crowd.

"Easy, baby." Jason dropped an arm about her waist as he guided her to the coffee urn. Jason knew the chaos within her.

"You were great!" Betsy Arnold said effervescently while the teenager eagerly drew coffee for Nadine and Jason. "Everybody's hoping you'll come to us again."

"Thank you." She flashed her quick, shy smile at her stepmother. "It's a beautiful school. The kids must love it."

"My husband always says it doesn't matter how the school looks, it's what goes on inside that counts. Of course, we're lucky," Betsy Arnold continued. "We have the best school system in the state." She lifted her head with a pleased gesture of recognition, smiling at someone across the room. "There's Cliff," she said, waving a hand to attract his attention.

Nadine fought to control her hands. She was holding hot coffee! But Jason was reaching to take the plastic cup from her hand while she half-turned to gaze at the man approaching them through the thickening crowd Her father.

"Coffee, Cliff?" Betsy asked.

"Sure." He smiled at Nadine with lively interest.

This was her father. This young man. Jason's age, her quick mind computed. Her stepfather's age, but her stepfather was an old man.

"It was great to be able to attend a concert and not fall asleep," Cliff Arnold told Nadine with warmth. She hadn't expected him to be so good-looking! Fair hair like hers. Brown eyes with an oddly wistful quality. Like hers, Nadine acknowledged, her throat tight at this outward indication of their relationship. "Usually Betsy keeps nudging me, to be sure I'm awake."

"What about some food, Nadine?" Jason suggested, after some informal exchange between the Arnolds and himself. His hand at her elbow. Taking charge. "Will you excuse us, please?"

Jason prodded her toward the buffet table. He was scared to death she'd say something disastrous. She'd expected to hate her father on sight. But she was obviously drawn to him.

"We'll leave soon," Jason promised, piling a plate high with food for her. Remembering she'd barely touched her dinner. "They'll understand you're bushed." Compulsively, her eyes sought out Cliff Arnold while she ate at Jason's exhortations, smilingly replied to the onslaught of compliments coming at her from every side. All her life she'd waited for this moment. To get him out of her system.

"All right, Nadine," Jason decreed gently.

"Let's cut out."

She didn't want to leave, Nadine realized with astonishment. She wanted to stay here, near the man who was her father.

"Let's go," Nadine agreed, shaken with conflicting emotions. "It's hot in here!"

Nadine lay awake in the darkness. Too keyed up to sleep. She'd seen her father. She mustn't leave without seeing him again. It wasn't enough, those few minutes tonight, with people all around them!

She stared fixedly into the darkness above, her mind racing.

She would see him again. Alone. Without Jason. At the office, she could go to his office.

What was the firm name? She squinted in concentration, trying to visualize the detective's report. Melton Industries! That was it. She groped in the darkness for the night-table lamp, switched it on. Instinctively glancing at her watch. Past three. In six hours she could climb into a taxi, head for her father's office.

Hands unsteady with excitement she pulled the phone book from its resting place on a shell beneath the night table, began to rip through the pages. She dug out a pencil, a scrap of paper, scrawled down the address. Tomorrow morning, long before Jason would be awake, she'd go to her father's office. Confront him. Spill out the years of silent fury.

With the address safely stored in her wallet, she clicked off the light, lay back exhausted. But now she would sleep.

Nadine awoke with a disconcerting sense of

falling through space. She leaned over to inspect her watch. Not yet eight. Early.

With nervous anticipation she showered, dressed, called room service for breakfast. Not because she was hungry but it would be something to do. She stood at the window, gazing down at the morning traffic, her throat tightening as she envisioned the confrontation with her father. But this was something she must see through.

The waiter arrived with creamy scrambled eggs in a protective casserole, crispy hot toast, fragrant coffee. She ate with unexpected gusto. Her eyes moving compulsively to her watch. No rush. She mustn't arrive at the office before nine-thirty.

In the elegant hotel lobby she inquired at the desk about a taxi, waited while one was called. The clerk looked at the address, explained that it would be close to a twenty-minute ride this hour of the morning. She pandered about leaving a note for Jason. No need, he was sure to sleep until noon. She'd be back at the hotel before Jason awoke.

In barely fifteen minutes the cabbie was pulling up before a starkly modern, two-storied building at the edge of town, with immaculately trimmed lawns and an extravagant display of foundation plantings. In the adjacent parking area perhaps sixty late-model cars were parked. Her father had done well for himself. His wife said last night that he was a vice-president

Fighting for an outward cool, Nadine entered the building, paused before the receptionist's desk in the lobby.

"Do you have an appointment with Mr. Arnold?" the girl behind the desk inquired. "Is it about the secretarial position?" Her eyes said that Nadine's way-out casual garb would never do.

"No, it isn't," Nadine said crisply, her face hot. "Please tell Mr. Arnold I'm here. Nadine Scott."

The name registered. The girl's eyes widened with startled respect.

"One moment, please"

A few minutes later a mini-skirted secretary came out to lead Nadine to an office far down a side corridor. Following the girl Nadine came to grips with the first touch of panic. Now that she was here, what was she going to say to him?

"In here, please," the secretary indicated an open door.

"Thank you."

In a vise of unreality Nadine walked into the expansive office. The carpeting lush beneath her feet. The oversized walnut furniture obviously expensive.

"Nadine, hello." Warmth in Cliff Arnold's eyes as he rose from behind his desk to walk toward her. His secretary quietly closed the door to the executive office. His eyes were surprised. He couldn't imagine why she was here.

"I may as well be honest," she said, faintly defiant. Her eyes holding his while color grew in her cheekbones. "Last night's concert was planned so that I could meet you."

"I don't understand." With polite curiosity in his smile, he gestured her to a chair. Yet Nadine sensed a wariness rising up in him.

"It took a while to find you." She clung desperately to her cool. "The last information I had on you, you were a student at Lincoln High."

"Hey, that was a long time ago!" He chuckled,

watching her without comprehension.

"I'm Indian," she reminded him. Half-Indian. That was well publicized. "My mother is Grace Goodfriend."

"Grace!" His voice was suddenly mellow. His eyes tender. "You're Grace's daughter? How is she?"

"She's still on the reservation," Nadine said tightly. "Things are better, now that I'm singing."

"Grace was so pretty, so sweet." Nostalgia shone from him. He was seventeen again, back at Lincoln High. "She was the loveliest girl in that school. I was so unhappy when Grace dropped out of high school, but we could all understand it, of course. The kids in that high school could have won ribbons for intolerance." His eyes were angry. "I'm afraid they gave Grace a rotten time."

"Mama left school because she was pregnant," Nadine said tautly. Her eyes holding him, commanding him to remember. "Because she was pregnant with me," Nadine repeated. "By you."

Nadine saw the anguished comprehension on his face. The realization that this was his daughter, his oldest child standing accusingly before him.

"Grace never said a word," he stammered, his eyes dark with shock. His face ashen. "Nobody knew. Not ever." He took a deep breath. "Grace never told me. Not a hint. One day I came to school and she wasn't there. I called the boarding family, and they said she'd gone back to the reservation. Just that." He shook his head in dismay. "Nadine, I swear, she never told me."

"Would it have mattered?" Nadine challenged. "Would you have married her?"

He shut his eyes for a moment of private

torment. "I was seventeen. I couldn't have married without my parents' consent. Grace knew they were furious because I was seeing her away from school."

"You never bothered to find out why she left!" Nadine lashed at him. "You let her go back home to face her shame alone. You never tried to reach her!"

"Nadine, I never knew. I never guessed."

"You should have!" Her voice shook. "You should have gone to her!"

"Nadine, we were two kids. What could we have done?"

"You should have gone to Mama," Nadine reiterated. "You didn't care." Her voice broke.

"Nadine—"

He stumbled toward her, his hands unsteady, reaching out to pull her to him. They clung together, both quietly crying.

CHAPTER NINETEEN

Nadine stared stubbornly at the magazine which lay open across her lap. A pretense of reading excused her from conversation.

"Nadine," Jason intruded with an attempt at jocularity, "you've been looking at that page for twenty minutes."

"I was thinking about the session," she lied. Jason was uptight because she had gone to her father and had spoken little about it to him. Jason felt himself shut out. Jason had a lot riding on her, Nadine reminded herself, he was scared of her flipping out. "Maybe you ought to try to postpone the session a week. I'm not sure I'm ready for it."

"You're ready for the session," Jason said matter-of-factly, but he was watching her closely. "It's all set up. You're not going to start being a hard-to-handle artist,'" he chided. "That's not your bag."

"Okay, so we do the session." Her voice was edged with rebellion.

"Look, honey, don't start creating hang-ups about what happened this morning." His eyes were worried. "Your father's a hell of a nice guy. Not a monster, as you expected."

"Don't keep telling me that," Nadine shot back, then fastened her gaze on her hands. "He wanted to take me home with him, right then," she confided after a moment, with a compulsion now to talk about it. "He wanted to tell Betsy and the kids. But I couldn't go with him, Jason." She swung to face Jason, her eyes anguished. "I said I'd come back later, when he'd had a chance to break it properly to his wife. I couldn't go there to his house, remembering Mama."

"It wouldn't be disloyal to your mother, Nadine," Jason pointed out quickly. "Don't think that."

"I promised her I'd let things be, I said I just wanted to see him. I would have nothing to do with him. Jason, I promised Mama! And then I saw him, and there was this feeling between us. Jason, he cried when he found out." She leaned back in her seat, suddenly emotionally exhausted. "Jason, I'm so mixed up."

"Baby, it's a traumatic experience," Jason soothed. "You have to expect to feel shook up. But you're trying to buy bad hang-ups. You don't need to feel disloyal to your mother because you're letting your father into your life!"

Nadine listened to Jason, wanting him to wash away her guilt. Yet she knew she teetered perilously atop a fence, with Mama on one side and her father on the other. No matter how strongly she felt about Mama, to be close with her father was to turn her back on her mother. Yet she wished to move into her father's life. Even to see him occasionally, to talk to him now and then on the phone, would fuse them into closeness.

"Before we fly out to the Coast in December, you can stop off and see your mother," Jason soothed warily. "You'll be an advance Christmas present."

"And then I stop off a day later at my father's?" she questioned with an undercurrent of defiance.

"Why not?," he challenged casually. "Everybody has two parents. They don't always live together."

For a moment his eyes held Nadine's.

"I don't know where I am, Jason," she whispered. "I don't know who I am."

Back in New York Nadine was swept up into the hectic pre-session routine. Jason and Claire, who had begun their marriage in Claire's apartment on East Seventy-third Street, were moving into larger quarters. Both were trying to persuade Nadine to take over Claire's apartment. Neither realized her deep attraction to West End Avenue, that it was so close to Seth's parents' apartment that Nadine knew she might be daily passing them on the street. Jason, who thought he knew everything about Nadine, knew nothing of Seth.

Late in October Jason flew out to the Coast to close the deal for the TV spectacular. A day later Claire was summoned home to North Carolina because her mother had suffered a heart attack. Feeling astonishingly alone in their absence, Nadine went across to the Drive on a cleanly crisp day to stroll along the river toward the boat basin. Frowning at the dirt of the Hudson, recalling the warnings of the ecologists. The world might yet have to go back to the Indian way of life to survive.

As she strolled, Nadine's eyes moved upward toward the uneven silhouette of apartment houses and brownstones that lined the east side of Riverside. Seth had loved Riverside Drive when he was a child. It was his playground. He fed the squirrels, watched the sea gulls, lay on the grass in the sun when the weather was good.

Nadine stared hard at the buildings above, knowing Seth's parents must still live there. They'd been there twenty-four years in their rent-controlled building. Nobody moved away from rent-controlled apartments in this city of insane rents.

She could call Seth's mother and lie about being in town for a few days. "I've lost his phone number, and I'd like to say hello." No. No, she couldn't talk to his mother. Words would freeze on her mouth if she tried.

If he were living in New York, and he must be, he'd have a phone. Suddenly she was half-running up the steep concrete path that led to Riverside Drive. Her hand already in her pocket, reaching for her apartment keys. She had to see him. She couldn't go on alone this way. Nothing was good without Seth. It was all make believe.

Almost a year and a half since she'd seen Seth! Yet, right now, this minute, it seemed as though she had just walked out of the pad on East Fifth, and now she must tell him how wrong she had been. Her hand was trembling when she dialed Information.

"Do you have a listing for Seth Coles," she said, her voice uneven. "C-o-l-es. I don't know the address. It's somewhere in Manhattan."

She waited, her breathing tense, until the Information operator returned. Hastily, she scrawled down the number the operator gave her. Seth was a phone call away.

Nadine called persistently, every half hour by the clock, with a growingly determined frenzy to reach Seth. At dusk she realized she had forgotten about lunch, went into the kitchenette to make herself a sandwich, a cup of coffee. The phone jangled discordantly. Frowning, she rushed to answer.

"Hello." Politely impersonal. Cautious, because even with her new unlisted number, there were calls from fans, from fellows in the music-business world who were out to make a pitch, and for whom Nadine had little interest.

"How're you doing, baby?" Jason wore his briskly cheerful voice.

"Okay," Nadine said casually. When she was uptight, like now, Jason's solicitude irked her. "How're things working out?"

"We're set," Jason reported. "All signed up. We fly out on the sixteenth. I'll have Claire line up some interview shows while you're out here." He took a deep breath. "I spoke to Claire a few minutes ago—she says she should be back in town sometime tomorrow evening. She'll call you."

"Jason, stop worrying about me," she said sharply. "I'm not psychotic, I can stay alone for a couple of days."

She listened, masking her impatience, while Jason filled her in on details about the coming TV taping, about which he felt jubilant. It was, he said, exactly what she needed at this point in her career. At last Jason was saying good-bye. Eagerly, Nadine dialed Seth's number.

Again the phone in Seth's apartment rang repeatedly. She sighed impatiently, her hand perspiring from the tightness of her grip on the phone.

"Hello."

"Seth—" Her voice unfamiliarly deep in her eyes. "Oh, Seth—"

"Nadine!" His pleasure obvious. "Baby, how are you?"

"I miss you," she said softly. "Seth, I never stop missing you."

"Where are you?" he demanded with an urgency that matched her own.

"At my place." Quickly she gave him her address.

"I'll be up in twenty minutes," he promised. "I'll go hogwild–I'll cab up."

They lay naked beneath the blankets, her head on his shoulder, her left leg thrown across his thigh. Radiators clanked with the final thrust of heat for the night. Both of them completely relaxed, satisfied just to be together.

"Seth, did you honestly search for me?" Nadine asked, eager for reassurance.

"Baby, I tore this town apart," he reiterated.

"But later you didn't try," she punished herself. "When you knew where I could be reached." Through the concerts, the recording company, the TV stations.

"Nadine, you didn't need me," he reminded wryly. "You were doing great. How could I come chasing then?"

"I needed you, Seth," she insisted. "I'm only half-alive when we're not together."

"Tell me more about this Friedlander guy," Seth asked, outwardly casual. He didn't like the idea of Jason's managing her.

"I told you everything, Seth. About how he picked me up at that festival. Jason's great," she said with warmth. "His wife handles my promotion." That was what Seth wanted to know. That Jason wasn't sleeping with her.

"Seth, it's been so awful without you. Every way."
She moved closer. "Seth, I haven't been with anybody else," she said with candor. "Never anybody
but you. She closed her eyes while Seth pulled her
to him again. Everything was going to be all right.
She was with Seth.

Seth stayed on in his East Seventh Street pad,
which he'd inherited from a classmate. Some nights
he slept over at Nadine's apartment. The other nights
Nadine went to his. They exchanged keys.

Jason was polite but wary when Nadine first
brought him face to face with Seth. Shaken because
there were important portions of her life that were
blanks to him.

Jason realized how much Seth meant to her,
Nadine told herself. Now he understood why she'd
staved off all the others who'd made pitches. To ease
the relationship between Seth and Jason, Claire
made a point of having them over to dinner at least
once a week.

Nadine realized Jason was not fully accepting
Seth yet, though he made a jovial attempt at friendship. Maybe Jason was scared she would marry, cut
out on the career. Jason would have to find himself
a new property.

But she was more than a property to Jason and
Claire. They were like family to her. And she would
never stop singing. Seth wouldn't expect that.

This was Seth's last year in medical school. He
was working with desperate earnestness to graduate
high in his class. He would soon be applying for his
internship. This unnerved Nadine because Seth

spoke seriously about forsaking the prestigious New York hospitals his parents favored to try for a place in Appalachia, where he'd worked all last summer.

It was disconcerting to visualize New York without Seth. She went off on concert dates at regular intervals, but only for a few days at a time.

Nadine was to spend Thanksgiving with Jason and Claire. Seth would go to his parents' apartment, with plans to meet Nadine at Jason's later in the evening. The night before Thanksgiving Nadine telephoned her mother, who was enthralled with the miracle of a phone in her house. Later in the evening, her father phoned her, and she talked with him and Betsy.

"The kids are dying to see you, Nadine. They listen to your records constantly," Betsy reported with warmth, "Can you come out for Christmas?"

Nadine hedged about making a definite date. She'd have to be in California on the sixteenth, she explained. She'd see how things worked out. On the way back from the Coast, Nadine reminded herself silently, she must stop off at the reservation. She clung to that determination.

She was anxious to spend the Christmas holidays with Seth. There was the long school-vacation period. Jason promised they'd be done with the taping by the twentieth. Seth kept saying he was going to take her to his parents apartment for dinner, let them get to know her.

Thanksgiving would have been the perfect time. But Seth kept stalling.

Nadine tried diligently to enter into the Thanksgiving Day festivities at Jason and Claire's smart new apartment. When she arrived, the apartment was rich with the savory aromas from the kitchen. This was a good marriage, Nadine recognized with tenderness. With both Jason and Claire scarred by bad marriages, this one was especially appreciated. Wistfully, Nadine watched the small exchanges between Jason and Claire that spoke so eloquently.

When the three of them sat down to the table, Nadine found her mind roving constantly to Seth. Holidays were important. Seth and she should be spending this one together. She felt the weight of Jason's troubled gaze, looked up, forced a smile. Jason, too, wondered when Seth would make this more than a bed relationship.

They were digging into second portions of Claire's deliciously spicy pumpkin pie when Seth showed. Good humoredly, he settled himself beside Nadine.

"Nadine, you'll have to carry me out," Seth warned, grinning. "I ate like a horse at home." Under the table, his knee moved to rest against hers.

"Oh, I got those tickets for *Hair* for Saturday night," Jason reported, rummaging in his pocket. "Despite the long run, it still took some doing," he chuckled, handing the tickets over to Seth.

"What do I owe you?" Seth was already reaching into his pocket for his wallet. "And thanks for the effort."

"Compliments of the firm," Jason said leisurely.

For a few moments, Seth argued with Jason, until Nadine intervened to back up Jason. Seth was uptight about spending any of her money. She'd warned Jason, Seth was not to pay for the tickets. He was on a stringent budget.

Not until much later, when they lay naked in bed together, with the record player a muted background for their togetherness, did Nadine broach what was paramount in her mind.

"Seth, when am I going to meet your folks?" This was becoming an obsession with her, she thought self-consciously.

"Soon. What's the big deal?" he jibed.

"I want to know them," Nadine insisted. "I'm dying to meet Audrey. They're going to he my family, too. Someday. Aren't they?" Her eyes held his, demanding.

"You know we'll get married," he said quietly, a hand moving to her breasts. "But I've got to get my degree. Let's not move past that, huh, baby?" He lifted one leg across her slender thighs, watching her face for reactions.

"Seth, just take me there one evening for coffee," she coaxed. "Say we were just passing by. They don't have to know how things are with us." But his bringing her home would tell them that.

"We'll think about it," he hedged, his mouth moving toward her small, high breasts.

It was always this way, Nadine thought with frustration, even while Seth was moving her, again, to desire. Seth settled every serious argument by making love. But their relationship was broader than being in bed together. That wouldn't be enough for a lifetime together.

Nadine slept late, waking to the aroma of bacon crisping in an iron skillet, coffee bubbling in the percolator. She yawned, propped herself up on one elbow. Seth, whistling in the cozy warmth of the studio apartment, poured a mug of coffee, brought it to her in the sleeping alcove.

"How'd you like to try Mom's sauerbraten Saturday night?" be inquired casually. Sitting at the edge of the bed. "Of course, you have to appreciate sauerbraten to dig it."

"Seth." Her eyes widened with astonishment

"Hey, easy," he admonished good-humoredly. "You want to send us to the emergency room instead? That's hot coffee."

"You mean it, about Saturday night?" she pressed, excitement spiraling in her.

"I buzz d Mom while you were snoring," he said gently. "I said we'd have to cut out early—we have theater tickets."

"Seth, did you tell her about me?" Her eyes searched his face. Meaning the reservation background.

"I said I'm bringing this chick over for dinner," he said calmly. "Why make a big thing out of it? Let them get to know you."

"Seth, did you tell them I'm Indian?" Of course, the easy way would be to mention her white father out in the Midwest, with his jazzy chemical engineering job.

"Honey, I said I was bringing Nadine Scott up for dinner," he explained slowly. Humorously. "Even my folks must have heard about Nadine Scott by now, with all the hoopla. Anyhow, Audrey will clue them in," he promised, grinning. "She's a real fan. She'll flip when she finds out you're coming to dinner."

"How're things working out for Audrey at home?" Nadine asked compassionately. Seth had told her about the bust.

"Audrey was shook," Seth conceded wryly. "I think she'd run at the mention of a pot party. But Mom and Dad still watch her with fear in their eyes. You know."

"Seth, what'll I wear?" she demanded with childlike nervousness. Her mind filing through her closet of St. Marks Place-bought clothes.

"What you always wear, you kook," he chuckled. "This isn't Buckingham Palace. Now get out of that bed and come eat breakfast before I throw you on your back again."

"You haven't got the strength," she jibed, remembering last night.

"You want me to show you?" he challenged, pinning her down on the bed.

"Tonight," she laughed. "Right now give me breakfast"

Seth was taking her to his home for dinner. The words ricocheted through her mind. She was going to meet Seth's parents tomorrow night. A knot tightened in the pit of her stomach as she considered this encounter.

Nadine was delighted that Seth had a four-day vacation from classes. Tonight they'd go somewhere jazzy for dinner and to a film. They didn't need other people. Seth was working so hard this last year of school that he had no time for socializing. Except for her.

All day long, Nadine's mind kept hurtling ahead

to the dinner at the Coles'. Because Seth and she had theater tickets, his mother was pushing dinner up to six-thirty. They would have to leave at eight sharp to cab down to the theater. An hour and a half wasn't very long to impress Seth's parents with her potential as a daughter-in-law.

Saturday, in a red corduroy shirt that belonged to Seth, Nadine tiptoed about the apartment because Seth seemed bent on sleeping away most of the day. When the phone rang, she raced to answer before the buzzing could awaken him. She talked lengthily on the phone with Jason about the coming TV spectacular. This was the biggest thing she'd done to date. Jason was nervous because she was scheduled to do a concert the night before they flew out. He didn't want her to be exhausted. He knew the concerts took a lot out of her.

"I'll be fine, Jason. Stop worrying," she urged, wishing he'd get off the phone because Seth was stirring.

"Okay, baby," Jason wound up briskly. "Claire and I are driving up to Connecticut for the weekend." That would be to visit with the record-company exec. "Talk to you Monday."

"Hey," Seth drawled sleepily. "You plan on letting me stay out cold until time to dress for dinner?"

"You look so bushed," she said tenderly. "I couldn't bear to wake you up."

"Come over here and I'll show you how bushed I am," he jibed.

"Seth," she reproached, unexpectedly hurt.

"Seth, is that all I mean to you? Somebody to throw into bed?"

"Nadine, when are you going to grow up?" he rebuked, reaching out a hand to bring her down to the edge of the bed. "You're my girl for the desert isle. My woman for all seasons."

This was the honeymoon, Nadine decided with a surge of pleasure while Seth drew her beneath the covers with him. These weeks since she'd gone to the telephone in her desperation and called him.

"We'll have to get up and dress in a little while," she warned.

"In a little while," Seth promised, his eyes anticipatory. "We won't be late for Mom's dinner."

Walking down the corridor Nadine miffed the savory, wine-drenched aromas of the sauerbraten. From behind a door—Nadine guessed it was the Coles'—she heard the sound of her newest release.

"Audrey," Seth guessed, with a conspiratorial grin, and pushed the doorbell.

Audrey opened the door for them. Smaller than Nadine. A diminutive replica of Seth. Nadine smiled with a rush of affection. She hadn't expected the resemblance between Seth and Audrey to be so striking. It made Audrey especially appealing.

"Hi." Audrey was striving to be cool, her excitement glowing from her dark eyes. "I was just listening to your new release. Groovy!"

"Tell me what you don't have and Seth'll bring them over;" Nadine promised, wanting the teenager's friendship. One for her side.

Within minutes Felicia and Jim Coles were

greeting them. His mother good-humoredly rushing them in to the dinner table because of their theater date. Nadine trying not to grow uptight because his parents were striving to put her at ease. Because she was a guest, Nadine thought ironically.

"Mom flipped when I wanted to see *Hair*," Audrey reported, mildly aggrieved. "I don't know why."

"No real reason, Mom," Seth backed her up, grinning. "She won't see anything she hasn't seen before." No false modesty in this house, he'd once told Nadine with amusement.

"Seth, don't be crude," his mother shot back in irritation.

Audrey jumped into an earnest discussion of folkrock music, and her mother frowned unhappily. Mrs. Coles didn't want Audrey to be drawn to her, Nadine realized, uneasy.

Unhappily, Nadine compared the formal dining room in the apartment where Seth's parents had lived for the past twenty-four years to the hogan where she had grown up. Compared Mama to Mrs. Coles with a swift surge of shame that she would make such a comparison.

Seth's father talked animatedly over dessert about the theater in the late thirties, when, as a teenager, he'd saved his nickels and dimes to buy second balcony seats for Group Theater productions. His eyes rested uneasily on Audrey, who pined to see *Hair*.

"Mom, we have to rush off," Seth said apologetically when they'd dutifully finished seconds of dessert and drained their coffee cups.

"I know." His mother smiled with synthetic

brightness. "At the cost of theater tickets these days you don't want to miss a minute."

Not one word had been said all evening about her being Indian. It seemed to Nadine, super-sensitive in this respect, that the subject had been deliberately avoided. She could imagine the agitated conversation when Seth and she walked out. Mrs. Coles would be bursting with comments. Nadine remembered the tic in Felicia Coles' left eye. She was a nervous wreck because her only son, the medical student, had brought home a girl from the reservation.

Not until Sunday in her apartment, when Seth and she were sprawled on the bed with coffee and the Sunday *Times,* did Nadine talk about dinner the night before.

"Your folks put on a good show last night," she said with seeming casualness. "But they were sure uptight."

"Baby, I told you how they feel about my being seriously involved with a chick," he reminded. "They've got this one-track bit on their minds, about my staying with medicine."

"They wouldn't have been half as uptight if I weren't Navajo," Nadine insisted, her face hot.

"Oh, come off it, Nadine." He frowned in irritation. "Bigots they're not. I told you, they wouldn't care if you're red, purple, or green." He was silent for a moment. "They were uptight about Audrey. They associate you with the music scene—to them, that's the drug culture. It bugged them that Audrey flipped out for you. They still hurt from that drug bust."

"Seth, you know how I feel about drugs!" Nadine exploded.

"I know, but they don't. Music and drugs—in their minds it's the same culture."

"Seth—" Suddenly, Nadine was trembling. "Seth, why can't we get married? Now."

He moved his eyes quickly away.

"Because, baby, I don't pick up my degree until June. Then we can talk. When I'm not dependent upon my parents."

"Seth, you don't have to be dependent upon them," she said urgently. "You know how much money I'm pulling in! I can see you through this last year with no sweat at all."

"No," he said abruptly.

"Why not?" Her eyes challenged him. "Plenty of wives work to see their husbands through school. It's not new."

"Baby, I can't take this away from them," he said quietly.

"Take what away from them?" She was bewildered.

"Nadine, the biggest thing in their lives is putting me through medical school. The whole scene. I can't deny them that at this stage, after all these years of sweating it out with me."

"Then let's get married," Nadine said passionately. "Tell them about us."

"Honey, they're bright people," he said tiredly. "They know. But we have to sit out taking my degree. How long is it? Another six months or so."

"Then they'll worry about your internship," she

shot back. "They won't want you to get married because it'll be a drain on you," she mocked. "You'll be short-changing your career. Then it'll be your residency. Seth, I can't wait all those years!"

"We'll talk this summer," Seth promised. "Baby, will you cool it?"

"No!" Nadine swept away from the bed, strode to the desk, fumbled in a drawer. "No, Seth, either we tell your parents we're getting married, or let's cut out right now. I can't play this scene any more. I have to be everything to you—or nothing."

"Nadine, that's ridiculous." Seth left the bed to cross to her. He reached for her shoulders. "We'll talk in the summer."

She shrugged clear of his hands.

"No." She was trembling so that she could barely bring the key out of the desk drawer. "Here's the key to your pad. I've had it, Seth. I don't want to go on being a bed-mate. I'm square. I want to be married."

She surged past him, leaving the key on the table for him, slammed the bathroom door shut, locked it. Leaning with her face against the door. Praying he would come to her.

In a few minutes she heard the door to the corridor open, slam shut. Seth was gone. Gone from her life.

CHAPTER TWENTY

The first days of December dragged painfully for Nadine. Each time the phone rang she rushed to answer with a wistful hope that Seth would be calling. Each time the doorbell rang she hurried to pull it wide without bothering to ask who was there. But Seth neither phoned nor showed at the door. She was relieved when Jason and she boarded the United Airlines 747 at JFK, bound for Los Angeles and the date to tape the Alan Faith spectacular. Jason, anxious because she was depressed and unable to hide this, kept telling her a change of scenery was exactly what she needed.

Nadine leaned back in her seat, stubbornly shut her eyes. She hadn't been sleeping these nights since the split-up with Seth.

The flight was uneventful. They landed on schedule at Los Angeles International.

"Move your watch back three hours, Nadine," Jason reminded casually when they were seated in the taxi for the drive into the city. "It's two-forty Los Angeles time."

Nadine professed a deep interest in the scenery while Jason talked enthusiastically about Alan Faith. Dull country, she decided impatiently, unimpressed with the montage of oil pumps that lined the highway.

"We're coming up to Century City," Jason said after a while, conscious that Nadine was restless. "It used to be the old Twentieth Century Fox lot. Now it's this enormous complex. Apartment houses, a huge shopping center, a twenty-story office building." He chuckled reminiscently, and Nadine remembered that Jason had lived on the Coast for three and a half years. "It's a gas, to see these tall buildings climbing up into the sky after you've seen miles of one- and two-story buildings sprawled all over the place."

Nadine listened with a determined show of interest to Jason's affection-laced travelogue as they moved on through the countryside into town. Jason had made reservations for them at the Beverly Hilton. He said it was a typical Hilton with palms in front. They'd have an early dinner at Trader Vic's and she'd go to bed early. She was scheduled to show at rehearsal at ten tomorrow morning.

Nadine had been self-consciously uneasy about meeting Alan Faith. But despite his super-star status, she discovered she could relax with him. He was younger than she'd expected, probably no more than three or four years older than she. Tall, slight, handsome, gentle. And, of course, immensely talented.

Nadine threw herself into rehearsals with an intensity that delighted Alan. In addition to her scheduled spot Alan insisted that Nadine be written in throughout the show. Jason was ambivalent about her instant friendship with Alan, though he acknowledged, with candid jubilation, that it was excellent publicity for her, the way items were popping up in the columns about Alan and her.

"Alan's shrewd," Jason said with approval. "He knows what this does for his image, to share his show with a chick from the reservation."

Nadine was taken aback. Hurt. "It won't do Alan any good in the South," she shot back defensively.

"It's not the South that shoots up Alan's rating." Jason grinned complacently. "So what do we care? It's terrific for you."

Nadine worked hard on the show, grateful to have these demands made upon her, flattered that Alan Faith was squiring her about after hours. Dinner together nightly in quiet restaurants. Visits to campus coffee houses, where Nadine felt so at home. Just fun being together casually. No pitches to make her uptight

Jo was away with a group from the college, on a speaking tour dealing with Indian problems. She was due back momentarily. Nadine was eager to see Jo, yet uneasy. Jo's whole life was the Indian problem. All she had done was contribute money. And that limited by the trust fund demands. Sure most of her material dealt with her Indian background but Jo would feel she was using her people.

When the show was taped and Jason was arranging for their return flight, Nadine nervously announced that she wanted to stay in Los Angeles for a little while.

"What do you mean, you want to stay here for a while?" Jason stared hard at her.

"I want to see Jo," she reminded.

"Jo's due in tomorrow. We won't leave until the end of the week." He was watching her closely, trying to read past her face.

"I'd like to stay here for a week or two with Jo," she explained, striving for casualness. "I don't have a date scheduled for three weeks." The coffee house in Chicago, which she dreaded. It would be the first time Jason had booked her into Chicago. God, she hated that town! Except for Bob Frazer. She'd want to look him up.

"Nadine, you're not building a hang-up about playing Chicago?" Jason reproached anxiously. "Honey, Chicago is past history to you.

"I'll live through it." Nadine shrugged this away, took a deep breath. "But really, Jason, I want to stay. Alan's got a string of bashes lined up that sound like they may be fun. It's all new to me, Jason."

Jason sighed. He was anxious about her state of mind.

"How long do you want to stay here?"

"Until after New Year's," she stipulated. She would flip out in New York on Christmas and New Year's without Seth. She hedged about flying out to the reservation, despite her earlier determination to stop there on the way back to New York. Her father and his wife had called, urging her to spend the Christmas holidays with them. She couldn't go to her father for Christmas without hurting Mama. She hadn't even told Mama she had seen him. "I'll fly back right after New Year's," she promised.

"Okay, baby." Jason grinned suddenly. "Anyhow, you can't get into any trouble with Alan."

"I'm having fun with Alan," she said defensively. "He takes me to bashes and I don't get uptight. I'm getting used to being with people socially."

"Claire and I figured you'd go down with us to Jamaica over the holidays," Jason reminded wryly.

"Oh, Jason," she clucked. "Isn't it about time Claire and you went somewhere without me tagging along?"

"Okay, stay till after New Year's," Jason approved, though obviously wary about this arrangement. "Alan will keep you busy. Like I said, it's good for his image." His smile was ironic.

Two afternoons later Jo was sitting in the sitting room of her suite, while they smiled happily at each other over the sandwiches and coffee Nadine had ordered sent up.

"Baby, I can't believe it," Jo said with affection. "The way you've made it big in their world."

"Our world, Jo," Nadine said quickly, sparring with guilt. "It belongs to us as much as anybody else. More."

"I knew, back in Chicago, that you could do it." Suddenly, Jo was serious. She seemed so mature, Nadine thought studying her. That came with dedication, with being jailed for a cause, being briefly suspended from college when she was fighting for the establishment of a school of ethnic studies on the campus. Fighting back. "Nadine, settle out here where you can work with us." Jo leaned forward, her dark eyes glistening with zeal. "When we sit in next time, sit in with us."

"I'd have to do some juggling," Nadine said uncertainly. "I'm based in New York, of course. That's where the action is in recording."

"You can record out here," Jo reminded. "Lots of singers do. You go all over the country for concerts—the planes fly out of LA, too. Nadine, this can be the next major locale for Red Power. Be part of it with us."

"Let me get squared away with the next session.

Finish off some dates on the East Coast," Nadine said. Terror riding herd over her. If she became involved with the Red Power movement, it would be the end of Nadine Scott, singer. She had to give everything in one direction. She wasn't big enough to divide herself up.

Jo's eyes were wise, evaluating her. Nadine shifted in her chair, feeling inadequate.

"I'm staying out here for Christmas, Jo." She forced an eager smile. "Can we spend it together?"

"I'm flying to the reservation." Jo was withdrawing behind a small, bitter smile. "I want to see my son." She was gazing at Nadine now with an objectiveness that brought color into Nadine's face. As though she were a stranger. But it was Jo who had urged her to try to make it in the white world to show them what a girl from the reservation could do. "He's quite a boy," Jo went on, her face soft with pride. When he's ready for school I'll have him sent to me. He won't go to any Indian school," she promised with contempt. "What they did to me they won't do to my child. I know how to fight." Their eyes met. Nadine quickly lowered hers.

With a mixture of disappointment and relief, Nadine walked with Jo to the door. Knowing Jo was cutting her out of her life. It would never be the same with Jo and her again. She didn't have Jo's kind of dedication.

It was amazing, Nadine thought with a flutter of warmth, how protected she felt when Alan was at her side. His hand holding firmly to hers, they circulated through the name-studded crowd at a posh bash at Malibu. Both of them aware that, even here, they were apart from the others. The young generation. The authentically young, in a society where youth was worshipped.

Alan, in a low, amused voice, gave names to the familiar faces, known to her mostly from the "Late Show" on TV. Here and there she saw a young star that brought back the memory of films she'd seen with Seth. She was flattered when a woman star of the Forties recognized her and spoke with lavish admiration, until she realized the star's real objective was to take Alan off to bed.

As soon as a bash showed signs of becoming rough, and Nadine recognized this as a regular pattern, Alan quietly took her away. Usually to his own Malibu house, where they listened to records and enjoyed a late snack served by Donnie, his impeccable, fortyish houseman.

Christmas Eve she had dinner with Alan at his house at Malibu. Afterward they walked barefoot on the sand, returned to the house to watch Donnie meticulously decorate the Christmas tree he'd brought home earlier in the day. Donnie kept inspecting his watch. Nadine guessed he was anxious to be home with his family for Christmas Eve.

"I'd better cut out," Nadine said abruptly.

"I'll drive you home," Alan said quickly, and Donnie seemed relieved. Her leaving meant he could take off, too, Nadine realized.

In the Ferrari Alan switched on the radio, A local gossip columnist was spewing forth her daily ration. Nadine stiffened, her face suddenly hot.

"...Nadine Scott, who made it so fast from

reservation to singing star, is seeing much of handsome young Alan Faith. The Indian girl, not strong for socializing, has been seen nightly on the Malibu circuit with our Alan, whose charms are sufficiently potent to revise any lass' thinking."

Nadine leaned forward, switched off the dial. Trembling. Eyes ablaze.

"Cool it, baby," Alan urged gently. "So the old bitch thinks we're shacked up. It makes jazzy copy. We're the new beautiful young couple," he jibed.

"I hate people talking about me that way," Nadine said fiercely. "It's none of their business."

"Yes, it is," Alan said calmly. "It's part of the whole scene." He smiled brilliantly. "Nadine, it's Christmas Eve. We're supposed to be thinking beautiful thoughts."

"What are you thinking?" she challenged, nostalgia riding high about her.

"Home," Alan said, his eyes narrowed. "I've got six brothers and sisters, all married. Christmas is a big deal back home. But I can't bring myself to go home. I'll call tomorrow, but I can't go back." His eyes, when they swung to Nadine's, were baffled.

"Why not?" But even as she asked, she understood.

"With Mom it would be okay," he conceded somberly. "My old man kicked off last year. But the others, my sisters and brothers, their husbands and wives, they'd look at me as though I were something under a microscope. I've moved myself right out of their world. Ever read Tom Wolfe, Nadine?" he asked whimsically.

"Yes," Nadine said. Alan was surprised.

"'You can't go home again'." Her eyes were pained. "Why not, Alan?"

"What are you doing tomorrow?" Alan said, changing the subject.

"Sleep till two, have breakfast in my rooms." She shrugged. "Phone home."

"I'll pick you up about three," Alan said. "I know a swinging bash in Holmby Hills that ought to be fun."

"Okay," Nadine accepted. She didn't want to be alone on Christmas Day. "Three o'clock."

Nadine woke early, despite her determination to sleep until two. Conscious, instantly, that this was Christmas Day. Christmas, in California. Christmas meant coldness, the hope of snow. Christmas meant being with those close to you.

Nadine left the bed, flipped on the radio with a need to pierce the stillness of her rooms. No! Not Christmas carols, she was in no mood for that this morning. In nightie and bare feet she trailed into the sitting room, switched on the TV. The Christmas parade. Settling for silence, she crossed to the telephone to order breakfast sent up, climbed into a robe, washed her face.

She ate her breakfast without tasting. Thinking, mainly, about Mama. She'd sent fabulous presents home. Mama said the mobile home was the talk of the village. She could have gone home. Kooky to be sitting here in a hotel room, when she could be with the family. Go now.

Her eyes luminous, Nadine went to the phone, dialed, impatient to get through to airline reservations. Wouldn't Mama be surprised, and pleased!

And the kids! They were so excited about her singing, about the good things that were theirs now. But even while she spoke to the girl on the phone, Nadine realized it was absurd to expect an empty plane seat today.

"I'm sorry," the clerk said regretfully. "We don't have one availability today, unless there should be a last-minute cancellation. Would you like to be called?"

"No," Nadine said, wrapped in disappointment. "No, thank you. Forget it."

After a final cup of coffee from the large carafe that had been sent up, Nadine sat down to make her phone calls. To the reservation. To Cliff Arnold's household. To the luxury hotel in Jamaica where Jason and Claire were billeted. For a while, she was caught up in the pleasure of holiday conversation, particularly pleased that Betsy had put the three kids on to talk to her. She must go out there, Nadine told herself sternly. She'd promised the kids, so delighted with their newly found sister. But again, she experienced the uneasy tag of guilt. She was betraying Mama by becoming close with her father and his family. Her other family.

Nadine was restless when the phone calls were over, when the oppressive silence settled over her rooms again. She glanced at the clock again. Wishing, with childlike impatience, for three o'clock. She felt so comfortable with Alan. He made no demands.

At three sharp Alan showed. He'd stopped en route for a few drinks, but he wasn't zonked.

"I've got the keys to my cabin up in the mountains," Alan said casually. "Let's forget the bash, drive up and make ourselves dinner there. Christmas isn't real without snow. We can be there in an hour." He smiled persuasively, waiting for her acceptance.

"All right." It was absurd to feel suddenly tense because Alan and she were driving up to his mountain home. She didn't turn him on, they just enjoyed being together. Alan had nobody serious in his life. He said that, right out. But on Christmas nobody should be alone.

Alan talked compulsively, as they drove, about the West Coast jungle, for which he had a mixture of contempt and admiration. Nadine was glad that he was on a talking jag. She could sit back and listen, no effort required of her. Occasionally, Seth intruded into her thoughts.

"We'll soon be there," Alan said finally, with satisfaction. A glint of anticipation in his eyes as he leaned forward over the wheel. "It's groovy to come up here for a while. Forget everything down there." He nodded back toward Los Angeles, far below them. "Up here, with the mountains around me this way. I feel like I'm rolling back the calendar. I'm a kid again, back home." His eyes were opaque now, caught up in yesterday. His smile faintly bitter. "When anybody talked about being in analysis in those days, I figured they were nuts."

Alan had been in analysis for two years. He said it had cost him over twenty thousand already. Claire had been in analysis after her marriage cracked up. Was she headed for that scene too?

The cabin in the mountains was a sprawling contemporary of redwood and glass, that had cost Alan close to two hundred thousand. He rolled the car right into the garage, and they walked up into the house via the basement.

"Alan, it's glorious," Nadine gasped, when they were upstairs.

She wallowed in the lovely silence, crossed with a sudden sense of peace to the expanse of thermopane that looked out upon an incredible view of mountains and snow and blue sky.

"I'd better start defrosting if we're going to eat," Alan said spiritedly, strolling off toward the kitchen. "Then I'll light the fire."

Nadine dropped onto the long, wide sofa, legs tucked beneath her so that she could take in the magnificence of the view. How far from the hogan could she get, Nadine asked herself with painful humor. This was what Claire called the ultimate luxury.

Alan returned from the kitchen where he announced the steaks were defrosting, concentrated on starting a blaze in the brick-faced, free-standing fireplace. Music from the hi-fi filtered into the room. The sun was in descent. Soon it would be night. The austere isolation here in the mountains brought the desert solitude into her mind. No, she didn't want to think about home!

With the birch logs in the fireplace crackling away, Alan crossed to the bar to mix drinks. Normally, Nadine drank nothing stronger than beer. But this was Christmas.

Her mind was a kaleidoscope, shifting from the reservation to New York, to the Midwest town where her father lived, to Jamaica where Jason and Claire were on vacation. Jo who considered her copping out. Feeling herself shut out from each. Alone on

Christmas Day.

"Baby, drink this down," Alan was saying gently, putting a glass in her hand. Reading her mind. Alan said once, "Sometimes I feel so alone I want to die, that's why I went into analysis." The drink was sweet, potent. She sipped avidly, glad for his presence. Glad not to be spending Christmas alone in a hotel room.

"Baby, have another," Alan prodded, his eyes compassionate. "You're so uptight you're about to explode."

"Okay." She forced a smile.

The second drink went down quickly. She began to relax. How beautiful the blaze in the fireplace! How delicious its warmth.

"Come on, lie down over here," Alan coaxed, stretching across the thick, white wool pile rug before the fireplace.

When Nadine, barefoot, crossed to where Alan lay, the floor seemed unfamiliarity distant. She walked cautiously, her head light.

"Hey, baby," he jibed. "You're feeling the vodka."

For a little while they lay silent, without moving listening to James Taylor sing "Carolina in My Mind." Then Joni Mitchell's "For Free." As Joni finished, Nadine saw tears in Alan's eyes. Impulsively, she reached a hand out to touch his face.

The touch of her hand was a catalyst. He sought her hand, brought it to his mouth. Their eyes met. Nadine was aware of the tumult of excitement in her when Alan raised himself up on one elbow, dropped his free hand to her waist.

"Baby, it could he right with us," he whispered

earnestly. "I know it could be."

His mouth was exquisitely gentle on hers, as though he realized how desperately she needed to he loved. Knowing, too, that one wrong move and she would run.

The hi-fi dropped another record into position. Taylor again. An almost happy lilt to words that were sad. Fitting their mood. Alan's tongue filled her mouth while his hands moved about her breasts. Her head was foggy. Her body alert. Moving beneath the gentleness of his hands.

"Baby, it's going to be all right," he whispered, an anguish in his voice. "You'll see.

She lay still while he removed her clothes with tender swiftness. She waited, impatient. Her mind in eclipse. Only the body speaking. He lay above her. His mouth moving down to her breasts. His hands delicately touching. For an instant she stiffened in astonishment. Wary, waiting. She hadn't expected it to be this way. A low sound of excitement pushed its way through her faintly parted lips.

Her hands tugged at his shoulders. Telegraphing her needs.

"Alan." Her voice oddly husky, strange in her ears. Pleading. "Alan."

His body rode above hers now with a confident swiftness. She felt his hot breath on her shoulder.

"Baby, help me," he whispered. "It's going to he great."

Her hands sought him, encouraged. She whimpered faintly, with pleasure, with anticipation, as he entered her. Yes! Alan was right. It was going to be great.

Nadine lay back on the sofa, relaxed, the wide expanse of glass undraped on all sides so that the stars spilled across the sky in full view. Alan insisted on preparing dinner for them himself, no help from her. He was whistling in the kitchen.

With lithe restlessness she lifted herself from the sofa, moved about the huge living room. Inspecting Alan's recordings, his books. All kinds of books on analysis. He was really deep in that scene.

In a few minutes Alan called her in to the dining area off the living room, to sit down to the elegantly laid table. He was in high spirits himself. The amorous mood in retreat. Friends again.

She was fleetingly uneasy when he suggested they sleep over, drive back next day.

"Pick your own bedroom," he said humorously. "We have four. You can sleep as late as you like. I'll bring you breakfast in bed." His eyes coaxed her.

"Groovy," she approved. They both wanted to stay. They talked much after dinner. None of it personal. Nadine was astonished by, respectful of, the deep mysticism in Alan, of which she had been completely unaware before tonight. Poor Alan, groping so desperately for something to make life bearable. With all his money, all his success, still lost. This was a special bond between them.

At noon next day, as promised, Alan brought her breakfast in bed, sat at the edge while she ate heartily. When she was dressed, they'd drive back into town. They'd take the long way round. He wanted her to see the valley.

Nadine expected him to make a pitch before they left, She was relieved when no pitch was made.

Feeling guilty because she'd slept with Alan. A stand-in for Seth. Jason would be delighted to have the columnists spend space on Alan and her. That was what sold records. Let Seth read about Alan and her. Let him hurt. The way she hurt.

Nadine and Alan were together constantly. The whispers loud and clear. But always with people. Never alone. Never in bed together. Not since Christmas Day. Holding hands. A casual kiss before the others, those names which made up Alan's Hollywood world. Once a passionate kiss that evoked desire in her, but he released her and there was no more.

Right after the New Year's weekend, Jason flew into Los Angeles. Gloriously tanned, five pounds heavier, concerned about her. Jason and Claire kept up on all the Hollywood gossip. He'd arranged for the new session to be taped on the Coast. In ten days. Then Nadine and he would fly back for the Chicago concert and the dates in the East.

As usual before a session Nadine threw herself completely into preparation. Sleeping until noon, breakfasting with Jason, going into a recording studio to work over the sides to be recorded. Three sides were set. She planned to write a new song for the fourth side. Increasingly tense because this refused to work out properly.

"You're trying too hard," Jason chided gently, when she blew up in the studio after hearing the playback of the new effort. "Lay off for today." He was anxious for these sides to be terrific. She'd hit her first golden record. To stay on top you had to keep delivering.

"Jason, we're recording in four days," she shot back. "I don't have time to lay off!"

"Claire's flying in tonight. Let's all get up at a respectable hour tomorrow, spend some time at the beach. That'll knock some of the kinks out of you. You'll come into the studio feeling human again." Nadine frowned querulously. Knowing Jason was right, "I don't have a swimsuit."

"So cab over to Magnin's and buy one. Buy half a dozen," he joshed affectionately. "You can afford it." He paused, watching her closely. "You busy tonight?"

She shook her head.

"Alan's shooting the new film. He's up at six, goes to bed at nine. You know my schedule." She shrugged the relationship away. Alan was a passing moment in her life. It was over.

"Drive out with me to pick up Claire," he coaxed. "We'll have dinner somewhere together." The familiar scene again. Jason, Claire, Nadine.

"Sure." She forced a smile.

"Meanwhile, cut out to Magnin's, buy that swimsuit" Jason ordered genially. "Meet me at the hotel about six-thirty. We'll drive out to pick up Claire."

Nadine strolled through the elegant corridors of I. Magnin, remembering how she'd felt the first time she'd walked into Marshall Field in Chicago. Half-expecting someone to come over to shoo her out of the store. The saleswomen staring at her as though they expected her to steal something.

In the swimsuit department she was recognized.

She heard the flurry of excitement, stiffened self-consciously. Damn, she had to go to the john again! She had been constantly running the last few days. Perhaps it was all that coffee.

In the inner area of the rest room, Nadine made her way into one of the stalls. The two young women at the mirrors had been too involved in their personal discussion to recognize Nadine Scott.

"Honestly, this is getting impossible," one of the pair outside said dramatically. "I can't go anywhere for an hour without looking for a bathroom! Between running to the john and falling asleep every time I sit down, I wonder how I'll get through the third month of this stinking pregnancy, let alone nine months."

Nadine froze. *Running to the john. Always sleepy*. She couldn't be pregnant. She hadn't been near Seth since the Saturday night after Thanksgiving. She'd had two periods since then. No. One.

She was late. Sweat breaking out on her forehead as she tried to remember the date. She was late. Eight days late! But eight days didn't mean anything, she tried to consider realistically. Except that, away from Seth, she'd dropped off the pill. But now there was this running to the john and the sleepiness and the funny feeling in her breasts. Alan. That one time with Alan.

Nadine hurried away from the restroom, from the pair of voices so earnestly discussing pregnancy. The swimsuit forgotten. Out to the elevators, impatient to be away from the store. Alan, she thought frenziedly. She must tell Alan.

She checked her watch. Almost five. He would

be leaving the studio in a few minutes, he was a bug about cutting out at five sharp. She could be at the Malibu house almost as fast as he.

She left the cab, overtipping the driver as usual, hurried up the long path to the long contemporary that was reminiscent of the mountain house. Alan was home, the Ferrari sat in the driveway.

Nadine walked into the foyer, aware of the gentle breeze from the Pacific which swept through the house. She hesitated indecisively. She beard the hi-fl. In Alan's bedroom.

Nadine, breathless from her pace, moved down to the corridor to the huge bedroom with its king-sized round bed. At the door she paused, not immediately comprehending the scene on the king-sized bed. Alan sprawled nude on his stomach, with Donnie humped above him.

"More, Donnie," Alan was pleading, his voice a blend of anguish and passion. "Give me more, Donnie!"

CHAPTER TWENTY-ONE

Nadine sat on a corner of the sofa in her hotel sitting room, legs beneath her, shoulders hunched together tensely, eyes terrified.

"Jason, what do I do now?" Her mind going back to that tenement in Chicago, when Jo was pregnant. She thought about Mama, pregnant, sent home in shame. "Jason, what do I do now?" Her hands ice-cold, trembling.

"Relax," Jason said calmly, though Nadine knew she had rocked him with the news. He was sifting it through his mind. "First, Nadine, let's make sure you are pregnant," he said, smiling to emphasize his own cool. "You have any idea how many kids think they are pregnant when they're not? A few days late, and zowie, they flip their lids."

"Jason, I'm pregnant," Nadine insisted. Not with Seth's child. With Alan's. "Just that one time, I swear, that's all." Her voice was husky with frustration.

"You sleep with a guy, it's not a national disaster, honey;" Jason reminded. "Now this is how we handle it. You take a test to make sure. Then, if the test is positive, we check you into some plush private hospital for a couple of days 'rest.' While you're there, they do the abortion. Under hospital supervision, it's like no risk. It goes on the records as a routine check. No sweat." He leaned back in his chair, thinking hard. "I'll have to make some phone calls–"

"Jason, no." She recoiled from the prospect of an abortion with childlike fear.

"You want the baby?" he demanded brusquely,

to shake her into reality.

"No!"

"Nadine, it's safe," he insisted, leaning forward earnestly. "In a hospital with a top-notch surgeon in charge. You won't feel anything. They'll put you out. It'll be over in a little while. A hell of a lot easier than going through a delivery. You don't want the baby, Nadine." Jason persisted.

Nadine squeezed her eyes tightly shut, wanting to blot out the memory of the night with Alan, and what she saw on the king-sized bed in Alan's bedroom this afternoon.

"Jason, what was Alan trying to prove with me?"

"That he's a man," Jason said softly. "The poor bastard." He smiled at Nadine's sudden look of wide-eyed astonishment. "Honey, didn't you know Alan was gay? Half the country knows."

"I didn't."

"Go in and wash your face," Jason ordered. "Fix yourself up. We're going out to the airport to pick up Claire. Tomorrow we'll book you into a jazzy sanitarium, for a test, and whatever is called for."

"If this were Seth's baby," she said with sudden ferocity, "I wouldn't let them do it. I couldn't let them take away Seth's baby."

"Nadine, the way you feel about that guy, why don't you patch things up? It was good. I admit I wasn't keen on your being so heavily involved with any guy at this stage of your career, but you are, whether you like it or not."

"I said to Seth, let's get married, I'll see you through school. Lots of wives do that with jobs. What would that money mean to me? And we could be together." Her eyes were dark with unhappiness. "But Seth said he had to let his parents do the whole bit. He couldn't rob them of that satisfaction."

"That makes him a man, Nadine," Jason said gently. "You have to respect him for that." Jason leaned forward seriously. "Seth'll have his degree in June. What's the big thing about waiting till then?"

"Because then it'll be his internship and his residency; his parents don't want him to marry until he's set up in practice. He won't do anything to take away their glory. He's dying to go down to Appalachia for his internship, and they're chopping away at that already. They want some prestigious hospital in New York. Besides, it's too late for Seth and me," Nadine said bitterly. "After this, it's too late."

Nadine and Jason drove to the airport to pick up Claire. They stopped at a plush, quiet restaurant for dinner. Claire looked tired from the flight. Concerned.

She suspected something was out of whack, Nadine realized. But Claire wouldn't ask questions. She'd wait until Jason was ready to tell her.

While they dawdled over second cups of coffee, Jason went out to make a phone call. Claire left to go to the powder room. Jason returned, gestured to Nadine to stay.

"You check in tomorrow morning," he told her quietly, when Claire was out of hearing. "No breakfast. There's a quick test. They'll know by lunch time. If it's positive, they do the operation right away. Two days later you'll be discharged." He didn't call her "baby" today, Nadine noticed with a flutter of hysteria. Today "baby" was a loaded word.

At nine sharp next morning Jason was at her door, as scheduled.

"Do you want Claire to stay with you?" he asked quietly. "She'll come if you like."

"No," Nadine said quickly. "You stay." Jason had been with her from the beginning. From that day at the rock festival till now. She wanted Jason with her.

They cabbed to the hospital. Nadine too overwrought to concern herself with luggage. A nurse led Nadine away for the test. In a few minutes she joined Jason in the lounge. He smiled reassuringly, handed her the current issue of *Cash Box*, settled down himself with *Billboard*. Jason was nervous, she realized, and oddly, this was reassuring to her.

Jason and she read, talked about the lushness of the hospital and its grounds, tried to ignore what might lie ahead of Nadine. The test would be positive, Nadine reiterated mentally.

At noon the doctor came out to report, as casually as he might have discussed the weather, Nadine thought with resentment, that the test was positive. A nurse at the doctor's elbow led Nadine away to be prepped for the "minor surgery." Jason smiled reassuringly, told her he'd cut out for lunch.

Nadine knew he'd deliberately mentioned lunch, to emphasize his confidence in the outcome of the abortion. Yet this was surgery, her mind insisted on pointing out. She wished, with childlike intensity, that Mama was here.

She lay back in the bed in the hospital gown while the nurse did all that was necessary. Back in Chicago, Jo had no money for an abortion. Jo had been scared of quacks. "I'm not going to end up on a slab DOA because of some butcher."

She wouldn't die, not with a team of doctors and nurses scraping away the seed in her under the best of hospital conditions. Yet fleetingly, panic brushed her. Sometimes a girl died of an abortion, you read about that in the tabloids. Even under the best of conditions. Something nobody expected happened, and the girl was dead.

While Nadine grappled with her own fears, she was transferred from bed to stretcher, wheeled up into the operating room. How unreal this was! She felt drowsy, not quite sure now what was happening. That needle the nurse had popped into her thigh a little while ago. She always hated needles. Remembering Eddie. Eddie was so long ago. Eddie had been so young.

"We'll take you up to your room now," a young nurse said with a smile.

Nadine recalled the emergency room at the Chicago hospital, when Joanna was delivering. "My baby's coming!" Joanna had cried out. "I'm holding his head in my hands!" Only then did Joanna receive attention.

In her room Nadine drifted off to sleep again, to wake up to the reassuringly familiar sound of Jason's voice, on the telephone.

"How do you feel, honey?" Jason was asking, his face anxious as he listened at the phone. "Okay, get some sleep. Have dinner sent up. I'll come up as soon as I've talked a while to Nadine. She's still under."

"I'm out," Nadine reported calmly. "Tell Claire 'hi'. I'm fine," she said firmly before Jason could ask. "Like you said, nothing to it." She snapped her fingers in a Jasonesque gesture and managed a smile. "I just feel a little sore."

"Nadine says 'hi'," Jason relayed the message to Claire, grinning at Nadine. "You can come over to visit with her tomorrow. Tonight she'll watch TV." He put down the phone, made himself comfortable at the edge of the bed.

"What's the matter with Claire?" Nadine inquired. "Virus?"

Jason hesitated.

"She's pregnant."

Nadine gazed at Jason, startled, shaken. She turned her face away quickly, fleetingly, tears pricking at her eyes. She'd denied her baby life. She'd allowed the doctor to go in there and scrape him away.

"Jason, that's gorgeous news," she forced herself to say warmly. Managing a smile.

"Can you imagine me with a kid?" Jason grinned broadly. "After all these years. But we've got plenty of time to worry about that; Claire's not due till August. Sweetie, you're checking out of here day after tomorrow," Jason said briskly. "We'll tape the session right on schedule, then fly to Chicago."

"What about the fourth side?" Nadine demanded unhappily.

"I've been thinking about that. You've never recorded the number about Jo at the hospital, giving birth," he reminded cautiously. "It goes over great at the concerts."

"Jo might be upset."

"Jo will be proud," Jason said firmly.

"You're showing what happens to minority

people. You know, I know, millions of people know. But there are millions more who've never seriously thought about it. Show them what happens in a big city emergency room, where human life has no dignity, little value, unless it's wrapped up in a fat bank book."

"Okay," Nadine said, faintly fretful. "So we're set for the session."

The session was taped as planned, with Jason jubilant about the results.

"Baby, you're right with the mood of the Seventies," Jason said with satisfaction after the session, while they devoured inch-thick roast-beef sandwiches and black coffee in a restaurant not far from the recording studio. "The whole mood is changing, and you were in at the start. Saying simple things in a simple way, but with terrific impact. It's what happened to you, baby, and they know it's real."

"Jason, keep me working hard," Nadine pleaded earnestly. "Plenty of concerts, more TV, maybe a movie. A movie shot in New York," she stipulated quickly. Her eyes skidded to Claire. "Claire, you're tired," she said compassionately.

"Darling, don't worry about me," Claire soothed. "I'll be yawning for another six weeks."

They went back to the hotel to pack. In the morning they would be jetting to Chicago. She couldn't wait to get out of this town, Nadine thought fiercely. Let Jason keep her so busy she'd fall into bed at night too bushed to do anything except conk right out

In Chicago she had a festive luncheon at the Palmer House with Bob Frazer, who was delighted with her success. He knew, too, about Jo's involvement in California, and spoke about this with pride. He came to the concert with Joyce as her guests, as Nadine had previously arranged, but they didn't come back after the performance. He sent back a congratulatory   message instead.

In New York Nadine threw herself into a frenzy of activity. She was nearing her second Golden Record. She was sure to be nominated for a Grammy. Jason was jubilant about the new material she was writing. As an artist, she was maturing. Her personal life, she conceded, was shitty.

In April she went into a movie being shot in New York. Jason utilized her performance in this to springboard a Nadine Scott TV special, to be filmed in August. On her concerts now she made a point of talking, in a low-keyed, unaffected way, about how it was on the reservations, in the Indian ghettos. She made a plea to her audiences to write their congressmen, demanding reforms.

Jo wired her to join her group in a sit-in on what Jo called a fishing-rights swindle. Jason firmly rejected this—Nadine was too solidly booked. Guiltily, Nadine mailed out a huge check. Jo didn't bother acknowledging the contribution.

By June, with Jo's group splashed across the front pages, Nadine was so strung out that Jason was cautiously suggesting analysis.

"Baby, you need professional help," he insisted gently. "Sometimes things get just too much."

"Jason, I want to take a year off." She hadn't meant to throw it at him this bluntly. She'd been thinking about this ever since they'd come back from the Coast. "It won't be too rough on you, will it? The royalties keep coming in from the records. You've got the two new people–" Jason hadn't taken on the two male singers until he'd talked to her about it she remembered somberly. Not until then had she realized how much she owed to Jason. Because of what Jason had done for her, every other beginning singer in the field yearned to be Jason's singer.

"Don't worry about me." Jason brushed this aside, but he was frowning. "But not a year off, baby, that'll knock the props right out from under you. Look," he said persuasively, "I'll push off the next session. You take a month off. Unwind. Go home to the reservation. Maybe you'll want to stop off to see your father."

"No," she said quickly. Sighed beneath Jason's sharp scrutiny. "Sure, I want to see him," she acknowledged. "I'm dying to spend time with him, I keep promising I will. But I can't do that to Mama. She still doesn't know I've seen him."

"Go home and tell her," Jason coaxed. "You keep erecting hurdles in your mind. Your mother will understand. Hell, you have a right to know your father."

"Jo thinks I'm a cop-out." Her voice was low. "I came off the reservation with determination to help my people, and I've only helped myself."

"Screw Joanna," he said. "From the moment you started singing publicly you've helped your people. Every time you get up on a stage, go into a recording session, you're spreading the word about them. You're giving them dignity by being Nadine Scott. Don't you let Jo make you believe you're copping out."

"Jason, I don't know where I'm going."

"You're going upward, baby," Jason said with conviction.

"You've got everything going for you, looks, talent, drive."

"Jason, I need time to be by myself. To think." Every time she walked the streets she searched for Seth. She wouldn't move from the apartment, knowing Seth's parents lived around the comer. Once, she'd spied Audrey on Broadway, hurried into a store to avoid a confrontation. Poor Audrey. She'd never sent Audrey the records she'd promised.

"Nadine," Jason intruded urgently into her introspection. "Play it like I say. Take a month off. Forget about work. Fly out to the reservation. Stay with your folks a few days. Break it to your mother about having seen your father. She'll understand, baby."

"I don't know." Nadine wavered. Wanting to run home. To be close to Mama. Dreading to leave New York where Seth might, just might, call her. "Jason, I don't know." Her voice was an anguished murmur.

"Then call Seth," Jason ordered with deceptive casualness. "You can cope with all the other problems when everything's okay between Seth and you." That was true, Nadine recognized. "He's out of school now." Jason's eyes were serious. He was fearful of pushing her. "Have a showdown with Seth, Nadine. Now's the time. Give him that chance."

Nadine sat very still. Deliberating. Her throat tight as she thought about Seth. She hadn't believed him when he said they'd talk about getting married when he had his degree. All right, like Jason said, give him that chance.

Trembling, Nadine crossed to the phone, dialed Seth's number. Bracing herself for the sound of his voice.

"I'm sorry, the number you are calling has been disconnected," a polite, disembodied, impersonal voice shattered her dream.

"He's moved." Nadine's eyes darkened with anguish.

"Call his house," Jason ordered, leaning forward to pick up the phone book. "If he were in another apartment, the operator would have given you the new listing. He must be home."

"You call him, Jason." She didn't want to talk to Seth's mother. "Jason, please."

Jason hesitated, grinned wryly.

"Okay, baby."

Nadine dropped into a chair, laced her hands in nervousness.

"Hello," Jason said casually, as somebody obviously replied at the other end. "This is Jason Friedlander, a friend of Seth's. I've just returned from the Coast and I tried to reach him. I gather he's moved. Could you give me his new phone number?" He frowned, while Nadine watched anxiously. "Thank you, honey." Jason put down the phone. "That was the kid sister. Seth left New York to begin his internship. She wasn't sure where—she said to call later and ask her mother."

"We won't bother," Nadine said swiftly. "Seth's gone." She rose from her chair in sudden decision. "I'll do what you said, Jason. Fly out to the reservation for a few days. After that, maybe I'll fly out to see my father. It'd be fun to meet the kids," she admitted wistfully.

"I'll have Claire make your reservations," Jason promised with a reassuring smile. "Go down to the department stores and splurge on some jazzy presents." Jason knew how she enjoyed buying presents for the family. "How soon do you want to leave, baby?"

"As fast as Claire can get me on a plane," Nadine said intensely.

She wanted out of this town. Seth wasn't here. For a moment she dallied with the thought of asking Jason to call back. No! No, she didn't want to hear that he'd accepted an internship at some prestigious hospital in Boston or Chicago or Miami. The kind of hospital his parents would choose. His parents' total victory.

Nadine shopped with defiant abandon in the air-conditioned Fifth Avenue department stores. In Altman's gourmet shop, she bought a staggering range of edibles which were suitable for shipment to the reservation. Visualizing the excitement the parcels' arrival would elicit. But, first, she would arrive.

She went to Claire and Jason's apartment for dinner, watching with tender amusement Jason's pride in Claire's flowering pregnancy.

"Isn't she as big as a house?" Jason demanded with satisfaction, affectionately petting the bulging belly. "I'm considering having half a dozen more. "

"You do and I'll report you to Planned Parenthood," Nadine joshed. "Haven't you heard about the population explosion?"

"This explosion I'm happy about," Jason said complacently, prodding Nadine to the sofa.

"Let me help Claire," Nadine protested.

"You sit and talk to Jason," Claire insisted, with a blend of warmth and efficiency. She was preparing dinner herself tonight, though there was a woman who came in part-time each day to take care of the apartment and prepare dinner. For Claire, this was a personal gift of herself to Nadine.

Nadine tried to relax as she talked with Jason. She wasn't telephoning home, she'd arrive as a surprise. Zowie, Mama's face would light up when she walked in! In a few days she ought to be able to bring herself to tell Mama that she had sought out her father. It wasn't loving Mama less to love him, too.

Next day, on the plane, she alternately dozed and wove fantasies about Seth, all of which ended with disturbing conclusions. No room in his life for her. Now he was a doctor, though the years of internship and residency sprawled ahead of him. But he could call himself Dr. Coles en route to that jazzy practice his parents wanted so desperately for him.

The sun was a glowing red ball, dipping low in the incredibly wide sky, when the cab left her off a short walk from the village. A bag in each hand, the suede purse her stepfather had fashioned for her draped over her shoulder, Nadine headed for the mobile home that was the wonder of the village.

Again, it was the children who spied her as she approached. They rushed forward in exuberant welcome, and her arms opened to them. Oh, wow, they were growing! Time moved with such startling speed.

"Where's Mama?" Nadine asked, an arm around

each of the two smaller children as they walked with her.

"Mama don't feel good," Teddy reported somberly. "All this week she just lies in bed."

Alarm charging through her, Nadine sprinted ahead to the door of the mobile home, pulled it open, walked inside. Jody stood at the range, pouring water into a cup.

"Nadine!" Jody's face lighted. With more than pleasure. Relief, Nadine pinpointed with soaring anxiety. "Oh, Nadine!"

"Why didn't somebody write and tell me Mama was sick?" Nadine reproached.

"Mama wouldn't let us," Jody reported. "I'm fixing her tea now. She won't eat. Just tea all the time."

Nadine hurried down the narrow corridor to her mother's room. Her mother lay against a mound of pillows, dozing. Her face flushed, her breathing heavy.

"Mama," Nadine said quietly, dropping to the edge of the bed. Leaning forward to kiss her. How hot she was! "Oh, Mama, I've missed you." She was shocked by her mother's appearance. How old she looked! Statistics about Navajo life expectancy shuttled across her mind, and Nadine turned cold inside.

Her mother slowly opened her eyes, taking a few moments to focus. Brightening with pleasure when she recognized Nadine. "My daughter," she whispered. "I told them not to send for you."

"I came, Mama, nobody sent for me." Her hand touched her mother's cheek. She was running a high temperature. From the labored breathing Nadine recognized a respiratory infection. "Why didn't the doctor send you to the hospital?"

"No place in town hospital for me, Nadine," her mother said tiredly. "If I die, better I die here at home. Frank, you remember him, he gave me herb medicine. Herbs to clear this fire in my chest. If I am to live, I will live." She reached to bring Nadine's hand to her face.

"I'll phone for a doctor from town," Nadine said quickly.

"Nadine, the doctors don't go to white folks' house unless they're important—you think they come for an Indian?"

"You're going into town to the hospital, Mama. You'll have a room of your own, we'll call in the best doctors. Only the best for my Mama," she said tenderly. "Don't you know that?"

Mama smiled, her eyes moving with pride about the room. Every gift from Nadine on display.

"Every day you prove this to me, my daughter."

"I'll phone the hospital and order an ambulance sent out right away. You'll be settled in a hospital bed in an hour," she promised.

"No," Mama said sternly. "I won't ride in an ambulance. I'll dress and go into town with you. Caleb Youngblood has a truck, he will drive me to the hospital." Her eyes clouded with dread. "Once I went to the clinic with Teddy. I promised myself then, never again."

"It'll be different this time, Mama." Nadine helped her mother into a sitting position, moved about to find her clothes. The kids watching anxiously in the doorway.

"Mama's going to be all right," she soothed. "Go find Caleb Youngblood. Ask him to drive Mama and me to the hospital."

With dusk settling about them Caleb Youngblood drove Nadine and her mother over the gritty desert road into town. Jody would explain to her father when he returned from his job. Nadine sat with one arm about her mother, painfully conscious of the labored breathing, the high temperature.

At the impressively modern, sprawling hospital only in service two years, Caleb drove his asthmatic truck to the emergency entrance. Nadine insisted he return to the reservation rather than wait for her. She would stay here with Mama. With Mama's hand firmly in hers, Nadine walked towards the emergency entrance.

"Maybe we shouldn't be here" Mama froze at the door, her eyes overly bright, scared. "Nadine, let's go home."

"Mama, no," Nadine insisted gently. "We'll stay."

They walked inside, to the stark-white, sparsely occupied waiting room. Three patients waited on the benches. The desk at the moment was deserted. They wouldn't have long to wait, Nadine told herself with relief. Hating the antiseptic scent, the impersonal faces of those who were moving about in the corridor just ahead. People came here with their grief, to be a number on a chart.

A nurse came down the corridor into the waiting room, to call for the couple with a fretful infant. The nurse's eyes scanned the room, lighted on Nadine's mother. She nodded crisply, made a brief notation on a book on the desk. A few minutes later, another nurse emerged, to lead an elderly woman, obviously in deep pain, who sat with a frightened, middle-aged daughter, into one of the small examining cubicles which flanked the corridor.

"We'll go in soon, Mama,'" Nadine whispered. "There's only one other patient before you now."

While Nadine soothed her mother, a young nurse with a solicitous smile came out to usher an older woman, watched over by an anxious husband, into another cubicle.

"You're going to be just fine, mom," the young nurse crooned, and shot encouragement at the woman's husband. "The doctor's going to examine you now."

"We'll be next, Mama," Nadine said, frightened by Mama's high color, her wheezing.

While Nadine spoke encouragingly to her mother, the emergency door swung wide and an expensively tailored, older man with a child in his arms strode into the waiting room. A beautifully groomed, fretful-faced young woman followed, gazed about with distaste.

"Dad, I think we ought to wait until Craig can locate Dr. Fredericks," the woman said sulkily. "I'm sure it's no more than a sprain.

"It could be a fracture," the man insisted firmly. A business executive, a lawyer, Nadine guessed. "I want X-rays immediately.'"

"Nurse," he called out peremptorily as a nurse moved into view.

"Oh, Judge Martin." The nurse moved forward, her eyes inspecting the quiet, scared child in his arms.

"He fell down a flight of stairs, there may be a fracture," Judge Martin said briskly. "We can't locate Dr. Fredericks, he's out on a case. Please find a doctor, nurse."

"Just a moment!" Her eyes blazing, Nadine leapt to her feet. "My mother is very sick, We were here first. If there's a doctor available, I expect him to treat my mother."

"Please, Miss," the nurse reproached coldly. "Judge Martin's grandson may have a fracture."

"Which can wait!" Nadine's voice rose stridently, despite her determination to retain control. "We are next—I want a doctor to see my mother. I want her admitted to a private room."

"Nurse." The quiet authority in the voice, the familiar, spun both Nadine and the nurse about to face the new arrival. Seth! Seth here! "Nurse, please take this patient." Seth nodded toward Nadine's mother, "into an examining room." He turned with a perfunctory smile to the judge. "Dr. Sachs will be with you shortly, sir." He leaned forward for a cursory examination of the child, questioned the mother, pegged the situation as not an emergency. Only now, when the judge and his daughter reluctantly seated themselves on a bench, did he look at Nadine.

"I heard your voice," he said, his own too low for anyone to eavesdrop. "I couldn't believe you were here."

"Oh, Seth." Her eyes clung to him, trying to assimilate the miracle of his presence.

His arm about her waist, he prodded her toward the examining room where the nurse was helping

Nadine's mother, now in hospital gown, onto the examining table. Nadine stood by, excited, happy. Seth was here. Not at Massachusetts General. Not at some lush country-club hospital. Here, near the reservation.

"Don't be frightened, Nadine, because we're going to give her oxygen," Seth said quietly. "That's to relieve her breathing." He turned to the nurse, issued instructions, and the tight-lipped woman left the room. "It's a mild case of pneumonia. Most Indians are particularly susceptible to respiratory ailments," he reminded. "But with oxygen and antibiotics we'll have it quickly under control."

"Seth, I want a private room for her," Nadine said quickly.

"And a jazzy doctor!" he rided her gently.

"Dr. Coles," Nadine whispered, and saw Mama watching them in bewilderment "Mama." She took her mother's hand in hers, "this is my friend from New York. He's going to make you well." The glow in her eyes told Mama the depth of the relationship between Seth and her.

The nurse returned with medication. Seth himself, to the nurse's disapproval, administered the hypodermic.

"Mrs. Scott is to be admitted," Seth told the nurse. "Please arrange for her to be moved to a private room in the West Wing." He smiled dryly at the nurse's glare of shock, turned his attention again to Nadine's mother. "Nadine and I will be up to check you out later," he promised her with an encouraging smile. "When they've got you more comfortable upstairs. Oh, nurse," he said calmly, "is Sachs seeing the kid?"

"Yes, Dr. Coles. Dr. Sachs is sending him up to x-ray."

"I'm checking out," Seth reported briskly, a hand at Nadine's wrist. "I was due off duty two hours ago." He drew Nadine out with him into the corridor. "Wow, am I glad I hung around!"

Seth's car, a nine-year-old Volvo, was parked in the adjacent area. Wordlessly, his eyes saying much, he helped Nadine into the car, strode around the front to slide in behind the wheel. Nadine's head cradled on his shoulder, they drove out into the desert. The heat of the day replaced by the night chill.

Seth parked in the beautiful solitude, reached for her hand.

"I came out to this town to he closer to you, Nadine," he began quietly. "To understand you better. To know how I failed you. I've been out to the reservation many times in these few weeks. I walked where you walked. I saw for myself, everything you'd tried to tell me. I looked, Nadine, and I was ashamed of myself for being white. I knew why you couldn't compromise, why you couldn't wait."

"But you didn't call me," she reproached. She laughed shakily. "I'm easy enough to find if you bother to read the entertainment pages."

"I know where you've been every minute. But I saw you were doing great without me. You didn't need me. I'd failed you, but you made it, anyway. You didn't need a doctor husband."

"I'm no good without you, Seth. I can't cope with problems. Awful things happen to me." Later she would tell him. "I want to be with you, Seth. To live forever where running waters meet."

She knew who she was now. She knew where she was going.

About the Author....

Julie Ellis was born in Columbus, Georgia. She moved to New York at age 16 with her parents, after her high school graduation. Julie studied drama, and was part of the mid-'50s Off-Broadway scene as actress/playwright/co-producer. Seven of her plays were produced Off-Broadway and presented on the summer hotel/bungalow colony circuits. She wrote 76 sides of children's records (hitting BILLBOARD'S Bestseller List). Her first paperback novel was published in 1960 and between 1960 and 1974 she wrote 143 contemporary, gothic, romantic suspense novels and 3 non-fiction titles that were published by major paperback houses.

Julie has written one hardcover/softcover bestseller per year (a number of early paperback originals now being re-published in hardcover in the United Kingdom). Ellis is published in thirteen countries. A favorite among library readers across the country, Julie regularly appears on LIBRARY JOURNAL'S "Pre-publication Bestseller Lists". In 1993 she made the United Kingdom's Registrar of Public Lending Rights List of the most-read authors in the United Kingdom Library System (minimum of 300,000 loans per author).

A single mother since 1972 (first separated, then widowed), Julie considers her major productions her daughter Susan and her son Richard. Julie is a passionate environmentalist whose convictions appear regularly in her novels (the devastation of our Northwest forests in LOYALTIES, the unnecessary deaths caused by the tobacco industry in LASTING TREASURES, gun control in COMMITMENT). Julie is a vegetarian with occasional lapses due to social circumstances. She alternates between her Manhattan apartment and beach house in Montauk.

ORDER FORM

More exciting titles from Moonlight Romances

❏ **#038-3 BIRDS OF WAR** by Jane Toombs. Daring pilots in the air, rivals on the ground, torn apart by Francis's love for Eileen.

❏ **#039-1 CANAL FEVER** by Shirley Remes Carroll. Sean's pride drives him to almost lose the love of his life, Anna Hess.

❏ **#040-5 CHAMPAGNE NIGHTS** by Nancy John. Melissa was torn between her feelings for Phil and the love of her children.

❏ **#041-3 COLTON'S FOLLY** by Renee Simons. Abby and Cat carved out a truce, but a kiss threatened to destroy that truce.

❏ **#042-1 DANGEROUS WATERS** by Vida Devlin. Cindy risked everything for paradise and passion.

❏ **#043-X DARING ALLIANCE** by Karla Hocker. Amidst the War of 1812, Lady Georgiana battled to gain the love Barrett Gray.

❏ **#044-8 EDEN** by Julie Ellis. Against a background of the legendary Old South, a powerful novel of tempestuous affairs.

❏ **#045-6 KNOW WHEN TO RUN** by Ida Hills. Erika's homecoming produces a tangled web of romance and murder.

❏ **#046-4 OAK HILL** by Jane Cox. Whitney dared not admit that the hatred she felt for the Union officer Reefe Preston was love.

❏ **#047-2 RELUCTANT LADY** by Alicia Rasley. Romance and royalty woven with devious treachery...Regency style.

❏ **#048-0 THE HEART'S REWARD** by Vella Munn. Rani's love for Scott had strength and passion, but she needed wisdom.

❏ **#049-9 WHERE RUNNING WATERS MEET** by Julie Ellis. Nadine could not forget her heritage...and the man she loved.

Send check or money order (no COD's) made payable to:

KAPPA BOOKS, INC.
Dept. MR, P. O. Box 1182, Fort Washington, PA 19034

Please ship my order for _____books @ $4.99 for the first book and $2.90 for each additional book, plus $1.50 shipping and handling per book to:
(Please allow 4 to 6 weeks for shipping)

NAME_____

ADDRESS_____

CITY_____ STATE____ ZIP_____

PUT A CHECK MARK BY EACH BOOK ORDERED, TEAR OUT PAGE AND MAIL